RUNAWAY

WOLFES OF MANHATTAN THREE

HELEN HARDT

RUNAWAY
WOLFES OF MANHATTAN THREE

Helen Hardt

✾ Created with Vellum

DEDICATION

For everyone who helped support my career in 2020.
Thank you!

Riley Wolfe is finally free from her past.

So why is she still running?

Coming to terms with her father's death and her own implication in his murder has sent Riley reeling, so she does what she does best. She runs. Not only from her home but from herself, ending up in a small town in Montana

Matteo Rossi lives a modest life, doing construction, making silver jewelry, and renting out the cabin he inherited from his uncle. He's happy and has no wish for anything else, until a beautiful renter from the east comes hurtling into his life.

Passion erupts between Matt and Riley, but Matt soon discovers his lovely renter isn't who she claims to be. When she disappears, he's determined to find her, even if it means walking through fire.

PRAISE FOR HELEN HARDT

STEEL BROTHERS SAGA

"*Craving* is the jaw-dropping book you *need* to read!"
~*New York Times* bestselling author Lisa Renee Jones

"Completely raw and addictive."
~#1 *New York Times* bestselling author Meredith Wild

"Talon has hit my top five list...up there next to Jamie Fraser and Gideon Cross."
~*USA Today* bestselling author Angel Payne

"Talon and Jade's instant chemistry heats up the pages..."
~RT Book Reviews

"Sorry Christian and Gideon, there's a new heartthrob for you to contend with. Meet Talon. Talon Steel."
~Booktopia

"Such a beautiful torment—the waiting, the anticipation, the relief that only comes briefly before more questions arise, and the wait begins again... Check. Mate. Ms. Hardt..."

~**Bare Naked Words**

"Made my heart stop in my chest. Helen has given us such a heartbreakingly beautiful series."

~**Tina, Bookalicious Babes**

WOLFES OF MANHATTAN

"It's hot, it's intense, and the plot starts off thick and had me completely spellbound from page one."

~**The Sassy Nerd Blog**

"Helen Hardt...is a master at her craft."

~**K. Ogburn, Amazon**

"Move over Steel brothers... Rock is *everything!*"

~**Barbara Conklin-Jaros, Amazon**

"Helen has done it again. She winds you up and weaves a web of intrigue."

~**Vicki Smith, Amazon**

FOLLOW ME SERIES

"Hardt spins erotic gold..."

~*Publishers Weekly*

"22 Best Erotic Novels to Read"

~*Marie Claire* **Magazine**

"Intensely erotic and wildly emotional..."
~*New York Times* bestselling author Lisa Renee Jones

"With an edgy, enigmatic hero and loads of sexual tension, Helen Hardt's fast-paced Follow Me Darkly had me turning pages late into the night!"
~*New York Times* bestselling author J. Kenner

"Christian, Gideon, and now...Braden Black."
~**Books, Wine, and Besties**

"A tour de force where the reader will be pulled in as if they're being seduced by Braden Black, taken for a wild ride, and left wanting more."
~*USA Today* **Bestselling Author Julie Morgan**

"Hot. Sexy. Intriguing. Page-Turner. Helen Hardt checks all the boxes with *Follow Me Darkly!*"
~**International Bestselling Author Victoria Blue**

BLOOD BOND SAGA

"An enthralling and rousing vampire tale that will leave readers waiting for the sequel."
~**Kirkus Reviews**

"Dangerous and sexy. A new favorite!"
~*New York Times* bestselling author Alyssa Day

"Helen gives us the dark, tormented vampire hero we all love in a sensual paranormal romance with all the feels. Be warned... The twists and turns will keep you up all night reading. I was hooked from the first sentence until the very end."

~*New York Times* bestselling author J.S. Scott

"A dark, intoxicating tale."
~**Library Journal**

"Helen dives into the paranormal world of vampires and makes it her own."
~**Tina, Bookalicious Babes**

"Throw out everything you know about vampires—except for that blood thirst we all love and lust after in these stunning heroes—and expect to be swept up in a sensual story that twists and turns in so many wonderfully jaw-dropping ways."
~**Angel Payne,** *USA Today* **bestselling author**

PROLOGUE
RILEY

The beauty of being my father's daughter was that he'd taught me from a young age to be a proficient liar. I could convince anyone of anything. All I had to do was smile, flutter my eyes a little, and wiggle my ass when I walked away.

Worked great on the runway.

All eyes on me.

Except when I wanted to disappear.

My father had taught me that, as well.

Not only could I make the marks on my skin disappear, I could disappear wholly.

Usually at his behest. This last time?

All me.

He was gone. Burning in the flames of hell, I hoped.

Still he saw me. I felt his nauseating gaze I felt his nauseating gaze on my body, his clammy touch on my flesh. That's why I burned myself sometimes.

After all, I'd been taught well how to hide scars.

Sometimes, though, even burning didn't help.

Sometimes, I wasn't sure anything ever would.

1

RILEY

I chose Montana because of Rock.

I had the address of his cabin, but of course I didn't go there. That would be the first place he and Reid would look for me. No, I chose a cabin in a remote little town in big sky country. I paid cash for a week's lodging.

I also paid cash for my rental car, and it was easy enough not to leave a trace. My father had outfitted me with two fake IDs as soon as I turned eighteen. He had his reasons.

His abhorrent, disgusting reasons.

As far as I knew, my brothers weren't aware of my aliases.

Chloe Mansfield.

Today I was Chloe Mansfield.

The GPS in the car led me to the small cabin. I chose small for a reason. I wanted to escape my life, and part of escaping my life was escaping the glamour and glitz. This week I wasn't Riley Wolfe, heiress and supermodel.

This week, I was Chloe Mansfield, regular woman.

I pulled my long dark hair back into a high ponytail, and I wore no makeup. My skin felt like it could breathe for the first time in ages. I liked the feeling.

I pulled up to the cabin and parked the car in the tiny drive-way. When I got out, I looked up at the big blue sky and inhaled.

Not only my skin was breathing. *I* was breathing for the first time in what felt like forever.

My father was dead.

Dead and cremated.

At this moment, my brothers were planning his memorial service. I had no qualms about missing it. Oh, I kept up with the family news. I knew full well we had all been implicated in his murder.

I also knew full well that none of my brothers nor I had killed the asshole. We all had reasons, but we weren't killers. Rock hadn't even been in the state when it happened.

Roy, Reid, and I had been in Manhattan, and none of us had alibis. Of course, I knew where I'd been, and it wasn't at my father's penthouse murdering him, although the thought certainly had merit.

I had been in my apartment, coked out. Not my finest moment, but I wasn't about to berate myself. My life, to this point, had been both blessed and cursed. To the outside world, all that was visible was the blessed part. I was born with beauty, brains, and a wealthy family. That was all most people ever saw. Even my brothers Roy and Reid only saw that part of me. They saw me as Daddy's little girl. Daddy's favorite. At least up until a day or two ago.

I *was* Daddy's favorite, all right. It hadn't cost me much.

Only my soul.

I inhaled again, relishing the clean air of mountainous Montana. Then I strode to the lockbox, used the combination sent to me by the owner, and let myself in.

A rustic little—and I did mean little—living room greeted me. It looked much bigger on the website, but that was okay.

I was here to disappear, and I didn't need vast space to do that.

The floors were dark hardwood, and a faux bearskin rug sat in front of the fireplace. Yeah, it was faux. I'd asked when I'd seen pictures. Lying on the skin of a beautiful animal didn't sound like relaxation to me. A few logs sat in a brass basket next to the fireplace. Strange, since it was summer. Part of me wished it weren't, though, because I would've loved a fire.

To the right of the living room was the kitchen, also small but perfect. Not that I had ever cooked a meal in my life. I laughed out loud. I'd have to go into the small town and hit up the tiny grocery store for some frozen entrées. Lean Cuisine, probably, and of course some brown rice and vegetables.

My mother had trained me well from the beginning. Only good fats, and we kept those to a bare minimum. No dairy, no fatty meats, and no white flour or white rice. Whole-grain breads only, and again, at a minimum.

I'd grown used to brown rice and quinoa. Used to celery, carrots, and spinach. Used to tilapia and cod braised in lemon juice. Not the tastiest fare in the world, but it kept my body thin enough for the runway.

Which meant, of course, I could see my ribs and my abdomen was concave. The camera truly did add ten pounds.

I walked out of the kitchen and into the bedroom. The king-sized bed took up nearly the entire room. Only a three-drawer dresser and mirror completed the ensemble. Off to the side was a small bathroom with a toilet, sink, and shower. No bathtub, but that was okay, because there was supposed to be a hot tub in the back. I planned to do some significant relaxing here, and that hot tub would be a big part of it.

Speaking of the hot tub, I left the bedroom and found the back door. There it was, tightly ensconced on the redwood deck.

The low whir of the motor drifted over to me. You know? Right now might be a great time to test it out.

I was in the middle of nowhere, and though it was summer, a refreshing breeze blew around me. Perfect for the hot tub.

I removed the cover, which was more difficult than I'd anticipated. But I got it off and was mesmerized as I watched the steam rise from the water. I hadn't even brought my bags in from the car, and my bathing suit was buried somewhere. I didn't want to bother with it. Who would see me? I walked back into the kitchen, stripped down to nothing, and then walked barefoot across the redwood deck to the hot tub.

I stepped in, and when the warmth and hydration enveloped me, I closed my eyes.

Oh, yeah... This was heaven. I seriously might never leave this place.

I breathed in and out slowly, letting the steam moisturize my face and penetrate my lungs.

"Yeah," I said aloud. "I could get used to this."

"So could I."

2

MATTEO

Chloe Mansfield jerked out of the water, arms around her breasts, and then submerged herself quickly.

Too bad. Already I could see she had a gorgeous rack. Her frame was a little thin, but still, I'd have liked a better look.

"Who the hell are you?" she demanded.

"I didn't mean to startle you, ma'am."

Her eyes widened at my use of "ma'am."

"I'm Matteo Rossi."

"And...you're here because...?"

Because I'd really like to get a better look at you.

"Because I own this place."

Her eyebrows nearly flew off her forehead. "Well, I rented this place for the week, so you have no right to—"

"Hold on, hold on," I said. "I just came to make sure you have everything you need. I brought you some groceries, in case you haven't had a chance to stock up."

"I was planning to go into town later."

"Honey, it *is* later. This is a small town. Everything closes at five o'clock so folks can get home to dinner."

She opened her mouth, closed it, and then opened it once more. "Oh."

"Where are you from, anyway?"

She wrinkled her forehead for a minute, which made her look adorably cute. "Pittsburgh."

"A big city girl? You're used to grocery stores that are open twenty-four hours, no doubt."

"Well...yeah."

I couldn't help a laugh. "We do things here a little differently in Sumter Falls, Montana. Everything opens at eight and everything promptly closes at five, whether it's the grocery, liquor store, or the apothecary."

"Apothecary?"

"Pharmacy, druggist. Whatever."

"I see."

"Except the movie theater, but it's only open on weekends. Last show's over by eleven."

"Oh," she said again. Then she looked around tentatively. "Could you get me...a..."

"Towel?"

"Yeah, that would be perfection."

"Seems a shame to cover you up, speaking of perfection," I couldn't stop myself from saying, "but sure. Hold on."

I walked back into the kitchen and then to the bathroom, where I grabbed one of the fluffy white towels. I brought it back to Chloe.

"Thanks," she murmured. "Now, do you mind?"

Took a lot of energy for me to turn around and look away. I really wanted to get a good look of that dark-haired gorgeousness. Her face was so beautiful it could've been carved by gods.

Seriously. And I didn't say that lightly. Because I didn't talk like that. Ever.

She cleared her throat. "Okay, I'm out now."

I turned around. She was tall. Really fucking tall. Not as tall as I was, of course, but I was six-five. Taller than all the women around these parts, though. She was tall and lean, and I swear to God her legs went on forever. She looked like an angel wrapped in a white towel.

"I hate to bother you," she said, "but my bags..."

"They're in the bedroom. I already brought them in."

"Wow, really? I didn't realize I had left the car unlocked."

"You didn't. I found the keys on the kitchen table and took the liberty of—"

"Of breaking into my car?"

I couldn't help a sly smile. "No. I used the key."

"Without my permission. That's called breaking in where I come from."

"In Pittsburgh, I suppose so. Here in Sumter Falls, it's called being a good neighbor. We don't even bother locking our cars. Our crime rate is really low, and we all know each other."

"That doesn't seem like a good idea to me."

"It's *not* a good idea...in Pittsburgh."

"How would you know? Have you ever been to Pittsburgh?"

"No, ma'am, I haven't. And I have no desire to go there. I'm just a small-town guy who is happy here in Sumter Falls."

A tiny grunt emitted from her. Yeah, all these big city girls were alike. They didn't all look like her, though. Man, she was the most beautiful thing I'd ever laid eyes on, and I really, *really* wanted to see what was under that towel.

"Well...nice to meet you, Mr. Matteo."

"First name is Matteo. Last name is Rossi. But you can call me Matt. What should I call you?"

"Riley."

"Riley? I thought your name was Chloe. Chloe Mansfield."

Her cheeks were already red from the heat of the hot tub,

but I swore they got even redder. "Right. It is. But I go by Riley. It's my...middle name."

"Okay. Riley it is."

"If you'll excuse me, Mr. Rossi."

"Matt, please. Mr. Rossi doesn't exist. Even my grandpa went by his first name."

"Fine. Matt. Please excuse me. I have to get some clothes on."

I couldn't help myself. I stretched my lips into a grin. "Ma'am, you don't have to get any clothes on at all."

She turned full-on beet red and ran into the kitchen.

Too bad she was only here for a week.

3

RILEY

Once I was safely in the bedroom, I leaned against the door, nearly hyperventilating.

I was used to being around attractive men. Blond, dark, redhead, all skin tones and colors, all races and nationalities, and all gorgeous.

Everyone was gorgeous in the modeling world.

But Matteo Rossi took gorgeous to a new level. First, he was light where I was dark. His hair was the color of fresh wheat, and though his skin was tanned, I could tell he was naturally lighter than I was.

And about that hair the color of fresh wheat. It was long—as long or longer than my brother Roy's. Golden stubble graced his jawline, and what a jawline it was. Square and masculine and perfectly sculpted. His eyes...the lightest blue.

Then his body...corded and muscular, with large hands and thick fingers, the broadest shoulders I'd seen in some time, and an ass that was perfection in Levi's.

I was used to being around perfection, and probably partly because of my past, rarely did I have this intense an attraction to another human being.

My heart thudded rapidly. So hard against my chest that I could see the movement on the white towel that still covered me.

Damn.

I wanted this man. I really wanted this man in a way that was completely new to me.

I'd been around the block, for sure, but not the normal block.

The intensity of my attraction to Matteo Rossi scared the hell out of me.

I inhaled and exhaled deeply several times, trying to slow my rapid heart rate. When I finally felt I had myself in a modicum of control, I let the towel drop to the floor. My suitcase sat at the foot of the king-sized bed, so I lifted it onto the bed and opened it. I grabbed my oldest, softest pair of jeans and a T-shirt and quickly threw them on, along with a comfortable pair of Crocs flip-flops.

I walked swiftly toward the door, and my heart started thudding uncontrollably once more.

Matteo Rossi might not even be out there. He'd said he dropped some groceries off for me since the store was closed. What other reason did he have to stay?

For God's sake, Riley. Calm down.

I inhaled slowly and exhaled, turning the doorknob and opening the door.

Then my heart started racing once more.

He was still there, standing in my kitchen—well, technically it was *his* kitchen—and peeling potatoes over the sink.

"Hey," he said.

"I didn't know you'd still be here."

"Yep, still here. The garbage disposal is a little finicky, so I wanted to show you how to use the plunger to unclog it if you need to."

"I think I can figure out how to use a plunger."

He didn't have to know I'd never used a plunger in my life. I wasn't even sure what a plunger looked like. The Wolfes had people to do those kinds of things.

"I'm sure you can. I'm sure you're quite capable of anything you put your mind to, honey. But like I said, the disposal is finicky, and there's a certain knack to it."

Honey. That was the second time he'd use the endearment. It warmed me all over, as if warm honey itself were coating me.

"Last time I checked, I'm not your honey."

"Nothing personal. I call everyone honey. But if it bothers you, Riley, I'll stop."

It doesn't bother me. In fact, I love it. It makes me want to melt into your arms and—

"It bothers me," I said flatly.

If there was one thing my father taught me, it was how to lie convincingly.

The perpetual smile that had been on Matteo's face since he arrived disappeared. "No problem."

I hadn't expected to feel any remorse. I turned my feelings off long ago for my own sanity. But sadness and sorrow slid through me. I'd hurt this man's feelings.

I hadn't meant to. Honestly, I rarely considered feelings, since I didn't have any myself. On top of that, I lied. I liked him calling me honey.

I liked it a lot.

And that freaked me out more than a little.

"Potato peelings are the worst," he said. "That's why I'm using them to show you this. Plus, then you'll have some potatoes to make for dinner tonight."

"I don't eat potatoes," I said, again flatly.

"Okay... Then I'll have some potatoes for *my* dinner tonight."

I was being so damned rude. I couldn't help it, and I hated myself for it. I liked this man. I was attracted to this man.

I'd come here to disappear. To be alone. Matteo Rossi made me want to *not* be alone.

I opened my mouth to speak but nothing came out. I could say so many things.

It's not that I don't like potatoes, but they're so starchy that I never eat them.

But then he would ask why, and I would have to tell him I was a model on a strict diet.

I'm allergic to potatoes.

Yeah, he'd believe that. I was a very convincing liar. But I'd never heard of anyone having a potato allergy before. Peanut butter? Strawberries? Mushrooms? Yeah, but never potatoes.

I was attacked by a potato as a young girl.

Right. I was a convincing liar, but that was just too much.

"Thank you for bringing me the supplies."

"I guess I'll just take the potatoes home with me," he said.

"It's okay," I said. "This is my vacation. I think I'll throw caution to the wind and eat a potato."

His lips quivered. Just a touch, but I noticed. He wanted to smile. And the fact that I had made him want to smile made me very happy. Very happy indeed.

"Go ahead," I said. "I know you want to."

"Want to what?"

"Smile."

That split his face into a wide grin. "Thank you. I'd say the same, but I haven't actually seen you smile."

Oh, boy. That was harsh. Problem was that it was also correct. Right on the money.

I wasn't a big smiler. Not a lot to smile about in my world, and of course, on the runway, we models were supposed to have that sullen look that top fashion designers found alluring.

Personally, I thought we all looked mad as hell.

Right now, though, I was so tempted to smile. The muscles in my cheeks itched to slide upward.

"Come on, Riley. You can do it."

My God, he had a sexy voice. Low and husky and smooth as silk.

So I did what he asked. I met his ice-blue gaze, and I smiled.

"That wasn't so hard, was it?"

How exactly was I supposed to answer that? It was a yes or no question. If I answered yes, I'd look like a hard-ass who never cracked a smile. If I answered no, I'd look like a silly little flirt.

I took the third option. I didn't reply at all.

Matteo shook his head with a sigh. "You are a tough nut to crack, Riley Mansfield."

He didn't know how right he was.

"I'm really glad you're here," he said.

"Oh?"

"Yeah, I am." He set the potato peeler down and looked me straight in my eyes. "I love this place. In fact, I live in a cabin almost identical to this one. Inherited both from my bachelor uncle who passed away a few years ago."

"I'm sorry," I said.

"It's okay. He lived a good long life. But that's not my point. My point is this place is magical. It helps a person realize what's truly important in life, and for some reason, Riley, I think you need to be here right now."

"That's kind of why I booked this place."

"Is it? Or did you just want to get off the radar for a while?"

"Well, I..." I...what? He was exactly right. I wanted to get off the radar. I wanted to disappear. I didn't really give a damn where I disappeared to, just that I'd be off the radar.

"As I suspected. Something drove you here. Some need to

escape something. That's all fine and well, but you could've escaped to a spa."

"Yeah, I thought about that." Truth.

"What made you choose Montana?"

"My brother, actually. He used to live in a little biker town outside of Helena."

"But he no longer lives there?"

"No, he had to move to New York for...work. He lives in Manhattan now."

"Manhattan... Quite a change from big sky country. I'll bet he misses it."

"He does. He didn't want to leave here."

"Why did he, then? You can always find work wherever you want to be."

"It's a long story." I sighed.

"Well, then, you're in luck, Riley. I love a good long story, and it just so happens I don't have any plans for this evening."

4

MATTEO

She lifted her perfectly sculpted eyebrows. Ms. Riley Mansfield was also from Manhattan. I was sure of it. She had that New Yorker look.

Of course, her reservation in the name of Chloe Mansfield showed a Pittsburgh address, and she said herself she was from Pittsburgh.

I didn't believe her. She had uptight New Yorker written all over her face.

But I'd play along. She was a gorgeous woman, and I *was* free tonight.

"I don't want to bore you," she said.

"You are the least boring person I've met in a while," I said. "And that's the God's honest truth."

That got a smile from her.

"I was right," I said.

"About what?"

"About your gorgeous smile. You should smile more often, Riley."

"There's not a lot to smile about in my world."

"I think you just made my point. You need this place. A week here, and I guarantee you'll be smiling a lot."

A week in my bed and she'd be smiling even more than that, but I wouldn't push. She had an outer shell that was harder than steel from what I could see.

What she didn't know was I was also the town silversmith, and I could melt anything.

"Let me show you how to unclog this damn thing." I opened the cupboard door beneath the sink, reached in, and pulled out the rubber plunger. Then I turned on the faucet and flipped the switch for the garbage disposal. I pushed the potato peelings down the drain.

She gasped. "Be careful! Push too far in and your fingers will be caught in the blades."

"Only if I'm a complete moron."

She bit her lower lip. "It's better to use the dish brush." She grabbed it out of the dish-drying rack and handed it to me.

I held up both my hands. "Haven't lost a finger yet."

"Indulge me, then. Just use the brush, at least while I'm here."

Indulge me. Hell, yeah, I'd like to indulge her. Indulge myself...

But I had to go slow with this one. Very slow.

Like clockwork, the growl of the disposal morphed into a whimper, and the sink began filling up with water clouded by starch from the potato peelings.

"See? Potato peelings always do it, but they're not the only culprits." I grabbed the plunger. "First you have to put the plug in the other side of the sink. It's right there." I pointed.

She grabbed it and placed it in the sink correctly.

"Now you need to place this plunger right over the drain where the clog is and give it three quick snaps. Watch." I plunged three times, and again like clockwork, the drain cleared.

"Looks easy enough, but if I don't eat potatoes..."

"I think you just said you might eat a potato, but it's not just potatoes. I've seen it happen with salad, spinach, carrot peelings. Potatoes are just the worst. The trick is the three quick snaps. Two won't do it. A lot of my renters call me to fix this, so I figured it was best to just show people up front how to do it because the damned thing *will* clog."

"Why not just install a new disposal?"

"Because this one works fine."

"Clogging up every other time you try to use it is not working fine," she said indignantly.

"Okay, then here's reason number two. Installing a new disposal is a big pain in the ass and it will cost me money."

"Then call a plumber to do it."

I couldn't help it. My jaw dropped. I seriously just told her that a new disposal would cost me money, and her suggestion was to hire a plumber? So that I could pay not just for the disposal but also for the installation?

Something wasn't computing between those pretty little ears.

"Uh... Riley, that would cost *more*."

Now *her* jaw dropped. Had she truly not realized what she had suggested? Interesting. I'd just learned something new and useful about Ms. Riley Mansfield.

She had no financial worries. Not a one.

"I'm sorry," she said.

"No need to be sorry. But I won't be paying a plumber when I'm perfectly capable of installing a garbage disposal myself."

"I understand. I'm sorry," she said again.

"Tell you what," I said, deciding to take a plunge. "Come out to dinner with me and we'll call it even."

"D-Dinner?"

"Yeah. You've heard of it. The evening meal?"

She nodded, blushing.

God, she was fucking hot.

"Why would going out to dinner make us even?"

"It's a joke, Riley. I'm using it as an excuse to take you to dinner. We have a few restaurants here in this tiny town, only one of which is any good. I'd like to buy you dinner."

"How can you buy me dinner if—"

"If I can't afford a garbage disposal? I never said I couldn't *afford* a garbage disposal. I said there was no need to replace it when this one works fine with a little nudging. Why waste the bucks when I don't have to?"

She opened her mouth but then closed it.

She did that a lot.

"So...about dinner?" I was nothing if not persistent.

"I don't know..."

"It's a public place. Nothing to be frightened of."

"I'm not frightened."

"Then what's the issue? You got a boyfriend?"

"No."

"Okay, then. It's a dinner invitation, Riley. Dinner. Nothing else."

"You...have a key to this place."

"Because it's my place. Do you really think...?" I shook my head. "You know what? Forget dinner. Forget everything." I turned, my body tense with anger, and walked toward the front door.

"Wait!"

I turned. She stood between the kitchen and living area, her lips parted.

"What is it?" I asked.

"I didn't mean to be rude. I just... I'm not used to strange men being nice to me."

I had to stop my jaw from dropping to the floor. I grinned instead. "I'd hardly call myself strange."

"You know what I mean," she said. "Not strange as in bizarre. Strange as in stranger. I don't know you."

"I knew what you meant. I'm just trying to lighten the mood here."

"Why?"

"Because you definitely need to lighten up, Riley."

5

RILEY

He wasn't wrong.

I'd come here to disappear, not lighten up. Unfortunately, lightening up wasn't in the cards for me. Neither was disappearing, apparently. Matteo Rossi seemed damned determined that I not disappear.

A dinner invitation? Innocent enough. It was a dinner date. Just a dinner date.

Problem was? I was terribly inexperienced at dating.

My father had gotten rid of any suitor who was interested while I was still living at home. Once I left and was out on my own, things hadn't changed much. I might steal a glance with a handsome man every now and then, only to find that same handsome man gone the next time I looked for him.

Even then, I'd never been attracted to a man the way I was attracted to Matteo standing in front of me.

No one knew I was here.

Not even my father.

He'd never know. Finally. He was in his grave, and though he wielded a lot of power, even he couldn't conquer the ultimate foe—death.

"Thank you for the invitation, Mr. Rossi," I said finally. "I'd be delighted to accept."

That gorgeous grin split his face once more. "Awesome. And it's Matt."

I nodded. "Matt."

"Let's go, then," he said.

"I should change into something more suitable."

"You look great."

"For dinner? I can't possibly—"

"You're in Sumter Falls, Riley, not Pittsburgh. You *are* dressed perfectly."

Interesting. I'd never gone to dinner wearing jeans and a T-shirt in New York. I had an image to maintain. I was Riley Wolfe, supermodel, daughter of billionaire Derek Wolfe.

But here I was no one.

Simply Riley.

Riley Mansfield.

Riley Mansfield wasn't a supermodel.

Riley Mansfield lived in Pittsburgh, and I had no idea what she did for a living.

She was...a teacher. Yeah, a teacher. She taught high school business classes. Perfect, I could converse with this mountain man about business on a high school level.

Riley Mansfield taught high school business classes in Pittsburgh.

Riley Mansfield was a nobody from a nobody home in nobody Pittsburgh.

Riley Mansfield's parents had a happy marriage and were living in their nobody home in middle-class Pittsburgh.

Riley Mansfield was a nobody. Invisible. And she liked her life.

The only problem?

Riley Mansfield didn't exist.

But I could pretend. I was good at pretending. For a week, I could be Riley Mansfield, business education teacher from a happy Pittsburgh family.

And maybe, just maybe...I could feel Riley Mansfield's happiness—if only just a little—this week.

"Okay, Matt," I said. "Let's go."

TRUDY'S CAFÉ was a homey little place situated in a large residential home. It had been remodeled inside and housed two separate dining rooms, both tiny.

"Matt, great to see you!" the hostess said. "Your usual table?"

"That'd be great, Trudy."

Okay, this was Trudy. She was a pert little thing, nearly a head shorter than I was, but then, I literally looked down on most women. She had a few silver streaks in her dark hair and wore vintage clothing—a prairie skirt and peasant blouse. Huge silver hoops hung from her ears. In spite of all this, she was striking. Not beautiful in a classic way, but something about her worked.

She led us to a side table right by a window. "Here you go. Menu's on the board as usual. Enjoy."

Matt held my chair out, which surprised me. Sure, I was used to such manners in the big city, but he'd made such a big deal out of this small-town life that I didn't expect such chivalry.

I liked it.

Being a gentleman suited Matteo Rossi. Sure, he was dressed in Levi's, a plaid flannel shirt, and his long hair was an unruly mass of blond waves, but he acted as though he were donning an Armani tux in the finest Manhattan restaurant.

In fact, he looked better to me than the finest dressed male models in New York.

"Trudy's food is the best," Matt said. "Believe it or not, she studied cooking in Paris. But about ten years ago, after a painful divorce, she ended up here and opened up this little café. She does amazing things with the limited stuff we get here. It's become a passion."

"I'm sorry to hear about her divorce."

"She doesn't mind talking about it. It's been ten years, and she's doing great here."

"So...what do you recommend?" I eyed the large chalkboard on the wall which, oddly, appeared to be visible from every table in the place. That must've taken some doing.

"I can't recommend anything."

"Then why are we here?"

"I mean, I can't recommend anything because Trudy never repeats the same menu."

My eyes popped into circles. "Seriously? In ten years she's never repeated a menu?"

"Well, she'll do the same dish, but it's never exactly the same. If that makes any sense."

"So every night is like the chef's special?"

Matt laughed. "I guess you could say that."

Three dishes were available tonight on the menu. Chicken breast with mushroom sauce, roast lamb chops, and pasta with sundried tomatoes and lemon. That was probably my best bet, though pasta was carb city.

"What sounds good?" Matt asked. "I can guarantee you they will all be delicious. I've never had a bad meal here."

I continued perusing the chalkboard. Salad was fresh baby greens with homemade balsamic vinaigrette, and the soup was tomato bisque with wild rice. That sounded interesting. Wild rice was a whole grain—always good for my diet—and tomatoes were high carb but also very nutritious with lycopene and lots of fiber.

I laughed out loud. Why was I worried about my diet? Chloe Riley Mansfield wasn't a model. She was a business ed teacher. Chloe Riley Mansfield didn't burn herself and do coke to deal with her life. Chloe Riley Mansfield hadn't brought any coke with her.

Matt cocked his head at my laughter. "Did I miss a joke?"

"No. Sorry."

"Something must've made you laugh, Riley."

"It was nothing."

"That's a shame, because you have a beautiful-sounding laugh, and your whole face lights up."

Warmth spread through my cheeks and down my neck.

"Why do I get the feeling you don't actually laugh a lot?" Matt said.

"I...don't know."

"Then you *do* laugh a lot?"

"I suppose not."

"Then I'm honored. I was witness to something extraordinary." He smiled.

And oh, was he handsome when he smiled. His teeth were perfect, of course, as was the rest of him. He had dimples on both sides, though the one on the right side was slightly bigger, making for an adorable lopsided effect. His icy blue eyes crinkled at the corners and seemed to speak right to my soul.

The eyes are the mirror of the soul.

One of my modeling instructors had told me that long ago, when I was a young teen just getting started in the business. We had learned to let our eyes do a lot of talking.

You can make anyone think he's the only person in the room with the right look from your eyes.

I seriously doubted that Matteo Rossi had any kind of modeling training, but boy, did he have that eye thing down pat.

"Can I get you two a drink?"

I zapped out of my hypnotic stare at Matt and looked up to see a young server. And by young, I meant very young. So young his voice hadn't totally dropped yet.

"Hey, Troy." Matt looked up. "I'll have a beer. Riley?"

"A...stinger, please."

"Sorry, ma'am, we don't have a full bar here. We have Guinness lager on tap, Stella in bottles, and tonight's wines are a red blend from Paso Robles, and a white Burgundy."

A white Burgundy? That sounded great. "I'll have the Burgundy, please."

After Troy had left, I said, "He can't possibly be old enough to serve alcohol."

"He's not, but we don't stand on ceremony around here. Troy is a good kid and he does good work for Trudy. Nobody here in Sumter Falls is interested in getting him in trouble." He nodded toward a table in the corner. "Including Buster over there. He's the sheriff."

"Interesting. Things are certainly different here than in New...Pittsburgh."

He laughed. "New Pittsburgh?"

"I mean Pittsburgh, of course." *Nice, Riley. You almost blew your cover.*

"Of course you did." Matt's eyes twinkled.

I was going to have to be a lot more careful.

6

MATTEO

S he was definitely hiding something. I wasn't one to pry, but Riley Mansfield had gotten under my skin in the five hours I'd known her.

I mean, *really* gotten under my skin. In an "I really have to fuck her" kind of way.

Not because she was beautiful, though she certainly was the most beautiful woman I'd laid eyes on in a long time. And not so much because she was challenging, although she certainly was.

No, it was something else. Something I couldn't quite put a finger on, but something that drew me in, nonetheless. I wanted to know her secrets. I wanted to heal her heart. She'd given me no indication that her heart had been broken. Hell, I didn't even know what she did for a living. But I knew why she had come here.

She was hiding.

And I wanted to know why.

How this quest for knowledge on my part necessitated a need for me to fuck her, I didn't know. I knew only that I wanted her. I wanted to kiss those full pink lips, suck on those pretty brown nipples—yes, I got a look when she was in the hot tub. I'm human, after all—and I wanted to sink myself into her lush body.

Hell, I could leave it at that. Riley Mansfield wouldn't be the first woman who'd rented my cabin who I'd wanted to fuck.

This one was different, though. I had no doubt. No doubt at all.

Troy came back with our drinks, and I took a long sip of my beer. This was an old house, so Trudy didn't have the biggest kitchen or bar area. She brought in kegs of whatever she could get the best deal on from the liquor distributor in Billings. When the keg ran out, she brought in a new one, and it was always different, but she made sure it was good quality beer. While Guinness was known for their stout, they also made a damned good lager. Trudy probably got a good deal on it. She always offered a bottled beer too. This week it was Stella Artois. What it would be next week? No one knew. Same with the wine. She got cases of decent wine at the best price she could, and when they were gone, she brought in something new.

Riley Mansfield was probably used to a wine list a mile long.

"What is a stinger, anyway?" I asked.

"I'm not quite sure. They taste kind of minty." She laughed. "And they sometimes make me drop my fork."

Another laugh from her. Oddly, I felt as though I'd been given a gift.

I smiled. Riley Mansfield was a true enigma, but I knew one thing.

She and I *would* be going to bed together.

I wanted her that much, and I was prepared to do or say anything to get inside that hot little body. Instinctively, I knew she didn't let just anyone in.

But she would let me in.

I'd make sure of it.

Troy returned to take our orders. I ordered lamb chops, of course. They would come with a potato or grain and a vegetable, whatever Trudy was able to get.

Riley paused a moment. "Is the pasta dish vegan?" she asked.

"Vegan?" Troy said.

"Yeah."

"It's vegetarian."

"I can figure that out by the description. I want to know if it's vegan."

Troy look to me, confused.

"Is there butter in it? Eggs or any other dairy product?" I asked.

"I'll have to check with Trudy," Troy said.

"Never mind," Riley said. "I'm not vegan. I was just wondering. I'll have the pasta. Oh, and a cup of the tomato bisque with wild rice."

"You know," I said, "that sounds really good. I'll have the soup too, Troy."

Troy nodded and left.

"He seriously doesn't know what vegan means?"

"I'm not quite sure myself," I admitted. "I just guessed on the dairy and egg thing."

"Really?"

"We're pretty meat-and-potatoes here in Montana. But Trudy does make one of her offerings vegetarian every night."

"Vegan is kind of vegetarian on steroids. It means no animal products at all, including eggs and dairy. Some vegans even insist on vegan wine."

"Isn't wine vegan by nature? Grapes and all?"

"Most wine is filtered using animal proteins, like egg white. True-blue vegans won't drink it."

"You're not vegan, then?"

"No, I'm not even vegetarian. Though I don't eat a lot of red meat."

"Then why did you ask if the pasta was vegan?"

"Because I care about what I put into my body, Matt. I like to be informed."

"But you ordered the pasta anyway."

"Yeah"—she looked down at her lap for a second and then met my gaze—"I figured I'm on vacation—just a high school business ed teacher on vacation. So what the hell?"

I raised my beer mug. "I will definitely drink to that."

I didn't get another laugh out of Riley, but I did get a gorgeous smile. She picked up her wine goblet and took a drink.

Troy brought our soup then, and I took a taste. Interesting. The nuttiness of the wild rice added a nice contrast to the sweet and savory of the tomato.

"This is delicious," Riley said after swallowing her first bite.

"Told you I've never had a bad meal here."

"I believe it. I'm excited to try the pasta. Not that I usually eat dessert, but I noticed that there's no dessert listed on her menu."

"Trudy likes to surprise us, but you can get an idea. Just watch the other diners. Someone will have dessert before we get to ours."

"You know? I might just have dessert tonight. A surprise sounds great."

"Surprises are always good." I couldn't help smiling. "Why don't you normally eat dessert?"

"I just don't."

"Honey—" Shit. I'd done so well. "Sorry."

"It's okay. It doesn't bother me so much anymore. What were you going to say?"

"All right then, honey." I chuckled a little. "I was going to say you need to treat yourself more. Dessert is one of the little treats in life."

"What about everything in moderation?"

"*Not* eating dessert isn't moderation, Riley."

She smiled and took another sip of her wine. "I suppose you're right."

"Hey"—I nodded toward the table next to us—"Troy just brought dessert to that table, and it looks chocolate and completely menacing."

She glanced over. "Oh my God. It's cake or pie or something, and it's nearly a foot tall."

"If it's too much for you, we can share one."

"All right." Then she glanced away from me and concentrated on her soup once more.

I wasn't sure I'd make it to dessert.

"I SO OVERDID IT TONIGHT," Riley said when I walked her to the door of the cabin.

"You took about two bites of our dessert. I'd say *I'm* the one who overdid it."

"Well"—she looked at her feet—"thank you for dinner. You didn't have to pay."

"I guess I'm a little old-fashioned," I said. "I invited you, so of course I paid."

"It was very kind of you. I...enjoyed myself."

"Glad to hear that, Riley, because I definitely enjoyed myself."

I touched her cheek, and though she winced a little, she didn't pull away. Her skin was so soft, like the finest silk.

"Why are you afraid of me?" I asked.

"I'm not afraid."

"Let me come in."

"I... I can't."

"Please." I leaned in and brushed my lips lightly against hers. God, already I was hard as marble.

"Matt, you seem like a really nice man, but I'm just not—"

I couldn't help myself.

I slammed my lips down on hers.

7

RILEY

He was kissing me. This gorgeous man was kissing me, running his tongue along the seam of my lips, coaxing them open.

I'd kissed before. This was nothing new.

What was new was that I actually *wanted* to kiss this man.

And that scared the shit out of me.

What would a kiss be like with someone I actually wanted to kiss? I could find out easily. I could simply part my lips and let him in.

He was so big, so strong, and though my feelings frightened me, I wasn't frightened of *him*.

I should have been. He could overpower me at any moment. He could take what another had taken so many times without my permission.

Yet I knew, somewhere deep inside myself, that he wouldn't do that. Matteo Rossi would not take anything I didn't give to him willingly.

What would it hurt to let him kiss me?

I relaxed my lips and parted them.

His groan vibrated through me when his tongue swept over

mine. My arms drifted upward, seemingly of their own accord, and found a resting place on his hard, broad shoulders. He was warm, so warm. I grasped his muscles. Then I moved one hand higher, let my fingers scrape across the blond stubble on his cheek. All the time he was kissing me, our lips sliding together, our tongues probing each other. And what a kiss it was. I wasn't recoiling in repulsion. No, anything but.

I wanted this kiss. I wanted this man.

In a way I'd never wanted anything in my life.

No!

Quickly I pushed at his shoulders, breaking the kiss with a pop of suction.

His blue eyes widened, and a look of sadness streaked across his handsome face. His full lips were pink and puffy from the kiss.

From *our* kiss.

My fingers slid to my mouth. I could still feel his phantom lips on mine. His strong hands on my cheek, caressing me.

"Look, Riley..."

"You don't have to apologize," I said.

"I wasn't going to."

"Oh." I wasn't sure why I thought he was going there. No man had ever apologized for kissing me. Why would Matteo Rossi?

"I don't think it's any secret that I'm very attracted to you," he said. "Are you attracted to me?"

Yes. No. Yes. No.

Yes, I'm attracted to you. But no, I don't want to be.

I didn't say any of this. Instead, I stood there like an idiot.

"What are you hiding, Riley?"

My mouth dropped open. Where had that come from? "I'm not hiding anything."

"Bullshit."

"Who do you think you are?"

"I think I'm a guy who would like to get to know you better. I think I'm a guy who is attracted to you. I'm talking majorly attracted, Riley. Surely you know what a beautiful woman you are."

Hell, yeah, I knew. I'd been beautiful my whole life. Most people probably thought I was lucky. Personally? I considered it a curse.

Riley Wolfe, supermodel. *Riley Wolfe brings back the days of Cindy Crawford and Naomi Campbell.* Yeah, that had been a headline. A headline I'd been forced to live up to.

Apparently I was good at modeling. Modeling took more than just a pretty face and a hot body. Yeah, I worked hard, but I was also a natural, according to all the experts.

I didn't say any of this to Matt. To Matt, I was Riley Mansfield, business ed teacher. And he was Matt Rossi, small-town guy who owned a few cabins and...was the most beautiful man —both inside and out—I'd ever met in my life.

"Sure," I said. "I've been called beautiful a few times."

"A few times?" He shook his head.

"Yeah? Well, you're the hottest thing walking around here as far as I've seen."

He smiled. "So you *are* attracted to me."

"I'm breathing, aren't I?"

That got a laugh out of him. "I suppose I could say the same thing. I'd bet no man on earth could resist you."

If he only knew how right he was...

There was no good answer to that, so I stayed silent.

"May I come in?"

"That's not a good idea." Even though I wanted it more than anything in the world.

"Why not?"

"I'm just not ready."

"Your kiss said differently."

He wasn't wrong. I had definitely kissed him back, and I'd enjoyed every second of it. But I had a harsh history as far as sex was concerned, and he deserved better. He deserved a whole woman. I was so far from that. I wasn't sure I could ever be wholly healed. But my father was dead now, and I was going to try. No more drugs. No more burns. Even if it killed me.

"I loved the kiss," I said truthfully.

"I'd love to give you another, then."

"Matt..."

"I have no idea what you're running from, but whoever hurt you? I'd like to fucking pummel him into the ground."

I shook my head and let out a light chuckle. "He's dead."

"Good. Saves me the trouble."

"You're a really nice guy, Matt. And I'm a fucking mess."

"You look pretty good from where I'm standing."

"If you could see inside my head, you'd rethink that statement."

"Hell, honey, we all have shit inside our heads. God knows I do."

"I'm sorry."

"Don't be. I'm okay. I'm happy here. I don't let the past control me."

Did he truly have a past? A past as horrific as mine? He couldn't possibly. "Then you're stronger than I am."

"Strength isn't really the issue. Perseverance is. It's the journey."

I sighed. "What if I'm tired of my journey? What if I'm just too fucking tired to persevere?"

"I think that's why you're here," he said. "You're running. You're hiding. And that's okay. It's okay for a week. It's even okay for two weeks, three weeks, a whole year. But eventually you won't be able to run any longer."

"I can run for a long time, Matt. I'm in great shape."

"I can see that, but you know as well as I do that I was speaking metaphorically."

I couldn't help a smile. "Yeah, I know."

"What are you running from, Riley?"

"A ghost," I said. "The phantom that I fear will haunt me forever."

"I understand, maybe even better than you think I do. Funny thing about ghosts, though. They can be exorcised."

8

MATTEO

"Can they?" she asked, her voice adorably childlike. "Can they truly?"

"They can. You'll still have the memories. Believe me, no one knows that better than I do. But you can come to think of them as another lifetime, one that was part of your journey but has no bearing on it now."

She let out a soft scoff. "I wish I believed that."

"You don't have to believe it. Not yet, anyway. Things take time, but the beauty of that is, you're young and you have all the time in the world."

She backed up then, settling against the wooden door. Then she met my gaze. "You seem so...together. So much more together than I could ever hope to be."

"Together is an illusion. No one is fully together, not even Dr. Phil himself. You can bet on that."

"That's old news. I've lived my life by faking it until I make it. I don't want to do that anymore. I can't."

"Fake it till you make it is bad advice," I said. "If no one knows you're struggling, no one will help you, and that can lead to horrible things."

I knew that better than most, for reasons I tried not to think about.

Shit. That was a boner killer.

Maybe tonight wasn't the night.

I brushed my lips over Riley's in a soft kiss. "Good night, honey."

She lifted her eyebrows. "You're leaving?"

"Yeah. You said you're not ready for anything more, and I respect that. I can't say I'm not disappointed, but I do understand. I'm here, at least for the next week while you're here. If you need some help chasing away the demons, I'm pretty good at that."

"I'm not ready, Matt. But I also don't want to be alone tonight."

"You came here to a tiny town where you don't know anyone. You came here to be *alone*, Riley."

She smiled shyly. "I did, but then I met you."

This time I lifted my eyebrows.

"I'm not anywhere near ready for anything, but I can't deny how attracted I am to you. And honestly, it's not just because you're gorgeous to look at. I think you're one of the good guys, Matt, and for a while, I was wondering if good guys still existed."

I kept my smile from splitting my face. This was serious, and I wanted to give her the respect she deserved. "Honey, good guys still exist. In fact, there are a shitload more of us than there are bad guys."

She sighed. "Not in my world."

"Then I think you need to find a different world."

"Like this one?"

"Not necessarily. You don't have to pack up and move. You just need to—"

She moved forward quickly and kissed my cheek, rendering me speechless.

"What if I want to? What if I want to pack up and move? What if I never want to go back there again?"

"Are you married?"

"Of course not! I would've told you if I were."

"Any kids?"

"Again, I would've told you."

"Then why can't you pack up and move?"

"I have a..."

"Job?"

"Yeah. A job."

"Quit. Without anyone depending on you and your paycheck except yourself, you can do whatever you want. Pack up, move, and find a new job."

She dropped her gaze to her feet. Yeah, definitely hiding something.

I tipped her chin upward, forcing her to look into my eyes. "Look, Riley. I get it. I do. There are times when I don't want to be alone either. And there's nothing more I'd love than to come inside and make love to you until the sun comes up, but that won't solve either of our problems."

Well, it would solve one of mine—the hard-on that had returned as soon as she kissed me.

She wrinkled her forehead. "You have problems?"

Had she not just heard me say I understood? I couldn't help it. I guffawed. "Honey, everyone has problems."

"I know. That made me sound really self-centered and privileged, didn't it?"

"Yeah. It did."

"I'm sorry. That was rude."

"It was."

I didn't mind, though. She'd just given me a big clue into what she was hiding from. Something really bad had happened to Riley Mansfield. Something really, *really* bad. And I'd also bet she wasn't a teacher from Pittsburgh. She'd used the word privileged to describe herself, and a teacher, who was most likely underpaid and notoriously *not* privileged, wouldn't have used such a word.

Who the hell was she? And what the hell had happened to her?

Walk away, Matt.

Good advice. Advice I'd taken from myself before. The last thing I needed was drama. I enjoyed my life and kept it as drama-free as possible.

Riley Mansfield? She would lead to drama. Big time.

Walk away. Do it. Walk the fuck away.

But my feet didn't move.

"I'm sorry," she said again.

"I accept your apology. Good night." I kissed her cheek lightly.

She nodded. "Will I see you tomorrow?"

"If you want to."

She smiled. My God, she was gorgeous.

"I definitely want to. Goodnight."

LUCAS, one of my best buddies and the late-night bartender at the Stein Saloon across the street from Trudy's, set a beer in front of me. "Who is she?"

I took a long draught of the beer. "Who's who?"

"The looker everyone's talking about. The girl you took to Trudy's tonight for dinner."

"She rented my cabin for a week. Her name's Riley. Riley Mansfield."

"And you took her to dinner? Since when do you take your renters to dinner?"

I laughed. "Since they started looking like her."

"Funny. When you get a good-looking renter, you don't usually take her out to dinner. You usually eat in and then take her to bed."

I couldn't fault his observation. Frankly, I probably could be making love to Riley Mansfield at the moment. She'd made it pretty clear she didn't want to be alone, and I knew exactly how to handle a needy woman, including one with a past. Hell, I'd done it before.

But Riley was different. I wasn't sure Riley was even Riley. Or rather, I wasn't sure she was Chloe. Perhaps Riley *was* her real name, and she'd given it to me by mistake.

"Maybe she turned me down."

That got a good guffaw out of Lucas. "That's great. Means there's hope for the rest of us."

"There's a story there," I said. "I just couldn't do it, Luke."

"There's another first."

I polished off my beer. "I'm out of here. See you tomorrow."

"Bright and early!"

I nodded and left the bar. Lucas and I had agreed to repair the fence over at Molly Carson's house. Molly was an elderly widow, and everyone in town helped take care of her.

Good hard labor was good for the head. I was looking forward to this project.

I had left my truck at my cabin after I said goodnight to Riley and walked into town for my nightcap. Now I walked home, enjoying the starry night, the half-mile to my cabin. In the distance, light shone from the windows in Riley's cabin. Temptation coiled through me. I could walk over there. I could knock on the door just to see how she was. Under the pretense that I was concerned.

Except it wouldn't be a pretense. I *was* concerned.

No. Don't do it, Matt. Give her the space she needs.

Damned good advice.
I started walking anyway.

9

RILEY

I thrashed in bed.

Images. Haunting voices. They all invaded my mind. I could deal with them. I had dealt with them for decades.

But since my father's death, the numbness had somehow dissipated. All those years, I'd forced my body to stop feeling, but now...?

Somehow, with his death, my body had awakened. Everything I had tamped down, everything I had forced to the very innermost crevices of my soul...

Now it was here.

He was inside me. Doing things inside my body. Things no father should do to a child. Things no man should do to a woman without explicit permission.

Those things...

Those abhorrent and horrific things.

His death shouldn't have made it worse. Indeed, I had rejoiced when I heard. Of course, that was before I'd been implicated.

I didn't kill him. I didn't kill the bastard, but if I was going to get blamed for it anyway?

I wished I'd been the one to pull the fucking trigger.

I wished it with everything inside me.

Why? Why could I still feel him inside me?

Why did—

I jerked at the sound of a knock on the door.

It was after midnight. Who would be knocking at my door after midnight? This was a small town, but small towns could have derelicts too.

I hadn't turned out the light, though. I always slept with a light on. I had since I was six years old.

Who knew I was here? No one but Matt.

It was Matt. It had to be.

I raced to the door clad in a tank top and pajama pants. Equally excited and frightened about opening the door.

I opened it anyway. Funny, I never opened the door not knowing who was on the other side in Manhattan or anywhere else. But I knew it was Matt, and I was right.

He stood under the porch light, looking just as delectable as he had when he bid me goodnight two hours earlier.

"Hey," he said.

"What are you doing here?"

"I saw the light in the bedroom on. Just wanted to make sure you were okay."

I swallowed. "I'm fine."

Except that I wasn't.

"Good. I'm glad." He smiled. "I'll be on my way, then."

Let him go. Just let him go. Don't drag him into your black world.

"Wait."

He lifted his eyebrows.

"Don't go. Come in. Please."

"Are you sure?"

"I'm asking you to come in, Matt. I'm not asking you to take me to bed."

"In that case, I'll be going." He smiled again.

"Seriously? You're really a big piece of—"

"Calm down. I'm kidding. My God, you big-city girls don't know how to take a joke."

"I can take a joke just fine. But jokes are usually funny."

He clasped his hands to his heart. "I'm not funny?"

"Just get your butt in here." I held the door open.

He entered, and I closed the door and clicked the deadbolt lock.

"I don't have anything to offer you accept water."

"Not true. There should be flavored seltzer in the fridge."

"Oh? Honestly, I haven't looked."

He walked to the kitchen, opened the refrigerator, and helped himself to a can. "You want one?"

"No thanks. I'm actually drinking water out of the tap. I never do that at home, but this is delicious. It's so fresh and cold."

"Sourced straight from the Rockies. Doesn't get much fresher than that."

"Then why do you drink that crap out of the can?"

"Because I like the crap out of the can. I like my water sparkling. Always have."

I shook my head. "You're something. That's for sure."

"I'll take that as a compliment." He took a drink of the seltzer.

Now what? Part of me wanted to throw caution to the wind and kiss him again, see what happened.

But I had so many demons. Was it fair to him to drag him into it? If only I could escape the demons, just for this week while I was here at his cabin.

If only...

How well I knew those two words. *If only...*

But my life was what it was. No "if only" could change it now.

"I don't have anything to offer you to eat. Unless you laid in supplies I don't know about."

"You have some snacks and some produce in the fridge, but I'm not hungry, thanks." He took another drink.

"Tell me," I said. "What should I do tomorrow? Tell me what to do in a small town."

"Honey, there's not a lot to do in a small town. Which is, I have a feeling, why you came here in the first place."

He wasn't wrong. "You're right, but sitting around alone in a cabin all by myself with my thoughts doesn't sound too great right now."

"Sounds pretty good to me," he said.

"Yeah, well, you don't have my thoughts."

"True. I only have my own." He set the seltzer down on the counter and looked me straight in my eyes. "Penny for yours."

If he only knew. "You'll need to pay way more than a penny for mine."

"Oh?"

"I only mean that… It's a mess in there. In my head, I mean."

"I doubt that."

"You'd be wrong." I picked up his can of seltzer and took a drink, wincing. "Ugh. How can you drink this crap?"

"It's a developed taste. Not everyone likes the bubbles."

"I don't mind the bubbles. I sure love a good champagne. Real champagne, I mean, from the Champagne region in France."

"You're not really a teacher, are you?"

My cheeks warmed. "Of course I am. Why would you doubt me?"

"I'd say most teachers don't drink a lot of champagne. Real champagne, that is, from the Champagne region in France."

"Why wouldn't they?"

"Honey, you exude champagne taste. Most teachers are most assuredly on a beer budget."

He was on to me. Not that I was overly surprised. I really didn't know how to put on an act. Why hadn't I said I was some kind of Hershey heiress from Pittsburgh? He might've believed that. Yeah, I'd had everything I could possibly want provided for me since day one.

I'd also had to deal with a lot of shit I didn't want. Shit I'd gladly live on a teacher's salary to be rid of.

"My parents are well-off," I said. "They're both lawyers, and they like champagne. I grew up with it, and even though I can't afford to buy the really good stuff myself, I still can drink it at their place."

The lie tasted bitter on my lips. I wasn't sure why, but I really didn't want to lie to Matteo Rossi. I felt transparent around him, as if he could see right through to my soul. I both liked and disliked the feeling.

"Oh." He nodded. "I guess that makes sense."

Good. Either he bought it, or he didn't and was going to let me think he did. I was fine either way. Just for a week I wanted to be no one.

He polished off the can of seltzer. "You sure you're okay here?"

"Yeah." Though I didn't sound too convincing. Even I wasn't buying it.

"I should go, then. I've got an early job in the morning."

"What do you do, anyway?" I asked.

"I do pretty well renting out this cabin," he said. "You know, people like you wanting to escape to a small town. I'm booked almost every week. I'm also the town silversmith."

Her brows lifted. "Oh?"

"Yup. Though it's more of a hobby. There's not a lot of call for fine jewelry here in Sumter Falls. Other than that, construction when it's available, and the occasional odd job around town. That's what I'll be doing tomorrow morning. My friend Lucas and I are helping out an elderly widow in town. She needs her fence repaired."

"That's nice of you."

"We all help each other around here. It's the small-town way."

I smiled. I couldn't help it. The crowds walking the streets of Manhattan didn't even want to look at each other, let alone help each other. I had a sudden inspiration.

"Do you need any help?"

"Lucas and I have it under control. Besides, it's hard work, Riley."

"Maybe I want to experience hard work."

He laughed. "Most teachers I know say there's no harder job."

Nice, Riley. You screwed that up. Truth be told, modeling was hard work as well. I was no stranger to hard work. But I *was* a stranger to pure manual labor, and for some reason, it sounded compelling to me.

"Teaching is very difficult. I won't deny it. Very challenging and rewarding, but I think I'd like to get outdoors and pound on things."

He laughed again. "Pound on things, huh?"

Oh, he had no idea. Pounding on things sounded like nirvana at the moment.

"Yes."

"You got it, then. I'll be by to get you at six sharp."

"Six in the morning?"

"You got it. Or have you changed your mind?"

I could easily get out of it. This was my vacation, after all. But damn, I wanted to spend time with Matt, and I desperately wanted to pound things. Like...*desperately*.

"I'll be ready."

"Perfect. Wear jeans and the toughest shoes you've got. Steel-toed would be best."

Steel-toed? Clearly my flip-flops weren't going to cut it. I did happen to bring a pair of old cowboy boots, though. They weren't overly fashionable in New York, but I loved them. I'd bought them on a whim during one of my princess trips with my father in Texas.

Despite the memories they brought to the surface, I never got rid of them. I always thought they might come in handy someday.

And tomorrow, they would.

10

MATTEO

How anyone looked so gorgeous at six in the morning was beyond me, but man, Riley Mansfield sure did. Surprisingly, she seemed to be dressed appropriately, except for a tank top, which wouldn't do. Luckily I had some old flannels in my truck. She could wear one of those over her tank. What surprised me most was her footwear. She was wearing cowboy boots—really broken-in cowboy boots. Surprising.

"Did you get anything to eat this morning?" I asked, once she had seated herself in the passenger side of my truck.

"Are you kidding? I barely rolled out of bed in time."

"Not a problem. Mrs. Carson always has breakfast burritos for us."

"I'm not sure if I've ever had a breakfast burrito."

"Then you're in for a treat. Hers are the best. Her mother came from Mexico. Mrs. Carson makes the best Mexican food you'll ever eat."

"Oh? I don't eat much Mexican food. Too much fat and carbs."

"You'll be wanting fat and carbs today, honey. You're going to be working hard. Pure physical labor."

"That's what I'm hoping," she said.

I laughed. Oh, she was definitely running from something. Running fast and far enough that she wanted to get up at six in the morning to help fix a fence. Her manicured nails sparkled in the early morning sunlight. I'd bet she'd never held a hammer in her life.

She would soon.

Lucas's truck was already in Mrs. Carson's driveway when we arrived. I pulled in and hopped out of the driver seat. I began to walk around the truck to help Riley out, but she jumped out on her own. She followed me up the walkway to the door of the house.

Before I could knock, Lucas opened the door, holding a burrito. "Hey, Matt." Then his eyes nearly popped out of his head. "Who's this?"

He knew damned well who she was. He'd seen me dining with Riley last night. Still, they hadn't been formally introduced.

"Riley Mansfield, Lucas Connors."

Lucas swallowed his bite of burrito and held out his hand. "My pleasure."

Riley took his hand. "Nice to meet you." When she took her hand away, she rubbed her fingers together.

I couldn't help a chuckle. Lucas probably had burrito hands.

"Come on in, you two. Mrs. C's got burritos ready and hot coffee."

"Just coffee for me," Riley said. "Very strong and very black."

I laughed again and then said quietly, "Mrs. Carson's coffee is more like light brown water. We can go into town and get you a decent cup if you want."

"Oh. No, that's okay. I'll just have some water."

"And a burrito," I said.

"Tortillas are pure gluten," she said.

"Tortillas are pure carbs, which are pure energy," I said, "and trust me, you're going to want pure energy this morning."

She gave me a semi-smile along with a sigh. "All right. I'll try one. I changed my mind on the water, though. I need some caffeine."

"Afraid you won't find that here. Tell you what. Luke, tell Mrs. Carson we'll be back in a jiffy. I'm going to take Riley into town to get her a decent cup of coffee at the Bean House."

"I'm not telling her that you can't stand her coffee."

"Shit. You're right. Yeah, don't tell her that. Just say Riley only drinks decaf or something."

"Her coffee's as good as decaf, and you know it."

"For God's sake, Luke, make something up. We'll be back in a few minutes."

Riley turned to me. "You don't need to go to all this trouble on my account."

"Coffee shop's a block away, honey. I'm telling you, it's no trouble at all. JoJo at the Bean House opens up at five for those of us in a small town who need some coffee."

"Okay, thanks." She smiled.

And when Riley Mansfield smiled, I felt like I could give her anything in the world. Way more than just a cup of decent coffee. She was that fucking beautiful.

Our quick detour to the coffee shop took no more than fifteen minutes. After we exchanged pleasantries with JoJo and I introduced her to Riley, she poured us each a cup.

"Just hot enough," JoJo said. "I've got this down to a science regarding temperature and brewing. You won't burn your tongue on my coffee."

Riley took a sip, and a dreamy smile split her face. "Now *this* is fabulous."

"Thank you kindly," JoJo said. "You come around anytime

while you're here. Coffee's always on from five in the morning to five at night."

"I'll definitely do that," Riley said. "Thank you."

We hopped back in the truck and rode back to the widow Carson's place. Luke had already finished his burrito and was out measuring the area we needed to repair. "Looks like we're going to need about sixty pickets," he said when Riley and I got out of the truck.

"I've got about thirty in my backend," I said. "We can head over to Jeb's to get the rest."

"One of these posts is going to need to be replaced as well," Lucas said. "It's rotted right here where it meets the cement."

I walked toward him took a look. Shit. He was right. That meant digging out the cement and replacing it, along with a new post. More work than I had in mind for today. "You got any concrete mix?"

"I do," he said, "but I didn't bring it."

"We can go ahead and replace the pickets on this other area here." I gestured. "Let's get that done, and then we'll deal with the post in the concrete." I looked at Riley. "You ever hammer a picket onto a fence rail before?" I smiled. I knew damned well what the answer would be.

She shook her head. "Not even once."

"It's pretty easy. You don't have to worry about lining them up so much on the top. I'll saw them off when were done so they're even."

"But don't they have to be even on the bottom?" she asked.

"As best as you can get it. The ground isn't particularly even, though. We just need to make sure Reggie and Mary can't get out."

"Who are Reggie and Mary?"

"They're Mrs. Carson's dogs."

"Oh? I didn't see any dogs in the house."

"They're probably out back in their dog run. You want to meet them?"

"I've never had a dog..." Her voice trailed off a little, as if she were wistful.

"Reggie and Mary are really friendly. You'll like them."

"Yeah, I think I would like to meet them."

"Not a problem." I nodded to Lucas. "We're going to go say hi to the dogs. Back in a minute."

He scoffed jovially. "Sure. Leave me to do all the work."

I grabbed Riley's hand—a spark jolted through me at the contact—and led her around Mrs. Carson's small ranch home and into the backyard. Sure enough, Reggie and Mary were in the dog run. Reggie wagged his tail and put his forepaws up on the fence as soon as he saw us coming. Mary was drinking some water.

Riley smiled. "They're so big! What kind of dogs are they?"

"I don't have a clue. They're rescues from a litter someone found in an old barn a couple years ago. If I had to wager a guess, I'd say a mix of German Shepherd and pit bull."

Riley stepped back a little. "Aren't pit bulls supposed to be dangerous?"

"Those two look dangerous to you? You won't meet two friendlier pups. Besides, pit bulls can be really sweet. They have to be trained to be assholes. Kind of like people."

"They are really pretty, aren't they?"

"They are. I had one of their brothers for a while."

"Oh?"

I still smarted when I thought of Herbie. "He got sick. Cancer. There wasn't anything the vet could do."

"I'm so sorry. How old was he?"

"Only two."

"I'm sorry," she said again. "Did you get another dog?"

"Nope. I will eventually. This only happened less than a year ago."

"So these guys are about three?"

"Yep. Gorgeous, aren't they? If you can believe it, Herbie was even prettier."

Riley eased gently toward the chain-link fence. Reggie bobbed his brown and black brindled head, his tongue hanging out.

"It almost looks like he's smiling," she said.

"Technically, dogs don't have the muscles to smile, but I agree. He looks darned happy, doesn't he?"

"Is it okay if I pet him?"

"Why do you think he's standing there wagging his tail? Of course you should pet him." I opened the gate. Reggie and Mary came running out.

"Down there," I said, keeping them from jumping on Riley. "They're both friendly, wouldn't hurt a soul."

She smiled as she timidly touched Reggie's soft head. "It feels like velvet."

"Herbie's head felt just like that. Mary's fur is a little more coarse." I gave the female dog a pat on the head.

Riley laughed. "I think they like me."

"Of course they do. They've never met anyone they didn't like."

"I've never had a dog," she said again. "I guess I never really thought I was an animal person. But if they like me, maybe I am."

Reggie and Mary liked everyone, but I didn't want to rain on Riley's parade. "I think maybe you are. You should get a dog when you go home."

"You know? I just might."

"We shouldn't keep Lucas waiting any longer." I wrestled the dogs back into their pen and shut the gate. "We can spend some more time with them once the fence is fixed."

"I'd like that." She smiled.

She looked happy. Genuinely happy. She might be running from something, hiding out in a small town, but a couple rescue pups had put a huge smile on her face.

At that moment, I thought I might do anything to keep that smile on her face forever.

11

RILEY

Matt showed me how to start a nail in the picket, place the picket so it was level and plumb—and I learned what plumb meant—and he demonstrated how to nail it to the two-by-four cross support boards that he and Lucas repaired.

Then he handed me the hammer.

It was heavier than I expected, but then I'd never held a hammer before.

"Watch your fingers, honey," he said. "If you hit one, you'll probably lose a nail. Oh...and it'll hurt like a mother."

My fingers were the least of my worries. Right now I wanted to pound that nail in good and hard.

Wham!

That one went through one of my dead father's eyes.

Wham!

I took out his other eye.

Wham!

His nose, that time.

Wham!

His mouth—that surly smile that meant one thing. He wanted...

Wham! Wham! Wham!

Each one gouged my father's body until it was a bloody fucking mess. All those years, I'd imagined his demise and how I could make it happen.

Now? Someone else had done it and I'd been implicated anyway.

Motherfucker.

More accurate—daughterfucker.

Such a complete sicko.

Wham! Wham! Wham!

There weren't enough nails in Matt's truck to do all the damage I wanted to do.

"Easy." He eased the hammer out of my hand. "That one's in, Riley. Time to start another."

I grabbed the tool back. "I'm done when I say I'm done."

"Hey." He cupped both my cheeks and looked into my eyes. "We've got plenty of pickets. Once the head of the nail is all that's visible, you're done. Okay?"

I nodded.

Fine. I'd hammered that one into my father's skull.

Time to start again.

~

BY NOON, we were done. And boy, was I beat. But wow, it felt good to pound those nails with a hammer. My father's corpse was full of a thousand holes.

A job well done.

"Mrs. Carson usually gives us lunch," Matt said, "but if you'd rather, we can go into town. I know how you feel about carbs and fat."

"Believe it or not, I'm starving," I said.

"Of course you are. You just worked your cute little butt off for five and a half hours."

"We should probably stay. I don't want to hurt Mrs. Carson's feelings."

"Carnitas and cheese enchiladas," Matt said. "That's what she always fixes for Lucas and me."

"What are carnitas?"

"Slow-cooked pork with onions and spices. It's to die for."

Pork, huh? I never ate pork. Beef and poultry only on occasion. I existed on fish and seafood, vegetables and brown rice. I wasn't sure what pork would do to my stomach. But I didn't want to be rude. Maybe if I just took a small portion.

"Does she serve any vegetables or anything?"

"Usually some rice."

Okay, I could work with that. A very small portion of pork and a big plate of rice.

I followed Matt to the doorway and entered the small house. My mouth watered when I inhaled. Something smelled utterly delicious. This wasn't any kind of pork I'd ever smelled.

"Come on into the kitchen," Mrs. Carson called.

At least I assumed it was Mrs. Carson. I hadn't actually seen her yet.

"Mrs. C," Matt said, "this is Riley Mansfield. She's renting my place for the week, and she helped us out today."

"Oh, my." Mrs. Carson trotted up to me. She was a spry old woman, and she reached up and patted my cheeks. "You sure are pretty."

"Thank you," I said.

"Mattie, this one might be a keeper."

Matt blushed. Seriously, he actually blushed. I held back a laugh.

"She's only here for a week, Mrs. C," Lucas offered.

Fredricka, blew a gasket whenever I put on so much as an ounce.

A sliver of guilt slid through me. In two days, I was supposed to fly to Paris for Dominique Cosmetics. I'd be calling Fredricka to have her smooth things over. She was a whiz with words. So the shoot would be postponed a week or two. I was distraught, after all. My father had just passed away. Not only that. He'd been murdered!

As far as the public knew, I was his little princess. So sad about his demise.

Yeah... I had to call her. I'd do it this afternoon. Right now, I planned to enjoy this delicious-smelling lunch.

And yeah, Fredricka, I'm going to gain a few pounds this week.

After all, I'm dealing with my daddy's death!

Ugh. The thoughts were beginning to nauseate me, and I really wanted to enjoy this lunch.

"Everything's set out," Mrs. Carson said. "Can I get you men a beer?"

"You bet," Lucas said.

"And for you, dear?" she asked me.

"I don't drink beer. Just some of the marvelous tap water would be great," I said. "I've never tasted such delicious water."

"We do have the best water. I don't suppose they have such good-tasting water in Pittsburgh."

"I should say they don't."

Not that I would know, but it sounded good. I never drank tap water at home. Always Evian straight out of a bottle. My brother Reid preferred Pellegrino.

The thought of my brother saddened me. They were worried about me, I knew. This wasn't the first time I'd taken off without any notice. Of course, it was the first time I'd taken off on my own and not gone into hiding at my father's request. Request? More like command. My brothers were used to me taking off for no apparent reason. This was on brand for Riley Wolfe.

I sat down at the table with Lucas and Matt, and Mrs. Carson slid a plate heaped full of meaty and cheesy delights in front of me. The initial plan had been to eat a little bit of pork and a big plateful of rice. I held back a chuckle. The rice on my plate was about the size of a golf ball. The rest of the plate was enchiladas and what looked like pot roast made of pork. That must be the carnitas. I couldn't help myself. I inhaled and closed my eyes.

How could anything truly smell this delicious?

A far cry from the nonexistent aroma of grilled tilapia and brown rice.

"Dig in," Mrs. Carson said.

I waited until Lucas and Matt each took a bite, and then I speared a piece of pork on my fork and slowly brought it to my lips.

Oh. My. God.

It was so tender and delicious. I had no idea what kind of spices she had used other than the onions. Probably some chili powder of some sort, maybe a little coriander? I wasn't a big cook, so I truly was only guessing.

"What do you think, dear?" she asked.

"It's delicious," I said after I swallowed. "You should be running a restaurant around here."

Lucas and Matt burst into laughter.

Had I said something funny?

"Everyone says that the first time they eat Mrs. C's goodies," Matt said. "It's like a ritual, you know? Every time I bring someone over here, they say the same thing."

He brought other people over here before? Just friends, maybe?

Or other women?

Did it matter? I'd just met the man, and I was leaving in six days. Still, it pierced my heart just a little. After all, Mrs. Carson had said I might be a keeper. That seemed to imply that Matt had brought other women here.

Why let it bother me? Right now, I was starving, and I had a plate of the most delicious food I'd ever eaten in front of me. I tried a bit of the enchilada next. It was a cheesy, corny, creamy delight topped with a red sauce that I'd thought might be tomato, but it wasn't. It was a mild blend of some kind of peppers.

"The sauce is divine," I said.

"I gave you the mild. The boys here like theirs spicier."

"I love spicy food," I said. "I eat Thai a lot at home."

"Do you want to try the spicy, then?" Mrs. Carson asked.

"Careful, honey," Matt said. "It's not for the meek."

That did it. "Yes, if you don't mind, I'd love to try it."

Mrs. Carson brought over a pot from the stove and spooned some reddish-brown sauce over the edge of my enchilada. "Best try a bite first, dear. It does pack a whopper."

I brought a bite of the newly sauced enchilada to my mouth.

It was delicious indeed. Almost smoky, and yes, very spicy, but I could still taste the flavor, which was remarkable.

I swallowed and cut off another bite with my fork, brought it to my mouth, and—

My jaw dropped. Heat invaded my mouth and throat. I grabbed my glass of water and drank half of it down.

Matt and Lucas were chuckling.

"Not for the meek," Lucas said.

I was certain my throat was on fire.

12

MATTEO

I couldn't help a raucous laugh. "We warned you!"

Riley coughed and sputtered as she downed her water. Mrs. Carson hurriedly brought her a new glass, which she downed as well.

"I'm sorry, honey," Mrs. C said.

"It's...okay," Riley choked out.

"It'll pass," Matt said. "Then you'll realize how good it is."

"It's already good. Delicious, actually. Just really"—she coughed—"hot."

"That's the best part." I smiled. "Mrs. C has it down to a science. Some food is just hot and you can't actually taste the flavor. With Mrs. C's you can."

She nodded and took another drink of water.

"It's best to start slowly," Mrs. C said. "I should have given you a mixture of the mild and hot."

"It's okay." Riley's voice was raspy. "It really is delicious."

"Thank you." Mrs. Carson winked. "I hope Mattie will bring you over again while you're here. When do you leave?"

"In six days," Riley said.

"Such a brief stay. That's not near enough time to get the full Sumter Falls experience. I wish you could stay longer."

"I have to get back to work," Riley said.

Back to work? This was summer. If Riley was a high school business ed teacher...

As I suspected all along.

Riley Mansfield was hiding things.

And I intended to find out what they were.

"I can't thank you boys enough," Mrs. C said to Luke and me.

"Anything for you," Luke said.

"Ditto." I downed the last of my beer and then looked to Riley. "If you've recovered, I'll take you back to the cabin."

She nodded. "I'm good. Thank you for the lunch, Mrs. Carson."

"Thank you for helping the boys, dear."

"It was my pleasure."

She wasn't lying. Riley had truly enjoyed pounding those nails. Talk about getting your frustrations out. Now I just had to figure out *who* she'd been pounding.

We walked outside to my truck.

An idea struck.

I had a little shop in town for my silversmithing. Normally I opened only by appointment, but during the summer, I hired a high school kid to man the store for me. In a small town there just wasn't a lot of demand for silver, but tourists loved it and I did a great business during the summer. Most of the items I crafted for sale were Native American designs, as those sold the best. But I also created my own designs.

Smithing was my passion, though it wasn't my main source of income. I did odd jobs, and my rental brought in a nice cushion as well. I'd grown accustomed to living basically. *Walden* by Henry David Thoreau had become my bible. I tried to spend as much time as I could outdoors and not get bogged down by the small stuff. I had a place to sleep, food in my belly, and a love of life.

My shop was ultimately me.

And I wanted to show it to Riley.

I pulled into the alley behind my little shop.

"I thought you were taking me back to the cabin," Riley said.

"I am, but we're making a detour. I want to show you something."

"Okay."

We got out of the truck and went into the shop via the back door. The kid I'd hired for the summer, Blue—yes, that was actually her name—sat behind the counter texting on her phone. She blew a huge pink bubble and let it pop over her lips.

"Afternoon, Blue. How's business today?"

"Hi, Matt. Not bad. Slow now, but people are still having lunch. I sold two pendants, four pairs of earrings, and a bolo tie this morning."

Earrings were always my biggest seller. "Nice. This is Riley."

"Hey." Blue cracked her gum.

"Hi," Riley said.

"This is my shop," I told her.

She widened her eyes. "Your shop?"

"Did I not tell you I work with silver?"

"You did. I guess I just never realized you actually sold it." Riley swept her hand over the glass encasing the finer jewelry. "This is beautiful work, Matt."

"I'm glad you like it. Pick one. Anything, and it's yours."

"Oh, I couldn't."

"Sure you can."

She zeroed in on a heart pendant with a pink sapphire accent on either side. "You made this?"

"Guilty."

"I can't believe it. That's more beautiful than anything I've ever seen at Tiffany's."

Tiffany's? How many business ed teachers were familiar with the fine jewelry at Tiffany's?

Riley Mansfield, what the hell are you hiding?

"It's yours," I said.

"How much is it?"

None of my finer pieces had price tags. Well, they did, but I made sure they weren't visible in the display case. That way, a person had to ask, and Blue would get it out and look at the price tag. Once the customer held the item, they almost always bought it.

"Doesn't matter," I said.

"It does to me."

"Why?"

"Because I want to pay you for it. That's why."

"But I don't *want* you to pay for it."

Blue unlocked the case from behind the counter and pulled out the piece. "It is gorgeous," she said. "I had a customer look at it this morning but—" Her cheeks reddened.

"It's okay, Blue," I said. "It's an expensive piece. I'm glad the customer didn't buy it, because it's perfect for Riley. Has her name right on it."

Riley blushed adorably. "No, it doesn't."

"Well, not yet, but I'll engrave it and then it will."

"May I look at it?"

I took the piece from Blue, hastily whisked off the tiny price tag, and handed it to Riley.

She fingered the delicate silver chain. "It's so lovely. I could almost swear it was white gold."

"It's rhodium-plated sterling. That's what I use for all my fine pieces. It resists tarnishing, which is why it resembles white gold. Not quite as sparkly, but a good substitute."

"I can't accept it." She handed it back to me. "We hardly know each other."

She was right. It was a generous gift, and we'd only known each other for two days. I gave it to Blue. "Put this in the back."

She nodded, placed the piece in a cotton-lined box, and went into the back where she presumably locked it in the safe.

Riley smiled. "You're keeping it for me?"

"Only until you leave. If you still won't accept it then, I'll put it back for sale."

"You're sweet."

Was it odd that she hadn't asked me what the price was?

Most women would have asked, especially if they'd offered to buy it, which she had.

But then...most women weren't familiar with the expensive pieces at Tiffany's. Most women didn't drink real Champagne from France.

Most women weren't Riley Mansfield.

Money didn't seem to be an issue for Riley. Yes, she'd said her parents had money...

Still, something wasn't adding up.

I was determined.

I'd solve the equation of Riley Mansfield.

And I'd do it in the next several days.

13

RILEY

I'd wanted to accept the pendant.

I'd really wanted to accept it.

But I couldn't.

As much as I wished I were a normal woman who might be able to have a normal relationship with a wonderful man like Matteo Rossi...I wasn't.

I never would be.

Taking the beautiful piece wouldn't have been fair to Matt. I'd certainly be willing to buy it. In fact, I'd wanted to.

It would be a beautiful souvenir of my week here in Sumter Falls, Montana.

"Is everything here one of a kind?" I asked.

"Pretty much," Matt said. "Sometimes someone will ask me to duplicate a piece, and I will, but I always make it just a tiny bit different. Even if I'm the only one who knows."

"Why?"

"Because it's art, honey. Every piece should be unique."

I nodded. "I get it. My brother's an artist."

"Oh? The one who lived here in Montana?"

Crap. First rule of disappearing—don't volunteer too much

information about yourself. "Yes. I only have one brother."

Actually three, but that was way too much information.

"What kind of artist is he?"

"A sculptor."

Rule number two of disappearing—if you inadvertently give away too much information, lie to cover it up. Roy was a painter. His preferred medium was oil on canvas. I doubted he'd ever sculpted anything in his life.

"What does he sculpt?"

Rule number three of disappearing—give only vague responses.

"A little bit of everything."

"What's his name?"

Rule number four of disappearing—never give names.

"He's not well known. It's really just a hobby."

"Yeah, that makes sense, since he had to move to New York for work."

Damn. Had I said that? I cleared my throat. "Yeah."

"I see." Matt gazed into my eyes.

I resisted the urge to look away. Not meeting a gaze was a sign of lying. I knew that. I was good at lying. Except lying to Matteo Rossi. Apparently I was really bad at that.

"Oh," Matt finally said. "Still, he has a name, right?"

"Sure. It's...Michael."

"Michael Mansfield. Maybe I'll google him."

"He doesn't have a website. He's a teacher. Like I am."

"Ah. An art teacher and a business teacher."

"Right."

"But he had to move to New York for work."

What the heck was wrong with me? Major mistake. Why would an art teacher have to move to New York?

"A friend of his from high school recommended him for a job at a private school." Nice save.

"I see," Matt said again. "Did your lawyer parents have a problem with the two of you going into education?"

"No."

"Good." He nodded.

I braced myself, ready to answer more questions. Ready to give out more misinformation.

But Matt didn't ask me anything else about my fake brother.

I was thankful, but surprised. Matt wasn't the type to give up on a quest for information. I'd already learned that in the two days I'd known him.

Blue returned to the counter.

"I guess I'll take you back to the cabin," Matt said.

I nodded, though I was saddened. I didn't want to say goodbye to Matt. I had no idea when I'd see him next, if at all.

"Can we walk around town a little first?" I asked.

"Sure, but I have a job in a couple hours."

"Oh?"

"Yeah. Just some handiwork for another resident. This one pays me." He smiled.

"What do you need to do?"

"Replace a pipe under the sink in her kitchen."

"Don't you have a plumber in town?"

"We do, but he's not always available, so I take the easier jobs."

"Replacing a pipe is an easier job?"

"It's pretty cut and dried, honey, and Leena pays me a hundred bucks for most odd jobs I do for her, so I rarely say no."

"I see." Leena? Sounded like a stripper's name to me.

"But I only need to get to that before six, so I can take a few hours to show you around town. What do you want to see?"

I smiled. "Everything."

He laughed. "Your wish is my command. Where do you want to start?"

"It's your town. What should I see?"

"All right." We walked out of his little shop and turned to view it from the street.

"The Silver Shoppe. Cute name."

"My mom suggested it."

"Oh? I'd love to meet your mom."

"You can't, honey."

"Does she live somewhere else?"

"No. She's dead."

"Oh." God, what an idiot I was. "I'm so sorry."

"It's okay. You didn't know. She died when I was a teen. Her brother—my uncle—raised me after that."

"What about your father?"

He cleared his throat. "Not in the picture."

"I see." Matt didn't know how lucky he was. My mother was a bitch, but my father made her look like a saint. How I wished my father had never been in the picture.

I'd be a lot more whole if he hadn't been.

"My uncle was a great guy. I think I told you I inherited the cabins from him. One gives me shelter and the other provides me with a nice income. All I have to do is pay the property taxes and insurance. And upkeep, of course."

"But you do most of that yourself."

"How did you know that?"

"You told me. You said you'd install a new garbage disposal when the one in the cabin finally died."

He laughed. "That's right. I did. No use paying a plumber for something I can do myself."

"Not to get too personal, but did you work with silver as a teen? Because you said your mom suggested the name for the shop."

He cleared his throat again. "She did, actually. It was always her dream to open up a shop, and that's what she wanted to call it. She taught me everything I know. When I opened my shop, I wanted to pay her homage."

"She was a silversmith too?"

"Yeah. A true artist, but she didn't do it for a business. She had a kid to feed. She waited tables over at the truck stop in the next town. Lousy hours but good tips, so I spent a lot of time with my uncle anyway when Mom wasn't around."

"I'm sure you must miss her."

"Always will." He didn't meet my gaze.

Was it hard for him to talk about his mother? It seemed to be.

"Here's something you'll like." He held the door open to the little shop next to his. "All antiques. Bess has a great eye. Dealers from all over Montana come here to look at her offerings."

I smiled. "I love antiques." I followed Matt into the shop and—

Tripped like an idiot over a step I didn't see.

"Honey, are you all right?"

"Just embarrassed."

Matt pointed to the sign outside the door.

Watch your step.

Nice. Too bad I hadn't bothered to read it.

My purse lay on the floor, and several things had fallen out. Shit. Matt picked up my compact, my change purse, and my pack of cigarettes, stuffed them back into my purse, and handed it to me.

"You smoke?" he asked.

"No. I mean...only sometimes. It relaxes me a little."

"Oh."

As much as I'd learned to be a proficient liar, thanks to Derek Wolfe, I'd never developed a taste for it.

I especially hated lying to Matt. Plus, I was really bad at it.

For some reason, I wanted to be ridiculously truthful with

Matt. Which was a stupid idea, because if he knew every bit of truth about me, he'd go screaming in the other direction.

Who wouldn't?

Half the time I wanted to run away from myself.

Okay, not half the time.

All the time.

"You should quit," he said.

"Trust me. It's not a problem."

Not at all. I never smoked. These cigarettes served a much different purpose.

"Then why do you carry cigarettes around in your purse?"

"What's with the grand inquisition?" I demanded...a little more harshly than I'd meant to.

"I'm sorry. My uncle was a smoker. Lung cancer is what killed him."

"Oh." I felt the size of a pea. "I'm so sorry."

"I'd hate to see the same thing happen to you."

"It won't."

I'd smoked maybe twice in my life, and both times it had made me want to puke.

"Then you won't mind if I take these." He reached into my purse and grabbed the pack.

"As a matter of fact, I do mind." I grabbed them back from him and stuffed them back into my purse. "You're out of line."

"Maybe. But I care too much for you to see you end up like Uncle Roger."

"I told you. I don't even smoke very much. It's not a problem."

He walked me out of the doorway of the antique shop and onto the sidewalk. He gripped my shoulders and turned me to face him. "Riley, what aren't you telling me?"

A loaded question if there ever was one.

What I wasn't telling him could fill volumes.

14

MATTEO

"N-Nothing."

Pretty much what I expected. She'd known me for two days, so she wasn't about to spill her guts. Not yet, anyway.

But I was nothing if not determined.

"All right. I'm sorry I overstepped my bounds. I just hated watching my uncle waste away. He was such a great guy. My hero, actually. He helped me get through..." Nope, wasn't ready to go there. Not with her. Not with anyone. "Everything. My mom's death. You know."

"I understand. It's okay."

But she clutched her purse close to her body, as if that pack of cigarettes inside were a security blanket she wasn't willing to part with.

Fine. Let her smoke herself to death.

Except that her wellbeing was important to me. More important than it should be at this early stage of knowing her.

Yeah, I wanted to get her into bed something fierce, but more than that, I wanted to know everything that made her tick. I wanted to know her favorite color. Her favorite flower. I wanted to know what made her happy and what made her sad.

I wanted to know her, and not just in the biblical sense.

"What's your favorite color?" I asked.

She cocked her head. "Pink. Why?"

"Just wondering. Favorite flower?"

"A rose."

"Let me guess. A pink one?"

"Pink or red, yeah."

"We're taking a detour."

"No antiques today?"

"Later, if there's time. Come on." I grabbed her hand and led her across the street to Kari's Flower Shop.

The bell dinged as I opened the door for Riley and I walked in behind her.

"Hey, Matt." Kari looked up from the magazine she was reading. "What are you up to today?"

"Did some work over at the Carson place this morning, and today I'm showing Riley around our little town. Riley, this is Kari Preston."

"Hi. Nice to meet you," Riley said.

"You too. Are you visiting Matt?"

"No, just renting his cabin."

"Got it."

"I want the most amazing pink rose you have, Kari," I said.

Riley blushed again. God, she was beautiful.

"I have some beauties." Kari walked over to her greenhouse and pulled out a vase full of pink roses. She brought it back to the counter. "Take your pick."

"My lady," I said to Riley.

"You don't have to," she said.

"I want to. Which one do you want?"

She eyed me oddly. A woman like Riley was probably used

to receiving two dozen roses at a time, and I was offering her a single bloom.

While Riley eyed me, Kari was eyeing her.

"You look familiar to me," Kari said. "Have we met before?"

"Not unless you've been to Pittsburgh," Riley said. "This is my first time here."

"Nope, never have. I've never ventured east of the Dakotas, actually. I prefer the openness of the west, you know?"

"It is nice," Riley agreed. "Nothing like...Pittsburgh."

"Still, there's something about you that seems familiar to me."

"Maybe I just have one of those faces."

I let out a laugh. Riley did not have "one of those faces." She was as beautiful and unique as women came.

Both she and Kari turned their gazes on me.

"Why exactly are you laughing?" Kari asked.

"No reason. Have you picked your rose yet?" I nodded to Riley.

Kari smiled. "If Mattie here is offering you a rose, I'd take it. All the girls around here would love to get a rose from him."

Riley blushed once more. "You're the expert," she said to Kari. "You pick one. They're all beautiful to me."

She withdrew a gorgeous dark pink bloom, wrapped it in tissue, and handed it to Riley. "That's two dollars and twenty-three cents," she said to me.

I dug two singles out of my wallet and laid them on the counter and then checked my pocket and pulled out a quarter. "Keep the change." I winked at Kari.

Riley buried her nose in the petals of the rose. "Mmm. I love that fragrance. It's so calming."

"Rose essential oil is a great relaxant," Kari said.

"I know," Riley said. "At home, I rinse my hair in rosewater. Keeps it really soft and silky."

I kept myself from widening my eyes. Rinsing her hair in rosewater? Again, didn't sound like any high school teacher I knew.

"Thanks, Kari." I reached toward the door.

"Anytime. Nice to meet you, Riley." Kari shook her head. "I wish I could figure out why you look so familiar to me."

Riley laughed nervously. "Nice to meet you too."

Once we were back out on the sidewalk, I turned to Riley and smiled. "You are something."

"What do you mean?"

"You're just...a puzzle. A puzzle, Riley Mansfield, and I'd really love to find all the missing pieces."

"Oh? Well, you're kind of a puzzle yourself."

"Me?" I guffawed. "I'm an open book. Ask anyone."

"Are you? Then tell me about your mother."

Wow.

That had come right out of left field and hit me right in the temple.

I didn't talk about my mother.

I didn't have to. Everyone in town knew my story. No one outside of town did. I never discussed it with visitors or renters.

I wasn't about to begin now.

After a painful minute of silence, Riley said, "Not such an open book after all."

I met her dark gaze. "Tell you what. I'll tell you all about my mother, if you do something for me."

"What's that?"

"Tell me what *you're* hiding, Riley."

She looked to the ground. "Nothing."

"Bullshit."

She brought her gaze back to mine and glared at me. "Nothing. Not a damned thing."

"You're a good liar when you have to be. You could fool most anyone else, I think."

She thrust the rose in my face. "I'm not a liar. If that's what you think of me, keep your damned rose."

I eased her arm down. "It's your rose, Riley. I want you to have it. It's beautiful, but it's not nearly as beautiful as you are. I want you to have that silver and pink sapphire pendant I made as well. I don't give gifts lightly, and I don't appreciate having them shoved back in my face."

"If you think—"

"I don't think anything. We both know there are things you're not telling me. For one, I don't believe for a minute that you're a high school business teacher."

"I am!"

"Okay, then. What classes do you teach?"

She opened her mouth and then closed it. Opened it again. "Business education."

"Okay. What specific classes?"

"Marketing. Merchandising."

"Merchandising? At the high school level?"

"Sure. Why not?"

"High-school-level business classes are things like accounting, keyboarding, entrepreneurship. Even business law. But not merchandising."

"My high school has an advanced curriculum."

"I see."

"Fuck you." She threw the tissue-wrapped rose down and stomped on it. "If you don't believe me, fuck you!"

"That's not the only thing I don't believe. I don't believe you're from Pittsburgh. If I had to guess, I'd say you were from New York."

"Oh? Based on what, exactly?"

"The fact that you have that uptight New York look."

She scoffed.

"Also the fact that you once referred to Pittsburgh as New Pittsburgh."

"I did not."

"You did, and what's more, you know you did. You're blushing again, and you're not looking me in the eye." I leaned down, picked up the now trampled rose, and handed it to her. "This is still yours, and I still want to know you. I just want to know the *real* you. Show me the real you, and I'll show you the real me."

She took the rose. For a split second, I wasn't sure she would, but she did.

"I want to go back to the cabin," she said.

"All right. The truck's parked behind my shop. Let's go." I grabbed her hand.

She didn't whisk her hand out of mine, though I half-expected her to.

We didn't exchange any more words until we reached the cabin.

I got out of the truck and walked her to the door.

"Thanks for the rose," she said. Then she unlocked the door and went inside.

So that was that. For now, at least. She was here for several more days.

I checked my watch.

Time to go. Leena was expecting me to replace that damned pipe in her kitchen sink.

15

RILEY

I couldn't stay here.

I had no right to be away from home and leave my brothers to the mess our father had left us.

Sure, I had my own issues with the bastard, but I was still a Wolfe sibling, and I had a duty to my brothers.

Not to my father. I owed him nothing.

But my brothers... We'd all been implicated in the asshole's murder, and they shouldn't have to deal with it alone.

Problem? I didn't want to leave.

I didn't want to leave Matt.

Of course, after my little sideshow in the street, he wouldn't want to have anything more to do with me anyway.

I could stay for the remaining days. I'd already paid for them.

But living here in Matt's cabin and not seeing Matt?

No. Not happening. I'd grown accustomed to him. In fact, I wanted to see him. Wanted to be near him. Wanted to feel his hand in mine, his lips on mine.

I even wanted *that* part of him.

That part that I never thought I'd want from a man.

Sex was supposed to be a wonderful experience between two people who wanted each other.

I'd never had that. I'd been forced. Violated.

Raped.

I was nearly eighteen before I could actually think the word, but yes, my father had raped me. Repeatedly. Since I was six years old.

Six fucking years old.

Rock had been sent away because he was trying to help me.

I hadn't understood at the time. Even though he was hurting me, I'd been devoted to my father. He called me princess. His little princess. He showered me with gifts, gave me whatever my heart desired.

Pretty soon, the only thing my heart desired was to be free from him.

My brothers never knew. I'd wondered on occasion, but my phone conversation with Roy a couple days ago proved they hadn't.

They hadn't known until now. Rock told them why he'd been sent away. Why he never came back.

I could be angry. Angry that he never came back and tried to save me again.

But how could I? He'd had the chance to escape Derek Wolfe for good, and he'd taken it. He'd taken it and run.

I'd have done the same thing if I'd been able to.

Of course, now Rock had been forced back into the family fold by our father's mandates. If he didn't return to New York and take charge of the family empire, none of us would inherit anything.

Rock had returned. He was now CEO of Wolfe Enterprises. He hated it, but he was doing it.

For Roy, for Reid, and for me.

In the end, Rock had returned.

I should expect no less of myself.

I carefully removed the torn tissue paper from my rose. The bloom hadn't been damaged and was still perfect, but the stem was broken. I was leaving anyway, so I couldn't put it in a vase.

Matt had given it to me, though, and I didn't want to part with it. I shot my gaze to the small bookshelf in the corner of the cabin's living room. Mostly old paperbacks, but among them stood a hardcover—a thick Stephen King novel. I grabbed it, opened it to the middle, and placed my flower between the pages. It would flatten and dry, and I could keep it forever.

That meant I'd have to take the book with me. It wasn't mine to take, but I'd leave a few twenties on the counter so Matt could replace it if he wanted to. It couldn't mean much to him, or he'd have kept it at his own place.

I fired up my laptop to get a flight out of here and back to Manhattan. I was hoping for a redeye, but none were available.

I took the first flight in the morning and booked it with my Chloe Mansfield credentials.

Now...what to do for the rest of the evening?

I was still full from Mrs. Carson's amazing lunch, but I'd be hungry later. Right. Matt had brought groceries. I'd make a salad or something.

Right now? I wanted to leave this day behind.

What better for that goal than a soak in the hot tub out back?

Except the hot tub wouldn't cut it. Hot soothing water worked for normal people. Sometimes for me. But not this time.

Only one thing would suffice.

I'd promised I wouldn't do it, but—

I reached for my purse.

And pulled out the pack of cigarettes.

This was my vice. My escape. I'd get into the hot tub later, but for now? Only one thing would put my mind at rest.

Physical pain.

A burn.

As a model, I had to keep my body looking perfect all the time, so I hid my burns well.

There was a spot at the top of my vulva that was always covered. I kept myself shaved for easy access.

My father had seen the markings more than once.

He'd never said anything. Not a damned thing.

I lit the cigarette and took a drag, mindful not to inhale even a tiny bit of smoke or I'd gag. Matt truly had nothing to worry about. I never smoked.

These cigarettes served a far more sinister purpose.

I always let the cigarette burn a few minutes. Had to make sure it wouldn't bend when I pushed it hard into my bare flesh. So I waited. This cabin was designated as a nonsmoking property, but I didn't rightfully care at the moment.

A few moments later, when a clump of ash fell off the tip and onto the hardwood floor, I still didn't care.

It was time.

I removed my cowboy boots and socks, my jeans, and then my panties.

Several scars marred my vulva. Sprouts of pubic hair had begun to grow in. My dark hair stubbled quickly. I'd considered getting laser hair removal, except the technician would see my scars, and I couldn't have that.

The middle scar was fresh. I'd burnt myself there a while ago, after I had dinner with Lacey Ward, who was now my brother Rock's wife.

Lacey was a stranger—a stranger who knew my father. She was his estate attorney and had read the will to us.

She'd seemed so nice, so easy to talk to, so I'd asked her to dinner.

But I chickened out.

When Rock had called her, I told her to have him join us.

I hadn't been able to divulge my secret to her.

So I left dinner early, went home to my Manhattan high rise, and burned myself.

Then I disappeared.

Again.

I'd been traveling for several days before I found this cabin. Luckily it was available at the last minute. Montana had been my plan all along. That was where Rock had gone.

That was where I'd go.

And I had.

You're stalling.

That voice inside my head.

I was indeed stalling. Going over shit in my mind that I already knew.

I pushed the cigarette and sucked in a breath as it burned me.

It hurt. It hurt like a mother.

Yet it hurt so fucking good.

The pain. The searing, burning pain.

The pain that made me forget, if only for a few minutes, the pain inside my head. My heart.

My soul.

When the smell of my own flesh burning reached my nose, I removed the cigarette.

The wound was perfectly round.

Just perfect.

A perfectly round burn for perfect Riley Wolfe.

Riley Wolfe, supermodel who was beautiful on the outside but a fucking mess on the inside.

When the wound had cooled, I covered it with antibacterial ointment. I always took care of myself. Couldn't risk an infection that might spread to someplace visible.

Calmness drifted through me like a soft breeze.

The physical pain removed the emotional.

Oh, it wouldn't last long, but for these few precious moments, I was whole again.

Whole inside.

Still naked from the waist down, I walked into the kitchen to fix myself something quick for dinner. Burning myself made me hungry for some reason. It always had.

I opened the refrigerator. Matt had stocked me with some fresh fruit and yogurt. Some salad greens and sundried tomatoes.

Normal food fare for me.

I didn't want any of it.

This was a small town. No one would deliver. At least I didn't think they would.

That Mexican lunch had spoiled me. I wanted something bready and cheesy.

Pizza.

I wanted an extra-large thick-crust pizza with a double dose of everything on it, even anchovies. Did Sumter Falls have a pizza place? I had no idea, but I could drive into town and find out. I hastily put my panties and jeans back on. Not the cowboy boots, though. Flip-flops would do just fine.

I grabbed my phone and searched...

Bingo!

Rosati's Pizza on Broad Street in downtown Sumter Falls.

Fredricka would be so damned angry, but I didn't care an iota.

Pizza, here I come.

16

MATTEO

L eena didn't ask me to do her odd jobs because I was cheaper than the plumber.

I knew it and she knew it.

She wanted me to fuck her.

She'd been coming on to me since she moved here two years ago. She was young and attractive, but not my type. Her arms were covered in tats, which wasn't my thing. Her hair was cut short and dyed light blond, which also wasn't my thing. She smoked, which was definitely not my thing.

Still, I would have bedded her. She had a body that wouldn't quit, after all, and I was human.

The deciding factor? She'd had a one-nighter with Luke shortly after she moved here, and she pretty much stalked him for a couple months afterward.

I wasn't about to go there.

She'd finally left him alone, but not until he sicked the sheriff on her and scared her shitless.

Leena was fine as someone to do odd jobs for, though. Luke gave me shit about it from time to time. He never set foot in her place for obvious reasons.

"Hey, Mattie," Leena said through the screen door as I approached. "Come on in."

I opened the door, let myself in, and knelt down to give her dog a pet. "Hey, Roscoe."

"Roscoe, leave Mattie alone."

"You know I don't mind."

"Still miss your Herbie?"

"Every day."

"Time to get another pup, I'd say."

"I will. Eventually. Herbie was just so young. It's hard. Losing a dog is hard no matter what, but all my other ones at least had long lives. It's still too soon."

Leena approached and patted my cheek. "You're such a softie."

Leena was always touchy feely. Normally I didn't mind so much. She never got anywhere. Today, though, it bothered me. I nudged away and walked toward the kitchen. "Everything ready?"

"Yup. I got all the supplies you requested. Help yourself to a beer in the fridge."

"No thanks. I'll take a seltzer, though, if you've got it."

"Yup. Next to the beer."

I opened her refrigerator, found a lemon-lime seltzer, opened it, and took a long sip. Good stuff.

"Excuse me," Leena said. "I've got to get ready for work."

"No problem."

The supplies lay on the counter. I took stock. Looked like she had everything I'd need. Good. I wouldn't have to get anything from my truck. I kept it stocked for my odd jobs just in case.

The job shouldn't take more than an hour.

A few minutes later, Leena strode into the kitchen while I was lying supine, my head inside the cupboard under her sink.

Her legs and feet were bare. She was a cocktail waitress at the saloon, not a damned stripper.

"Thought you were getting ready for work," I said.

"I am." She squatted down.

She was wearing a black bikini, giving me a bird's-eye view of her rack.

"Is it beach night at the Stein?" I asked.

She winked. "Nah. I'm actually off tonight. I figured I might scare you away if I came out here in a lace corset and panties."

"You don't scare me, Leena."

"I don't seem to do much of anything to you."

"We've been through this. You're not my type."

"Mattie, you don't have a type. I've seen you with all kinds of women. Skinny, curvy, tall, short, blond, brunette, redhead. Hell, you even dated a woman with a shaved head once."

She wasn't wrong. Drea Matthews had been one hot little number. She'd cut off her hair in solidarity with her twin sister who was undergoing chemotherapy for breast cancer. The feel of a bald head during sex had been something else. Drea had been passing through on a run. She was a trucker. We met at the Stein and had a night of amazing sex.

Then we said our goodbyes and never saw each other again. I hadn't thought of Drea in a long time. I hoped her sister had recovered.

"It's because of Luke, isn't it?"

"Leena, do you want me to fix your damned pipe or not?"

She sighed and stood, so only her legs were once again visible. They were pretty decent gams, too.

"All right. Can't blame a girl for trying. I suppose you have it bad for that new chick."

"Who might that be?"

"You know, the one who looks like she was born with a silver spoon up her ass? I saw you walking around town earlier today."

"Her name's Riley, and she's only here for a week." Or less. We hadn't exactly left things well.

Damn. It was my fault. I'd pried. I'd pushed.

Whatever she was hiding, she wasn't ready to talk about it. God knew I understood that sentiment. Why had I pushed so hard?

Fuck.

Because I cared.

I'd known the woman for two days, and I cared about her.

I hadn't even gotten her into the sack.

"One of your renters, huh?"

"Yeah." I grabbed a wrench and started loosening the pipe.

"You say I'm not your type," Leena said. "I'd have bet a million bucks that rich girl isn't your type."

"Rich girl?"

"Yeah. She exudes it. That one comes from money."

I'd had the same thought, of course. No way was she a teacher from Pittsburgh.

But who *was* she, exactly?

"She's a teacher from Pittsburgh," I said, knowing full well I was lying through my teeth.

"Really? Hmm. Didn't see that coming. I'd have sworn she's a blue blood."

"Leena, honey, I've got to get this done, okay?"

"Sure, sure. Let me take you to dinner as a thank you."

"The hundred bucks will be more than enough."

"Come on, Mattie. I'll still give you the money. It's my night off. Let me take you out. As friends."

"Fine." A guy had to eat, after all.

I'd wanted to see Riley tonight, but I doubted she'd see me. I'd let her cool off and go see her tomorrow. With a dozen of Kari's roses this time. And if she threw them on the ground, I'd grab her and kiss her.

"Awesome. I guess I'll get dressed, then."

"Unless you want to fly to Florida and eat at a beachfront bar, I'd say that's a good idea."

She let out a sarcastic laugh as her legs walked out of my view.

I usually went to dinner with her when I did an odd job. This was nothing new. Luke razzed me for it, but I wasn't interested, and I made it clear to her every time. We almost always ended up having a good time. Kind of like brother and sister, though I wouldn't really know, since I was an only child. To her credit, Leena hadn't gone all stalker on anyone since Luke. We all guessed she'd learned her lesson.

A half hour later, I'd finished the job. I stood, cracked my back, and turned on the faucet to check for leaks.

Good as gold.

Who needed a plumber, anyway?

Leena walked back into the kitchen, this time in ripped jeans, biker boots, and a black tank.

"All good," I said, turning off the faucet.

"Awesome." She handed me a crisp Benjamin. "Ready? I feel like pizza tonight."

17

RILEY

P arking was an issue in a small town. You'd think I'd be used to that, coming from New York and all, but in New York I never drove. I had a driver, and on those rare occasions when he was off duty and I needed to get somewhere, I took a cab.

Sumter Falls didn't have any designated parking areas other than on the side streets. I found a space and walked over a block to get to the pizza place. Not a huge deal, except my flip flops weren't exactly comfortable.

Why did I own a pair of shoes that wasn't comfortable?

I should be used to that as well. Some of those stilettos I paraded around in on the runway were lethal weapons, and none of them were comfortable. Discomfort seemed to be a requirement for high fashion.

I thought again of Fredricka and my contract with Dominique in Paris.

Not what I wanted to be thinking about at the moment. Besides, I was leaving in the morning. I'd call Fredricka when I was back in Manhattan and tell her to postpone the shoot in

Paris. My father had just died, after all, and I needed to pay my respects.

Yeah, I was good at lying. I could even shed a few tears if I had to.

I opened the wooden door to Rosati's. The robust aroma of tomato sauce and melted cheese drifted toward me. I inhaled.

Food. Food was good. Dominique might not even want me once they saw how much weight I'd gained on this little excursion.

I didn't rightfully care at the moment.

How much time had passed since my last pizza?

A year, at least, and probably more.

I walked toward the hostess.

"Good evening," she said. "Just one for dinner?"

"Yes, just me tonight."

I didn't mind eating alone. In fact, I enjoyed it. Problem was that back home, someone always recognized me so I couldn't enjoy my own company.

Not so in this little town. I'd only met a few people, and what were the chances of any of them being here tonight?

"Right this way," the hostess said, and then she looked over her shoulder as the door opened again. "Be right with you, Matt."

Matt?

Couldn't be. Matt was a fairly common name. Right?

Don't turn around, Riley. Just don't.

But I did.

Sure enough, there was Matteo Rossi, his long hair up in a messy blond man bun.

And he wasn't alone.

A blond woman stood beside him. She was attractive in an unconventional way, and she had a killer body.

Great. Just great. Should I leave? The thought had merit, but I'd be more conspicuous that way.

"Here you go." The hostess led me to a small table near the back of the restaurant.

"Thank you," I murmured, taking the menu she handed to me.

"Adriano will be with you in a minute. He'll be your server."

"Thanks." I sat down—in the chair facing the back so I wouldn't see Matt and his date—and perused the menu.

Out of habit, my gaze went directly to the "healthy options" portion. Rosati's idea of a healthy option was a thin-crust pizza with no cheese. Just their signature sundried tomato marinara, shredded roast chicken breast, and an array of veggies.

It actually sounded pretty good, but I hadn't come here for a healthy option. I'd come here for gooey, cheesy pizza.

"Hi there."

I jerked upward and met the gaze of—

Wow.

My waiter was freaking gorgeous. Short dark hair and dark eyes, he looked like a Mediterranean god.

He smiled, and he was even more dazzling. "I'm Adriano. Do you have any questions about the menu?"

"Nope. It's pretty clear cut."

He laughed. "Yeah, it is. Can I get you something to drink?"

"A glass of wine, I think. Do you have a list?"

He laughed again. "We do. It's a piece of paper with the words red and white on it."

I joined in his laughter. It was joyful and contagious. "I'll try the red." Then I shut my menu. "And please bring me the most ridiculously fattening pizza you have."

His eyes crinkled. "That'd be our mucho macho. Three meats, extra cheese, and five veggies."

"Is one of the meats anchovies?" I asked.

"No, of course not."

"Add anchovies, then."

He lifted his eyebrows. "Seriously?"

I smiled. "I'm always serious, Adriano."

"Got it." He smiled back. "What size? Extra large?"

"I think small will suffice."

"Our small is twelve inches. It's a lot with all those toppings. Want to try an eight-inch personal size?"

Not one more pound, Riley, Fredricka's voice echoed in my head.

"The small. If I can't finish it, I'll take it with me."

"Good enough. I'll be right back with your wine and a glass of water."

"Perfect."

I turned around and watched Adriano's perfect ass as he walked away. Maybe not quite as perfect as Matt's, but nearly as hot. Matt's friend Lucas was great-looking too. Was Sumter Falls home to only good-looking men?

Shit.

I shouldn't have turned around to watch Adriano walk away.

My gaze met Matt's. He was sitting a few tables away with his date.

I turned around quickly and pretended to be engrossed in my phone.

Don't come over here. Don't come over here. Except…please come over here.

I'd been horrible to him earlier. Why had I thrown his rose on the ground and stomped on it? So childish, and that rose meant everything to me. I wanted to keep it forever. That was why I'd pressed it in the Stephen King novel.

So he'd pushed me a little. What really upset me was that I was so transparent. My father had taught me so well to hide my emotions, to lie when necessary.

How had Matt seen through it all?

Disappointment swept through me when he didn't come. If he hadn't said anything when I looked back and saw him enter, why would he now?

He wouldn't. I was the one who'd been a bitch. The first move would have to be mine.

No. I was here to eat a disgusting and glorious pizza. After all, I was leaving in the morning. No reason to start something I couldn't finish.

Besides, he was with another woman...which was slicing into my heart like a serrated steak knife.

That one's a keeper, Mrs. Carson had said.

Which only meant one thing.

Matt had brought other women to her place. Matt probably screwed every single woman who rented his cabin.

I was definitely better off without him.

Besides...

The thought of sex terrified me...and excited me.

How I longed to experience sex with someone I actually wanted touching me. Someone I felt something other than complete hatred for.

My father.

So many things he'd done to me. Sometimes he even let others watch. But they never touched me. Never touched his princess. Sometimes they begged him to let them, and many times I'd feared he'd allow it.

But he never did.

I suppose I owe him a small bit of gratitude for that.

Fuck. What the hell was I thinking? I owed him nothing. A big fat *nothing*.

He'd ruined me.

Because of him, I'd never be able to have a real relationship with Matt or anyone else.

Which didn't matter anyway, because Matt had already moved on.

Oh, but his kiss...

When I'd stripped away all my baggage and allowed myself to enjoy it...

It had been nirvana.

True nirvana.

Could sex with Matt be even better?

Could I forget how ruined I was and live in the moment?

Again, didn't matter.

Matt had moved on.

Adriano set my wine down next to me. I smiled and thanked him. Then I took a long sip.

Not bad for a house red. Basic and flavorful.

Just what I needed tonight.

Now, if I could just enjoy the rest of the evening and forget that Matt and his date were a few tables away.

18

MATTEO

"She's not going to turn around," Leena said to me.

"I don't know what you're talking about." I closed my menu. Pepperoni and mushrooms, my old standby. I never wavered from it.

"You've got your eyes glued to the back of her head, Mattie."

"No I don't." I purposefully looked down at the napkin in my lap.

"I get it. She's gorgeous. But she's not your type. She doesn't even live here."

"So? That's never been a requirement."

"If it's a romp in the hay you want, I can give you that."

I resisted an eye roll. "Not interested, Leena. We've been through this ad nauseam."

I couldn't help it. My gaze strayed back to Riley's head. Her hair was up in a high ponytail, and her neck...so long and silky, so ready for my kisses...

For fuck's sake. If there'd been one place I thought I *wouldn't* run into Riley Mansfield tonight, it was Rosati's. She was hardly the pizza type. Then again, she'd gorged on Mrs. C's carnitas and enchiladas.

"Hey, Mattie. Hey, Leena." Adriano strutted up to our table. "What can I get for you tonight?"

"You can tell Mattie here that his silver spoon at the back table over there isn't on the menu." Leena laughed.

Adriano met my gaze. "You know her?"

"She's renting my cabin this week," I said.

"Man, she's hot." Adriano smiled. "I think she might be into me."

Jealousy's green head speared into my gut. Most women were into Adriano, including Leena. He was number two on her list, after me, and she made no secret of it. He was half-Italian, same as I was, only he looked the part. My ancestors were from Northern Italy, and I had my Swedish mother's coloring.

"She's only here another few days," I said.

"Have you tapped her yet?" he asked.

My hand curled into a fist seemingly on its own. *Easy, Matt.* Hell, Adriano and I talked about women a lot. No reason for him to think this particular one was off limits. But thinking of anyone "tapping" Riley made me want to pound some skulls.

"I have not, and you won't, either."

"Man, if I can I—"

I stood, exercising every ounce of control I had not to grab Adriano's collar. I was taller and more muscular, and I could easily pummel him.

"She's *not* on the menu," I said so only he could hear. "Not tonight, and not ever."

"Easy, Mattie. I'm working here."

"You're working, all right. Just don't work her. She's been through some shit." Of that I was certain. I just had no idea what it was.

I sat down. "What do you want, Leena?" I asked.

"What did little miss silver spoon order?" she asked Adriano.

Anger threatened me again, but Leena was harmless. Adriano, however, was not. I didn't want him bedding Riley. No fucking way.

"She ordered a small mucho macho."

Leena's brows nearly flew off her forehead. "She's so thin!"

"I guess she's hungry," Adriano said. "She said she wanted a ridiculously fattening pizza. I believe those were her exact words."

"Sounds good, huh, Mattie?" Leena said.

"No way," Adriano said. "Matt's never ordered anything but pepperoni and mushroom in the three years I've been working at this place."

"Bring me a beer," I said. "And then we'll have a large mucho macho."

"Perfect," Leena agreed. "Make that two beers."

Adriano wrote down the order. "Got it. I'll be right back with your beers."

"What the hell is on the mucho macho anyway?" I asked Leena.

"Pepperoni, Italian sausage, pancetta, mushrooms, black olives, onions, green pepper, and fresh tomato. Oh, and lots of extra cheese."

"Sounds like heartburn on a platter."

"Little miss silver spoon is—"

"Riley, Leena. Her name is Riley."

"Geez, Mattie. I'm just teasing. You've got it bad."

She wasn't wrong. Riley Mansfield had gotten under my skin. Very rarely, I'd tried bedding a woman and she turned me down. I never gave it a second thought.

But I was giving Riley a lot of second thoughts, and I hadn't even tried to bed her.

This was my fault. I'd pushed her too hard. I rose.

"Where are you going?" Leena asked.

"I'm going to talk to her."

"Little miss—"

I glared at Leena.

"Okay, okay. Riley. Tell me, Mattie. What does she have that I don't?"

"She's not a stalker, for one."

"Neither am I. Luke just took my interest the wrong way."

"Leena, you followed him around for months."

"Like I said, I was interested. Apparently he wasn't. I learned my lesson. I've never done that to another guy."

"Good for you. Now, if you'll excuse me—"

She grabbed my forearm. "Sit down, Mattie." Her eyes were serious. "If there's one thing I've learned, it's don't go chasing someone who doesn't want you."

I chuckled. "You haven't learned that lesson with me."

"Hey, I give it my best shot when we're together. That's just who I am. But I don't chase you the way I did Luke."

I couldn't fault her observation.

Still...something about Riley called to me. It felt almost like...she needed me.

I pulled my arm away from Leena. "I'm just going to say hi."

"She knows you're here. If she wanted to say hi, she would."

"Maybe she doesn't want to, but I do." I walked to her table.

Riley swallowed a sip of wine and met my gaze.

"Hi," I said.

"Hi."

Neither of us spoke for what seemed like an hour.

Finally I cleared my throat. "I just wanted to say hi."

She nodded. "Well, you did."

Okay, then. This had been a huge mistake. I turned—

"Wait," Riley said.

I turned back. "Yeah?"

"I'm... I'm really sorry. About the rose. I shouldn't have thrown it down and stomped on it."

"Oh. Sure. Okay."

"I hope you'll accept my apology."

Something in her voice made me pause. She sounded sincere, but it was something more than that as well—something that made me sit down in the chair across from her.

"Listen," I said, "I'm sorry too. I'm sorry I pushed you. We hardly know each other, and I had no right to—"

She reached forward and touched my hand.

Sparks shot through me at the subtle contact. Real tingles that I hadn't felt in a long, long time.

"It's okay," she said. "In fact, it's nice that you cared enough to prod a little."

"Still, I shouldn't have."

She smiled, and the world was suddenly right again.

"You're right. You probably shouldn't have, but I shouldn't have reacted so strongly. I loved the flower. Truly."

I returned her smile. How could I not? Her smile was something amazing, and I got the feeling not everyone got to see it.

I felt privileged.

Even in the darkness of the restaurant, I could see her blush a little.

I couldn't help myself. "You're so damned beautiful," I said.

Her smile widened. "So are you."

I couldn't help a chuckle. "I'm not sure anyone's ever called me beautiful before."

"You are. I could say handsome. It's accurate. I could say gorgeous and magnificent. Also accurate. But beauty is the basis for all of those, and you *are* beautiful, Matt."

Her hand still rested on mine, and I entwined my fingers with hers. I didn't know what to say. I was having dinner with someone else, and I was a gentleman. I'd see the date to its conclusion. But I desperately wanted to see Riley later tonight. I didn't care what we did. If I never got her into the sack, I didn't care. I just wanted to be with her, in her presence.

"May I see you later?" I asked.

She frowned. "What about your date?"

"It's not a date, really. I replaced a pipe for Leena and she's buying me dinner."

She smiled again. Was that relief in her eyes?

"I'm glad, but there's something you should know."

I shook my head. "I don't need to know anything, Riley. I'm not pushing you for answers. I just want to be with you. We can do anything you want. Get a drink at the Stein. Go home and put a DVD in the player. Play a game of cards. Sit and do nothing. It doesn't matter to me."

"But—"

"Shh. It doesn't matter."

Adriano arrived with Riley's pizza. "You eating over here now, Matt?" he asked.

"No. Just saying hi." I laughed. "That's a lot of pizza for one person."

"I plan to make a big dent in it," Riley said.

"I've no doubt." I winked at her. "Let me finish my dinner and I'll see you back at the cabin, okay?"

She nodded. "All right."

19

RILEY

Was it fair?

I'd tried to tell Matt I was leaving tomorrow, but he kept shushing me.

I supposed it didn't matter. If it weren't tomorrow, it would be several days later. Matt and I had no future, anyway.

I couldn't escape my life, as much as I wanted to. My brothers deserved better. They were back in Manhattan dealing with the fallout of our bastard father's death. They needed me. And truth be told, I needed them too. Now that they knew the truth about me, maybe we could become closer. They no longer had any reason to envy me.

Indeed, I had reason to envy them.

In the meantime, a pizza the size of the Titanic awaited me.

Yeah, it was only twelve inches in diameter, but the crust was thick and the toppings were mountainous.

And the aroma was divine as I inhaled.

I couldn't help a chuckle. Fredricka would have a coronary if she could see me now.

I picked up a piece and took a bite. A little hot but not enough to burn the roof of my mouth.

And absolutely delicious.

After two pieces, though, I was full. I should have listened to Adriano and gotten the individual size.

"Another glass of wine?" Adriano asked after walking back to my table.

"I'd better not. I'm driving."

"How was the pizza?"

"Delicious, but I should have listened to you. This was way too much."

He picked up the tray. "I'll just box this up for you."

"I'm actually leaving tomorrow," I said. "So don't bother. Why don't you take it?"

"We're not allowed to do that," he said. "Health laws and all."

"I won't tell if you won't."

"Good enough." He winked. "It'll make a nice midnight snack. I'll be right back with your check."

I itched to look behind me, to see Matt's face, maybe get a better look at his date.

It wasn't a date, he'd said. He just helped her with a sink pipe.

He'd forgiven me for being such a bitch earlier, and I was thankful for that.

A new feeling swept through me—something I hadn't felt in a long time.

Anticipation.

I was looking forward to seeing Matt tonight.

Adriano brought my check. I paid in cash, of course. I had one credit card in each of my aliases, but I used them only for travel. I left a handsome tip, as well.

Then I rose and turned.

Matt and Leena were still eating their pizza, and I whisked past them quickly, forcing myself not to meet Matt's gorgeous blue gaze.

I'd see him later.

I couldn't wait.

THE KNOCK on the cabin door made my heart race.

I hadn't changed clothes, though I'd considered it. I was still wearing the jeans and tank I wore to the pizza place. My bones were tired from the work I'd done this morning, but the anticipation made my adrenaline surge.

I opened the door.

Matt stood there, his blue eyes burning two holes in my flesh.

"Come in—"

He grabbed me and slammed his mouth onto mine.

I opened.

I wanted to kiss him, remembered how amazing it had been.

But kissing might lead to—

No. Let it go. Surrender to his kiss. He won't force you into anything.

Just. Let. It. Go.

I heeded the advice of my subconscious.

I couldn't let Derek Wolfe color my whole life, let him keep me from something that could be beautiful. So beautiful.

I parted my lips, and Matt probed his tongue between them.

We'd kissed before, but this seemed different in a way I couldn't quite understand.

And I knew...

I knew at that moment that I'd let him make love to me.

I was leaving tomorrow, so I could be Riley Mansfield tonight. Just Riley Mansfield, who didn't have any of Riley Wolfe's problems.

I could suppress all my troubles—all my demons—just for this night.

I cupped his blond stubbled cheeks, letting my fingers scrape along the roughness. I wanted to pull him closer to me, so close that we were one being with this kiss.

I let my hands wander down, over his broad shoulders, down his upper arms. So big and muscled. I drew in my courage and then touched his butt—his amazing butt—and squeezed. He groaned into my mouth, pushing his clothed erection against my belly.

And I didn't back away.

Because I was Riley Mansfield tonight, not Riley Wolfe.

He broke the kiss, inhaled, and then trailed wet kisses over my cheek to my ear, where he softly nipped the lobe. I shuddered, his breath against the wetness an icy cold yet comfortably warm delight.

"I want you," he said softly, pushing his erection against me once more.

I want you too.

The words hovered on my tongue, begging to be released.

"I...want you too."

He growled into my ear and then pushed his tongue inside. Tingles shot through me, and my body couldn't decide if it wanted to be warm or cold.

And I throbbed between my legs. That secret place that I never thought could feel anything again.

"I want to make love to you in the hot tub," he rasped.

God. The hot tub. Naked. With Matt. In the hot tub.

"Then," he continued, "I want to come inside and make love to you in bed. All. Night. Long."

My nipples hardened, extending and yearning for his lips, teeth, tongue. Fingers, anything.

My body had never responded this way. Many times, I'd wondered if it actually could.

He moved from my ear, then, and met my gaze as he licked his swollen lips. "What do *you* want, Riley?"

A soft sigh escaped my throat. "I want all of that. All of it, Matt."

"Thank God," he rasped. "I couldn't think of anything else while I was finishing dinner. Then, you left, and you didn't look at me—"

I placed two fingers against his lips. "I didn't want to interfere with your dinner. I was afraid if I looked at you..."

"Afraid of what?"

"I don't know, exactly. I almost felt like I couldn't control myself."

He smiled. "Would that have been such a bad thing?"

"In the middle of a restaurant? Yeah."

"Doesn't matter. I'm here now. I'm here, and you're here, and I'm going to explore every inch of you by morning."

I closed my eyes and moaned. My body was responding in weird fluttery ways—ways I'd read about but never imagined.

Matt kissed my neck and then my bare shoulder. "Your skin is so beautiful. Like a pinkish-yellow rose." He dropped a kiss between my breasts and then he slid the strap of my tank off one shoulder and then the other. Kisses and more kisses, all over my chest and the tops of my breasts.

My breath caught and wouldn't let go. I wanted... Needed...

"Matt..."

"Hmm?" He nipped my shoulder.

"Undress me. Please."

"My pleasure." He pushed my tank down to my waist and over my hips. Then he unhooked my bra and I shimmied out of it. My breasts fell gently against my chest.

"Fuck. Beautiful," he breathed.

I flipped off my sandals while he unbuttoned and unzipped my jeans.

A slice of fear—or was it apprehension?—threatened me, but I waved it away. I wanted this more than the fear that wanted to control me.

Derek Wolfe was dead.

He had no more control over me.

And damn it, that would be the last time I thought of Derek Wolfe while Matt undressed me.

He eased the denim over my hips and down my thighs until I stepped out of the jeans and they lay like a blue puddle at my feet.

Only my pink lace boy shorts lay between Matt and me.

He stared, looked me up and down as if I were a side of beef hanging in a butcher shop.

And I liked it.

My God, I liked it a lot.

"You look so sexy, Riley, in those panties," he said. "I almost don't want to take them off you."

Good. I wanted them on. He could take them off when we got into a dark bedroom. But here? In the light? He'd see... He'd see my secret. I closed my eyes and whispered, "Please..."

"Please what." His breath was hot against my neck.

"Please. Let me keep them on. I want to look sexy for you."

"God," he rasped. "You're so beautiful. So damned beautiful."

I opened my eyes and met his gaze. "I want to see you. Please, Matt."

He smiled. "Undress me, then."

Undress me, princess.

No!

Fucking no!

Not now. You will not ruin this beautiful moment for me!

I hurled the unwanted images from my mind.

I trailed my fingers over Matt's broad shoulders. I wanted to see what was underneath his T-shirt, but something stopped me.

"Riley?"

I inhaled, gathering every sliver of courage I could find, and I slid my fingers down to the bottom of his T-shirt and inched it up.

His skin was so warm. So warm against my tingling fingers.

Slowly I moved it farther upward, concentrating on how much I desired him. And with each new inch of flesh I exposed, my heart beat faster.

His lighter skin contrasted with mine. I was tan, of course. Spray tanned. Part of the job.

Matt's chest was nearly bare but for a few blond hairs scattered over his pectorals. His nipples were dark pink, and when I slid my finger over one, it hardened under my touch as he sucked in a breath.

I had power over him.

Power I never knew I could wield.

It was thrilling.

I pushed the T-shirt over his head, and he lifted his arms to help me along. Soon it joined my clothes on the floor.

He kicked off his sneakers.

Now only his jeans separated me from *that* part of him. The part that both scared and excited me.

It bulged, and I stared.

Though I knew it was my imagination, I saw it beating in time with my heart.

Faster, faster, faster...

Until finally Matt took the reins from me. He unbuttoned and unzipped his jeans and removed them.

And he was naked.

Naked before me.

I averted my eyes.

I was used to it, always averting my eyes, until *he* forced me to look. Forced me to touch...

"Riley." Matt's voice. "Look at me."

I can't. Just can't.

Until finally, his warm fingers touched my chin.

"Please," he said. "Look at me, Riley."

Something in his voice made me obey, and I looked at him. Truly saw him. Indeed, truly saw *any* man for the first time.

His beauty astounded me. A god from Mt. Olympus couldn't look better than Matteo Rossi. He took my hand, then, and led it to his cock. "Feel this. Feel me. Feel what you do to me."

I gripped him, as if shaking his hand. He was warm and hard, yet his skin was like silk under my touch.

He closed his eyes and let out a low growl. "God, what you do to me. One touch from you is better than a homerun with anyone else. I swear to God."

I dropped his cock.

He opened his eyes and tilted his head.

He was questioning something, and I knew exactly what it was.

"I'm sorry," I said.

"Sorry for what? What's going on, Riley?"

"I'm...frightened." True words. The last time I had sex was with...

God, I couldn't go there right now. I just couldn't.

Matt reached toward me. "Baby?"

I forced myself not to cower backward.

He had hated it when I cowered. In his mind, I was supposed to want him as much as he wanted me. He never understood the two-way street of sex.

Fuck. What we had wasn't sex. It was abuse. Molestation. Fucking incest.

I was forever tainted by Derek Wolfe.

He wasn't the only one. Some of his friends fucked their daughters and sons. Sometimes he made me watch.

I supposed he deserved a little credit. He never let any of them touch me. Some of them passed their children around like the newest toy.

"Baby," Matt said again.

I wanted to answer him. Truly, I did. But my mind was now polluted with images and memories that I could never erase, no matter how hard I tried.

I wanted so much to be with this man. This beautiful man.

I was leaving tomorrow, and I'd never see him again.

Can't I have just one night? One beautiful night that isn't marred by my father?

I squeeze my eyes shut.

"Okay," Matt said. "I get it."

Clothes rustled.

He was getting dressed.

My eyes pop open. "Matt..."

"It's okay. We have the rest of the week. I won't rush you."

Except we *didn't* have the rest of the week. If I wanted this—and I did—I had to act now.

I forced the unwanted garbage from my mind, advanced toward him, grabbed both his cheeks, and pulled him toward me.

I kissed him.

I melded our mouths together and kissed him—all tongue, teeth, and lips.

A glorious kiss.

A kiss not just of passion but of need. Of my need for redemption.

For that was what I truly wanted—to be redeemed for my part in my father's madness. Once I turned eighteen, I could have stopped it all. I could have run.

But I didn't, and by everything I believed in, I had no idea why I hadn't.

Perhaps I couldn't have controlled what he did to me when I was young and weak. My brother had tried to stop him and had been sent away, never to return.

At the time, I didn't even know what was happening to me. I knew only that my father was hurting me, but he was still my daddy, and Rock was trying to hurt *him*.

If only I could turn time backward and relive those precious moments. Somehow get away and help Rock complete his task.

I could have saved myself the next two decades of horror. I could have saved my brother.

You were six, Riley. Six. A child. A child doesn't need redemption.

But an adult did.

Could Matteo Rossi offer me redemption? No. But he could make me forget for a few precious hours.

Except he couldn't.

Even as I kissed him, these thoughts pervaded my psyche.

I pulled away.

20

MATTEO

"Riley?"

"I'm sorry, Matt. I'm just…"

"Just what, baby?" I cupped her cheek, her skin so smooth beneath my rough fingers.

"I want this," she said.

"God, so do I. So what's the matter?"

She stepped backward, away from me, averting her gaze. Her cheeks reddened.

"Riley, please. Tell me what's wrong."

"I told you. I'm…frightened."

"Of what? Me?"

"No. Not you. I trust you, Matt."

"I'm glad. I promise not to harm you."

"I know you won't. It's just… It's been a long time."

A long time? She must have been kidding. This woman was the most gorgeous creature I'd ever laid eyes on. Surely men crawled out of the woodwork to bed her.

"We'll go slow, then," I said. "Let's just go out to the hot tub. That's all we have to do for now."

She met my gaze and nodded.

"Tell me how to put that beautiful smile back on your face, Riley."

She closed the distance between us and melted into my arms. "Hold me. Please."

I could do that. Holding her was no hardship. Except on my dick, no pun intended. If she was truly out of practice—and I had a hard time believing that—my big-ass cock might be intimidating her. One way to deal with that. I hoisted her into my arms, so my cock wasn't burrowing against her, carried her through the cabin, and outside to the deck.

"Matt! We're naked."

"Baby, there's no one around here close enough to see anything."

"I can see your cabin."

"That's all you see, and I'm here."

"True." She laughed. Kind of nervously, but it was a start.

"I'm going to put you down so I can get the cover off the tub," I said.

"Okay."

I set her down gently, my cock still hard as marble. I walked a little stiffly to the tub and got the cover off. I checked the temperature. Ninety-eight. Perfect. Anything over a hundred and we wouldn't be able to stay in for long.

I'd stay in the tub all night if I had to. Anything to get Riley relaxed.

"Go ahead and get in," I said. "I'm going to get us some water. And by the way, you may want to take those panties off now or I may have to rip them off you."

She nodded, looking slightly nervous. I walked back into the cabin, grabbed a seltzer for me and a bottle of water for her, and returned.

She'd gotten into the tub, and her perfect breasts were floating on top of the bubbly water.

My dick reacted instantly. I set the drinks in the drink holders and stepped into the tub.

The water whisked around me, warming me. Not that I needed warming. I was hot as blazes for Riley. This woman had a profound effect on me, and I was beginning to realize her physical beauty wasn't the cause.

Yeah, she was gorgeous with a rocking body, but Riley Mansfield was so much more than a pretty face.

Something hid inside her—something that disturbed her. Something that disturbed her so much that she pretended to be something she so clearly wasn't.

A teacher from Pittsburgh?

Not so much.

My goal tonight wasn't to make her tell me her backstory. No. My goal tonight was to make love to her. To show her some beauty in this world. Okay, so I wasn't completely altruistic. I wanted the sex for my own prurient reasons. But it would be good for her too, in more ways than one. Tomorrow we could talk about her real story.

I sat down next to her, a jet massaging my back. I didn't try to touch her, though I wanted to very badly. I simply sat. I'd let her make the first move. If we ended up just sitting in the hot tub all night, that'd be okay. We still had several days together.

Maybe I could talk her into staying longer.

Damn!

I didn't want my time with this woman to end.

Talk about scary.

Except not so scary, at least not in a bad way.

I wasn't in love with her. No one fell in love in two days. But I was definitely interested in pursuing something with her that I'd never pursued.

A relationship.

I wanted a bona fide relationship with this enigmatic woman I barely knew.

Yeah, scary.

We sat quietly for about fifteen minutes. At least I thought it was fifteen minutes. I didn't have my phone or a watch to check. Once I'd drained my seltzer, I rose. "I'm going to get another. You want one?"

She shook her head. "I'm still good. Thanks."

I was good as well, but I also had to pee, so I didn't have the option of staying. I walked back into the cabin and hit the can. While I was pissing, I zeroed in on a wallet sitting on top of the toilet tank. Hmm. Why was her wallet in the bathroom?

I had no idea. I finished my piss and washed my hands, ready to get back to the tub, when my gaze darted to the wallet again.

Don't do it, Matt. None of your business.

I did it anyway. I picked up the wallet and opened it. A Pennsylvania driver's license was tucked into the plastic-covered window.

Chloe L. Mansfield, with an address in Pittsburgh.

My eyebrows shot up.

Chloe *L.* Mansfield? She'd said her middle name was Riley.

I dug further. An American Express platinum card in the same name. And—

"What the fuck?"

Hundred-dollar bills. Fifteen of them, to be exact. Who the hell carried around fifteen hundred dollars in cash?

Not a schoolteacher.

I eased my rage. I already knew she wasn't who she claimed to be. No reason to be angry, and I was snooping anyway. This was on me, not on her.

Well, on her too. She shouldn't have lied to me, though I'd

already figured it out. Knowing for sure that I was right, though... That was a bummer.

I sighed and placed the wallet back on the toilet tank. I'd continue as planned. I'd make love to her tonight, show her some beauty in whatever fucked-up world she came from, and then tomorrow...

Tomorrow I'd get her to tell me the truth.

21

RILEY

Matt returned with another seltzer for himself. I took the last drink of my bottle of water and set the empty bottle back in the drink holder while Matt got back in the tub.

Darkness had fallen, giving me the cloak I needed for my scars. Relief swept through me, though only a little. Still I was flooded with apprehension. With fear.

How long had we been sitting in here? He wasn't rushing me, and I appreciated that. Truly.

But I was leaving tomorrow.

If I was going to do this—and I really wanted to do this, despite my apprehension—I had to get out of my own head and let myself go.

Sex could be a beautiful thing. Indeed, it was *supposed* to be a beautiful thing.

That I'd had a shitty introduction to the act was not going to color my enjoyment of this magnificent man.

I wouldn't let it. I *couldn't* let it.

I was leaving tomorrow, so tonight was my only chance.

He'd go slow. I knew it already. He'd stopped inside to give me the space I needed. I could have asked him to leave, and if I had, he would have. I knew that in my heart.

I had nothing to fear from Matteo Rossi.

Once he sat down in the water, I snuggled up to him, letting our bodies touch. He eased his arm around my shoulders, pulled me close, and kissed the side of my head.

Was he going to kiss me?

He didn't make any move.

It was up to me. He was letting me go at my own pace.

The problem? I didn't know what my own pace was. I'd never had sex when I wanted to have sex.

I was truly a virgin in some respects.

Every way except physically.

We'd kissed many times. Seen each other naked—well, almost, in my case. What next? What do I do?

"Matt?"

"Hmm?"

"I... I don't know what to do."

His eyes popped open. "What do you mean?"

"This. Sex."

"You're not a...virgin, are you?"

"No. I'm just not all that experienced, like I said."

"Just do what you feel, baby. Do whatever makes you feel good."

"I need you to... To kind of take the lead. Is that okay?"

He smiled. "I wanted to go slowly. For you."

"I know that. You're very sweet, but if you wait for me, I'm not sure anything will happen."

Right on target there. I had no idea how to seduce a man. No clue.

"Okay, Riley. But you tell me if you want to stop, like you did inside."

"I will. But I'm not going to want to stop."

"You did before."

"I know. Except that I didn't. Not really. I'm just a little scared."

"Why?"

Why? What a loaded question. I couldn't even begin to tell him why. He'd go screaming for the woods, and I wouldn't blame him.

"Just my inexperience. That's all."

"All right." He cupped my cheek and turned me toward him. "Kiss me."

I leaned into him and met his lips with my own. I parted, and he gently twirled his tongue around mine.

Very slow and sweet compared to our previous kisses, and soon I was throbbing, wanting more.

Unwanted thoughts, unwanted images, tried to force their way in.

No!

I won't let him destroy this beautiful moment. I won't!

I deepened the kiss, giving over to Matt. Matt was everything. All of my thoughts, all of my feelings... All Matt.

Matt, and nothing else.

Nothing else except this beautiful moment between us.

We kissed.

And we kissed.

And when he trailed one hand down to cup my breast, instead of dreading the touch, I embraced it.

Enjoyed it.

I *wanted* Matt to touch me.

And that made all the difference.

I broke the kiss, panting. "Let's go in," I said.

"You sure?" He cupped my cheek, skimming his thumb across my lower lip.

Am I?

"Yeah, I'm sure."

Please, let's go now before I chicken out.

"Good enough." He helped me out of the water, wrapped me in a towel, and led me inside.

We'd both pulled our hair into messy buns for the tub, and a few strands had come loose, sticking to our necks and shoulders.

Matt pulled the tie out of my hair so it flowed over my shoulders and down my back. "You're so beautiful," he said.

"Bed," I said. "Please."

"This isn't a race, Riley."

No, not a race. But I was so afraid I'd freak out if we didn't just get to it.

"I know that. I just want you."

"I want you too."

"Let me get a condom out of my pocket."

"Don't need it. I'm on birth control."

Shit. Another reminder of my past. My father made sure I was on birth control as soon as I blossomed. He didn't want any evidence of his transgressions.

"Still, we just met."

"I'm not very experienced. I told you. So unless you have something you're hiding—"

"Me? I'm an open book. I don't hide things."

I widened my eyes. "What do you mean by that?"

"I don't know, Riley. What could I possibly mean?"

I cocked my head. Was he...*angry* with me? "Matt, please. Don't ruin this."

"I have no intention of ruining anything."

"Take me to bed. Please."

"Fuck." He pulled the tie out of his own hair, and his locks cascaded over his shoulders like a lion's mane.

Matt was a lion, and I was his prey.

Oddly, I was okay with that.

"I don't know what you're hiding, Riley," he said, "but I know it's something."

"I'm not—"

He quieted me with two fingers on my lips.

"Stop it. I don't care. Not tonight. I've wanted you since I first laid eyes on you. You do something to me. Something different. I feel like..." He shook his head. "Fuck." Then he crushed his lips to mine.

That earlier kiss in the tub? The one that was gentle?

This one was anything but.

He devoured my mouth. Took, like a lion taking what was his.

Surrender to it, Riley, I begged myself.

Let your body lead you. Forget your mind for one fucking minute!

I leaned into his kiss.

Melted into his arms and surrendered.

His dick was hard, and it throbbed against the towel still covering me.

Tonight. Tonight I'd find out what all the fuss was about.

Tonight was for me.

For Matt and for me.

He trailed his fingers over my shoulders and down my arms, sending tingles racing through me.

My nipples stiffened, and I pushed into his chest, wishing I could whisk away the towel but knowing I had to get to the dark bedroom first.

My body was on fire. Truly on fire, and—

No!

When unwanted images tried to surface, I tamped them down.

Nothing would ruin this night for Matt and me. Nothing.

I was going home tomorrow. Going home to help my brothers deal with the fallout of my father's murder.

Going home, where I'd have to reveal the ultimate truth of my relationship with my father, for my brothers still didn't know everything.

That would be difficult.

I deserved this. This one night of passion and desire and nirvana with this wonderful man.

And damn it, I would have it.

Matt broke the kiss with a loud pop and inhaled deeply.

"Bedroom," I said. "I want to be in the dark."

"Why?"

"I just...do."

"Whatever you need." He pulled me to the bedroom and didn't turn on the light.

I let the towel drop to the floor.

My open suitcase lay on the bed where I'd begun to pack it. He set me down and closed the bag, tossing it to the floor. Then he joined me on the bed, his body covering mine.

He was kissing me again. He held his weight on his arms so as not to crush me, but the kiss was full of passion and need. So much need.

He rolled over then, pulling me with him, until we were lying side by side, our mouths still joined.

His erection nudged hot against my flesh.

And yes, I wanted it.

I wanted it inside me.

I wanted *him* inside me.

Such a new feeling, but dwelling on its newness only invited other unwanted feelings and images, so I didn't dwell.

I surrendered to the moment and nudged him. "Please."

"Not yet," he said.

"Now. Please."

"But I want to explore every inch of you, baby. We have all night."

Explore? Even in the dark, if he explored too much he'd find my burns. I couldn't let that happen. "You can explore me later. Right now I want you inside me, Matt. Please."

"Fuck," he groaned. Then he rolled on top of me and slid inside me. He groaned again. "God, you're tight."

Tight, yes, and he burned. But it was a good burn. A necessary burn. A burn I craved.

For when Matteo Rossi entered me, I reclaimed my body.

It was mine.

Not anyone else's.

Just mine.

I wanted this. This was *my* choice.

And I reveled in it.

"Trying to go slow," he gritted out. "Trying—"

"It's okay," I said. "Do what you need to do."

"I'll make this up to you, Riley." He pulled out and then thrust back in, hard this time, his dick burning through me like a flaming spear.

He pulled out quickly and thrust back in. *Again. Again. Again.*

Sweat emerged on his brow, making his hair stick to the sides of his face.

He fucked me hard. He fucked me fast.

He fucked me so damned good.

I locked on his face, his beautiful light-blue eyes, as he pumped. Focused on his beauty, on his body joined to mine.

I focused, sealing my mind from all other thoughts and images.

His beauty. His manliness. His pure, raw masculinity.

"I'm going to come, Riley," he panted. "Can't hold off. I'll... I'll... Fuck!" He grunted as he pushed hard into me, banging on my pubic bone and nudging the new sore.

I relished the ache, relished his release.

Relished our joining.

This was what sex was supposed to be like.

Finally, I could see beauty where before I'd seen only pain and self-loathing.

Finally, I could see light at the end of my dark tunnel.

22

MATTEO

F uck.

That release was like nothing I'd experienced before.

And I'd had a lot of experience.

I was clean, though. I always made sure of that. I always used a condom, and I got tested every three months for all STDs.

Fuck! The condom...

How had I acquiesced so quickly? I believed Riley. I believed she was protected and that she posed no threat to me otherwise. But how...? How did she believe *me* so freely? Most women weren't so trusting.

Very surprising, considering we both knew she was hiding something.

Damn. How much time had passed since I'd experienced a woman without a condom?

Too damned much time, that was for sure.

Riley had been tight as a virgin, too. Tight and ridged and perfectly gloving my cock.

I was already hardening again, aching for her, and I hadn't even withdrawn yet.

I rolled over and lay on my back, one arm covering my sweaty forehead. "Damn, baby," I said.

She let out a soft moan.

"I'll make it better for you next time," I said.

"It was wonderful," she breathed.

"But you didn't come. I didn't kiss you all over, suck on your beautiful pussy. I want to do all that and more."

"Mmm. Sounds great, but truly, Matt, it was wonderful."

She really was inexperienced.

"Give me a few minutes to recover," I said, "and then we're going to start again.

She turned and snuggled next to me. "Sounds good." Soon, though, she was snoring softly.

I couldn't bear to wake her.

In the morning.

I'd make slow sweet love to her in the morning. We had all the time in the world.

THE SUN'S rays streamed in through the window of the rental cabin. For a minute, I thought I was at home, but then I remembered.

Riley.

This morning I'd make love to Riley. Kiss every inch of her velvety body and make her come. Hell, I'd make her come twice. Maybe three times.

Except...

Where was she?

Her side of the bed was rumpled. What time was it, anyway? My phone was in the other room in the pocket of my jeans. Heck, it had probably died overnight. I really needed to invest in a new phone. My battery hardly lasted a full day. I charged it every night.

No clock in the bedroom, either. Was there even a clock in this house?

My watch. I'd taken it off to get in the hot tub. Where was it?

And for that matter, where the hell was Riley?

She must be in the other room.

I rose and headed to the can to take a leak. Hmm. Her wallet no longer sat on top of the toilet tank. She was obviously up, so she'd probably moved it back to her purse.

I walked into the living area, expecting to see her sitting on the couch or in the kitchen making coffee. Did she even drink coffee? Yeah, she did. She'd enjoyed JoJo's coffee. She liked it dark and rich.

Still, I really had no idea who she was.

"Riley!" I called.

No answer. I hastily put on my jeans and walked into the kitchen. No Riley there either.

The hot tub. Of course! I hadn't bothered covering it last night, so she probably got back in for a morning soak.

I ambled out onto the deck.

Sure enough, the tub was still bubbling...

But no Riley.

Okay, this was getting weird. I walked around the side of the cabin. Only my truck sat in the drive. Her rental car?

Gone.

I hurried back into the cabin to take a closer look. Nothing seemed amiss in the living room or kitchen, so back to the bedroom I went.

And it hit me.

The suitcase I'd moved off the bed?

Gone.

And in the bathroom? Not just her wallet was gone. Her toothbrush, toothpaste, moisturizer, hairbrush... Everything that I'd seen last night...all gone. How hadn't I noticed when I took a leak earlier?

Easy. I wasn't looking.

All I noticed was her missing wallet, and that was only because I'd snooped in it last night.

She was gone.

Riley Mansfield—or whoever she was—had left without a trace.

I ran my fingers through my disheveled hair. I still had no idea what time it was. I found my watch sitting on the coffee table.

Fuck. Eleven a.m.! Since when did I sleep this late?

Good thing I didn't have a job today. My phone had indeed died. I got the rest of my clothes on, left the cabin, and got into my truck. I needed a cup of black coffee and something in my belly.

Fortification. Only with fortification would I be able to take the next step.

The next step.

Even as I let the words form in my mind, I couldn't believe I was thinking them. I'd never chased a woman in my life, but that was indeed my next step.

To find Riley.

23

RILEY

I arrived in New York late in the afternoon with the time change. My limo was waiting, and within an hour, I was back at my luxury apartment in Manhattan.

Time to call my brothers.

I wasn't close to any of them. I hardly knew Rock, since he'd left when I was six, and Roy was so quiet he didn't get close to any of us. As for Reid? He was outgoing, quite the partier in some circles. Also the closest to me in age. He and I might have been close but for our father.

My father had kept me distanced from my brothers. He was probably afraid I'd tell them the truth. He needn't have worried.

I kept the truth buried far beneath my surface. I had to in order to exist.

To the outside world, I was Riley Wolfe, supermodel.

On the inside, I was a void of darkness.

Last night, though... Last night I'd seen the light. Matt had given me a precious gift, one I wished I could return. Leaving him had been one of the hardest things I'd ever done.

But this was where I belonged. Here. In Manhattan. Despite

the horror that had taken place here, it was my home. My brothers needed me.

Derek Wolfe was gone and he wasn't coming back. I thanked God on a daily basis for that one. I'd stopped praying long ago, but now I was free. Did I even believe in God? I wasn't sure, but I thanked Him nonetheless. I thanked Him for finally freeing me.

I was a mess inside, for sure, but at least I didn't go to bed every night wondering whether Derek Wolfe would show up and demand...

I didn't even want to think about it.

I looked around. The décor was modern, with clean, crisp lines and simple colors of brown, beige, and white. Steel sculptures sat on the mantle, and the coffee table and end tables were covered in clear glass.

It was the envy of many in my circles.

And I hated it.

It was sterile.

Now, I longed for the hominess of the cabin in Sumter Falls.

Time to put this place on the market and move.

But not until I helped my brothers solve the murder of our father. We'd all been implicated, and the only one of us with an ironclad alibi was Rock, who'd been in Montana at the time. The police might try to say he'd ordered a hit, but with what? Rock had been living a modest life in Montana, working construction. He didn't have the kind of money required to order a hit.

No, Rock hadn't done this.

None of my brothers had, though they all had a motive.

The strongest motive, though?

That belonged to me.

I'd suffered the most at Derek Wolfe's hands, and no one had known.

Until now.

Rock had told Roy and Reid why he'd been sent away all those years ago, and I'd told Roy in a phone call before I ran away to Montana.

God...Montana.

Montana and Matteo Rossi.

I absently brought my fingers to my mouth. I could still feel his lips on mine.

Lucky for me he'd turned out to be a sound sleeper. I'd tiptoed through the cabin this morning, packing up and getting out of there. Had he woken up, I didn't know what I'd have said to him, but I'd have thought of something.

Lying came very naturally to me, thanks to my father, although lying to Matt was a challenge.

Good thing he hadn't woken up.

I'd choked back tears as I left the cabin, as I got into my rental car, as I drove into Billings, as I got on the plane.

Finally, now that I'd kept the tears at bay all day, I was myself again.

Riley Wolfe, who buried her emotions inside. It was the only way I could exist.

Time to let my brothers know I was back. I called Roy. He was the one I trusted the most, though I couldn't tell you why. Of all my brothers, I felt the most like Roy would "get" me.

"Sis?" he said frantically into the phone.

"Yeah, it's me." I cleared my throat. "I'm back."

"Thank God. Where are you?"

"At my place."

"Are you okay?"

"Better, anyway." Thanks to Matt Rossi.

"We're here for you. All of us. What do you need?"

I sighed. "Right now I just need for all of this to be over, you know?"

"God, do I. I have news. When can we see you?"

I was exhausted. But this needed to get resolved.

"Tonight," I said.

A FEW HOURS LATER, I sat in Rock's hotel suite. He hadn't moved into the penthouse because it was still considered a crime scene. His new wife, Lacey, was there, along with her assistant, Charlie Waters. Apparently she and Roy were an item now.

I smiled. Roy looked happy. Actually happy. I wasn't sure I'd ever seen him that way before.

Once Reid arrived and room service had been ordered, we settled in for a long night.

"The memorial service is tomorrow," Rock said. "I know the thought of acting like children destroyed by our father's death makes us all want to hurl, but we all need to be there and do it."

No one said anything.

"You feeling me?" Rock asked.

"Yeah, of course," Reid said. "It just sucks, is all."

"No shit. But we have to be there."

"Any news on Zinnia?" Roy asked.

"Zinnia?" I said.

"Yeah. She's a woman who entered into some kind of settlement with Dad and Father Jim."

"Father Jim?"

"Shit. There's a lot you don't know," Rock said. "Lace, you want to fill her in, since you uncovered this part of it?"

"Sure." Lacey cleared her throat. "When I was an associate at my old firm, I found the signature page of a document in the copy room. All I know is that it was some kind of settlement and confidentiality agreement, and your father was one of the signatories. The other one was someone named James—we think it was probably Father Jim, but I can't recall the last name—and the third one was a woman named Zinnia. Again, I can't remember the last name. It took a lot of doing just to remember that much."

"Father Jim?"

"Yeah, Father Jim," Roy said. "He's not the paragon of the church he'd like us to think he is."

"Did he ever..." I gulped.

"No, no. He's not one of *those* priests." Roy shook his head. "At least as far as I know, though it wouldn't surprise me. His victims seem to be adult women."

"But Dad..." I gulped again.

Lacey, who sat next to me, touched my forearm. I whisked it away.

"I'm sorry," she said.

"It's okay. I just..."

Don't like to be touched. The words were true, but also contradictory. I'd let Matt touch me. In fact, I'd craved it.

"Dad liked little girls," Rock said. "We all know it now."

I shook my head.

"Riley?" Roy asked.

"Dad didn't like little girls," I said. "I mean, only me. He never..."

"Wait, wait, wait... What are you trying to say?" Rock asked.

"I'm saying that... Sometimes Dad and I... We were with... others. And he only touched me."

Roy shook his head. "Riley. Fuck."

"It's okay," I said, though it wasn't okay at all.

"We all know the truth now, Riley," Reid said, "and we're all so damned sorry."

"It's in the past," I said. The recent past, but still the past.

"We're going to get you all the help you need," Rock said. "The best there is. Roy and Lace have been working with a psychologist they really like."

"I'm not sure I'm ready for that."

"It's okay. We're on your time," Reid said. "You call the shots."

I laughed. Actually laughed.

"What's funny?" Rock asked.

"Just the idea of me calling my own shots. Totally laughable. He controlled me my whole life."

"Well, the bastard's dead and buried," Rock said. "From now on, you're in charge of your own life, and we're all here for you. Got it?"

"Got it." I smiled. Actually smiled like I'd smiled with Matt. "And damn, it feels good."

24

MATTEO

Mid-afternoon the next day found me wandering around town, visiting all the places I'd taken Riley. After a visit to Mrs. Carson's—where she fed me a Mexican lunch of posole and rice, which tasted like sawdust—I walked by Trudy's. She was closed, getting ready for the dinner rush, but I waved to her through the window and she motioned for me to come in.

"How's tricks, Matt?" she asked.

"Okay."

"You seem blue. That's not like you."

"Nah. I'm good."

"Ha! I've known you for too long. What's going on?"

Telling her I'd fallen for a woman in two days and that she'd left without a trace made me sound ridiculous, so I just said, "You're imagining things."

"If you say so. Want some iced tea or something?"

"That'd be great. Thanks."

She headed to the kitchen and came back with two iced teas and then gestured to a table. "Sit."

"Something smells great. What's on for tonight?"

"Coq au vin. I got a shipment of burgundy yesterday, so I'm making good use of it."

"Awesome. Maybe I'll come by for dinner." If I was hungry, that was.

"Great! Bring your lady friend."

I lifted my eyebrows. "You mean Riley? She's gone."

"Oh? I thought she was here for the week."

"She was. Her plans changed, apparently."

"So that's what's got you down in the dumps."

I took a long sip of iced tea. "Don't be silly."

"I could tell the other night you had it pretty bad."

"I'd just met her the other night."

"So? Don't you believe in love at first sight?"

I scoffed, nearly spitting out tea. "Of course not."

"I do," she said. "And trust me. That look on your face the other night? I've seen it before."

"On me?"

"Hell, no, not on you. Matt Rossi the heartbreaker. Usually on women you bring in."

"And this time?"

"I saw it on you."

"I'll say it again, Trudy." I finished my tea and stood. "You're imagining things. Thanks for the drink."

"Anytime. See you tonight for supper?"

"Yeah. Maybe." I walked to the door and walked back out onto the street.

Love at first sight. What a crock.

I walked past Bess's antique shop. Hmm. We'd never ventured in there. I'd meant to, but then Riley tripped and dropped her purse.

Her cigarettes. I'd admonished her for smoking.

Strange. I'd been with her nearly nonstop for two days and I'd never seen her light up.

Very strange indeed.

A few doors down stood the flower shop. I'd bought her a pink rose...which she'd subsequently thrown on the ground and trampled. But she apologized, and I forgave her.

At the time, I'd have forgiven her anything.

Could I forgive her for leaving?

A moot question, to be sure. If I never found her, I couldn't forgive her. So I'd find her first, and then I'd decide whether to forgive her.

I opened the door to the flower shop, ringing the bell attached to the handle.

"Just a minute," Kari called from the back.

"It's just me," I said. "Matt."

"Oh, hey, Mattie. Be right out. I need to talk to you."

"You do?"

"Yeah. Give me a minute."

"Okay."

What did Kari need to talk to me about? Probably had a job for me. I'd fixed some plumbing for her in the past and made some repairs to her refrigeration unit. Great. I could use the cash.

I perused the flowers she had available today. Front and center was a large vase full of pink roses, just like the one I'd given Riley.

Fuck.

I looked away quickly and checked my watch. A minute passed. Then another. Finally, Kari came bustling out front, rubbing her hands together.

"Thanks for waiting. Did you need anything today, Mattie?"

"No. Just came in to say hi."

"I'm glad you did. I have something I want to show you."

"What?"

She walked behind the counter. "Remember when you came in with that woman and I said she looked familiar?"

"Yeah."

"I figured out why." She pulled a magazine out from under the counter and set it down. "Take a look."

My heart raced and I widened my eyes. It was a copy of something called *Elle*, and on the glossy cover was none other than—

"Riley."

"Yup. That's why she looked so familiar to me. She's a super-model, Mattie. Riley Wolfe."

"I've never heard of her."

"Doubtless because you don't keep up with women's fashion and makeup. She's huge. The daughter of a billionaire named Derek Wolfe."

"Now him I've heard of."

"Yeah. Everyone has. He just died recently. Big murder case in New York."

I mouth dropped open. "Her dad is dead?"

"Yeah."

"Oh my God. She must be distraught. No wonder she..."

"She what?"

"She went home. She left early from her vacation. But why would she...?"

"Why would she what?"

Why would she use a fake name? I didn't ask the question. Kari wouldn't know the answer anyway, except it was becoming obvious to me. She'd wanted to escape for a short time. Escape the sadness and trauma of losing her father.

And she was famous. She wanted to be incognito. That was why she'd used a fake name, but she'd screwed up and given me her real first name and then covered her tracks by saying it was her middle name, when her fake ID showed her middle initial as L.

Poor Riley. Poor sweet Riley.

Kari picked up the magazine. "She really is gorgeous. Even when you guys came in here and she wasn't wearing any makeup or anything. She was beautiful."

"Yeah, she was," I said, nodding. "I can't believe this."

"Neither can I."

I grabbed the magazine from her. "Do you mind if I keep this?"

"Not at all. I'm done with it. Read it cover to cover."

"Thanks, Kari." I grabbed my wallet out of my pocket and took out a ten-dollar bill. "Buy yourself a few roses on me. I owe you."

"For what?"

"Trust me, I do." I walked out of the shop, the bell ringing once more.

I owed Kari big time.

Now that I knew who Riley really was, I could find her.

25

RILEY

"Riley, darling," Fredricka whined, "what am I supposed to tell them *this* time?"

I felt bad putting Fredricka in this position. It was all me, this time. I couldn't blame it on my father. Not that I ever did before. "Tell them I'm sorry, but I need to stay in New York for now. My father's memorial service is tomorrow."

"Couldn't you have told me this a week ago? Instead of just missing the shoot in Paris?"

Yeah, I could have. I *should* have.

From now on, I vowed to be different.

"If you didn't make me so much money," Fredricka said, "I'd drop you like a hot potato."

"And I wouldn't blame you."

"What?"

"I said, I wouldn't blame you."

She laughed. "I just wanted to make sure I heard you correctly. I was expecting one of your 'any agent in New York would be thrilled to have me' speeches."

I sighed. I'd behaved so badly in the past. Sure, my father was to blame for my disappearances. Or was he? I was over eighteen. I could have—*should* have—taken control. He'd also instructed me on how to handle Fredricka.

"I'm sorry, Fredricka," I said. "Things are going to change."

"Darling, that would be wonderful. But I always love you anyway."

"You've done a lot for me," I said. "I'll never forget that."

"Thank you, darling. I'll make your excuses to Dominique. I'm sure I can talk them down and get them to reschedule. How much time do you need to mourn your father?"

Mourn my father? Ha! About zero seconds. But I did need to stay in town to help my brothers solve his murder and get us all out from under the detectives' eyes. "Would a month be too long to ask?"

"I'll make it happen, darling. Talk to you soon."

"You're the best. Thanks, Freddie."

She laughed off the use of her hated nickname and we ended the call.

She'd been good to me, had gotten me tons of work over the years and a lot of money. I vowed to treat her better and not put her in uncomfortable positions anymore. Time to woman up and be a professional.

Tonight I was meeting my brothers and their significant others for dinner in the private banquet room at the Gabriel LeGrand restaurant to discuss our situation further. The chef had promised a gourmet feast for us. Yeah, the Wolfe name was pretty powerful here in Manhattan.

I laughed out loud.

I doubted anyone had even heard of the Wolfes in Sumter Falls, Montana.

Rock had existed under the radar in a similar Montana town for over a decade.

Being invisible for a few days had been fun. Exhilarating, even. Of course, Matteo Rossi had helped as well. More gorgeous than the handsomest male models and so muscular. Plus, he was a nice guy. A really nice guy. The kind of guy I hadn't believed actually existed.

Maybe they were all out west.

It didn't really matter how many nice guys existed, though. I'd found the one I wanted. Too bad we had no future.

I'd just have to deal with that.

Compartmentalize, Riley.

I was good at that. I'd had to be, to exist before the death of my father.

No thinking of Matt right now. Not until my brothers and I had figured out this whole Derek Wolfe mess.

Yup. Compartmentalize.

I took a quick shower and changed into a dinner outfit of black capri pants and a pink silk shirt. Black Louboutins completed the look. I fluffed my hair and decided to let it air dry. What the heck? Just a little lipstick, blush, and mascara, and I was ready to go. My skin was relishing being free of heavy model makeup.

My driver was waiting downstairs to take me to the restaurant.

Yeah, I had a driver. What a privileged world I lived in! A couple days with Matt had made me realize so much. Things I took for granted were such luxuries to most people.

Damn. I was thinking about Matt again. I missed him terribly. And why? I hardly knew him, yet we'd shared something so beautiful. So magnanimous. So precious.

How could I live without him now?

Damn it! Compartmentalize, Riley.

I arrived at the restaurant and thanked my driver. He cocked his head, looking at me oddly.

Had I never thanked him before?

My God, I hadn't. Things were going to change.

Roy and Charlie were already seated in the banquet room. The others hadn't arrived yet. I was glad to have the chance to talk to Roy alone. I didn't know Charlie at all, but if Roy trusted her, I would.

"Hey, Sis," Roy said.

"Hey." I glanced to Charlie. "Nice to see you again."

"You too." She smiled.

Charlie was quite pretty. Her brown hair and round face were understated, but her eyes were spectacular indeed. A stark light blue-gray that really mesmerized me.

I looked away when I caught myself staring.

"They're amazing, aren't they?" Roy said.

"What's amazing?"

"Her eyes."

Charlie blushed. "Roy..."

"It's okay," I said. "He's right. I'm sorry for staring."

"I've tried to capture them on canvas," Roy said. "It's not possible."

"Can we talk about something other than my eyes?" Charlie asked. "You're making me self-conscious. I'm sitting here with the most beautiful supermodel in the world."

My cheeks warmed. I was used to compliments. I'd gotten them all my life on my beauty. But for some reason, Charlie's words embarrassed me. As if she were nothing compared to me.

Which wasn't true. She was lovely. All her average features combined together to make something very striking.

"My sister is beautiful, for sure," Roy said.

"Of course you think so," Charlie laughed. "She looks exactly like you."

This time Roy blushed. The two of them were just so sweet together. It was kind of sickening.

"Do you two want to get a room?" I asked.

"That sounds pretty good to me," my brother replied.

"For God's sake, Roy," Charlie said.

Man, I was really missing Matt.

Compartmentalize.

"Where were you the past several days?" Roy asked me.

Finally, a change of subject, even though it wasn't one I wanted to talk about. Better than listening to the two of them fawn all over each other, though.

"Nowhere, really."

"Riley..."

"I ran away. I'm sorry. It... It won't happen again."

"Sis, it happens all the time."

"You don't understand."

"I'm sure I don't. Enlighten me."

I chewed on my lower lip. "The other times... They weren't my fault."

"Oh?"

"Dad... He'd take me..." I gulped, nausea clawing up my throat.

"Roy, please," Charlie said.

"No, it's okay." I swallowed down the acid. "I do owe you an explanation. My life hasn't been pretty, but that doesn't excuse me leaving the rest of you in a lurch."

"Riley," Roy said, "I'm not accusing you of anything. None of us are. We wish we'd known. We'd have stopped him. Please believe we would have."

"I'm not sure you could have."

My quietest brother grew red in the face. "Oh, we would have. Trust me."

"Rock tried, and look where it got him."

"He was a kid. This last decade, we were all adults. If we'd known, we'd have stopped him. I swear to you."

My soft-spoken brother was angry. Rage emanated from his pores. I believed him. They would have rescued me. More likely, they would have tried but failed, making their own lives miserable in the process.

It wasn't their fault they hadn't known.

It was mine.

Derek Wolfe had me trained well. He'd stripped me of my sense of self to the point that I did whatever he told me.

That wasn't my brothers' fault. Was it even my father's, once I reached the age of majority?

No.

It was mine.

My own fault. I could have broken away and begun healing long ago, but I hadn't. Why?

Did I have some sick case of Stockholm syndrome?

I shuddered at the thought.

"I know, Roy," I replied softly.

Rock, Lacey, and Reid entered the banquet room then, bringing this conversation to a halt, thank God.

Or so I thought.

Rock, never one to mince words—at least as much as I remembered—dived right in.

"You all right, Riley?"

I nodded.

"You sure? People who are all right don't disappear without a trace."

"Rock..." Roy began.

"It's okay," I said to Roy. "This time was all on me, but the others..."

"That bastard," Rock said through gritted teeth.

My cheeks burned. All gazes focused on me. All five of them.

"Hey," Reid said. "We didn't know."

"I know that."

"We would have stopped it. We would have found a way."

"I already told her that," Roy said.

"It merits repeating," Reid said. "He was a motherfucker."

"You mean daughterfucker." Then I clamped my hand over my mouth.

How had I said that? How had those horrific words spewed out of my mouth?

"Hey," Roy said. "Easy."

"I don't know why I said that. I mean, it's true, but..."

"It happens," Rock said. "Sometimes things are so awful that you can't help but put them in the crudest terms possible. Trust me. I've been there." He shook his head. "No, I take that back. I never went through anything like you went through, but there *are* things you don't know about my life."

Reid nodded. "Buffington. Yeah, we've heard stories."

"I don't know what you've heard"—Rock took a sip of his water—"but I'd imagine it's all true."

I fidgeted with my napkin for a few seconds, and then I met my oldest brother's gaze. My brother, who'd been sent away because he'd been protecting me. Trying to keep my father from hurting me. Trying to save me from the life I was ultimately condemned to.

His eyes were clear and green. Gorgeous eyes, actually, but filled with not only rage but also sadness and regret.

What had happened to Rock? Because of me?

Lacey touched his arm lightly, as if offering him comfort.

Rock cleared his throat. "We didn't come here to rehash old news."

"Maybe not," Reid said, "but I think we need to. What happened to you and what happened to Riley is important. We can't forget those things, because those things represent exactly who our father was."

Roy, who was usually quiet during these family meetings, cleared his throat and regarded me. "You and Rock weren't Dad's only victims."

"I know," I said. "He was tough on you and Reid too."

"No, that's not what I mean."

This time it was Charlie touching Roy's arm.

"I have something to tell you," Roy continued. "Something I learned through my work with Dr. Woolcott." He cleared his throat again. "And it's not pretty."

26

MATTEO

Taking a redeye from Billings to New York hadn't been in the plans. I'd decided to drive, but the transmission in my truck went kaput before dinner. I hightailed it over to Mary's auto repair shop, but she was booked solid for the next week.

"Sorry, Mattie. I really need to get another mechanic in here. It never rains but it pours!"

"Can you move me to the front? I'll pay extra." I had a few dollars tucked away for a rainy day. This was well worth it.

"No can do," she said. "I have to order your parts. That'll take a few days in and of itself."

"Shit."

"Just leave her here."

"Yeah. All right." I raked my fingers through my hair and pulled out my phone to call Luke. "Hey, man," I said when he answered. "I need you to meet me at Mary's and drive me home. And then to the airport."

A half hour later, Luke waited patiently at my cabin while I threw clothes into a duffel.

"I hear she's a famous model," he said.

"Yeah. Apparently."

"You really think you have a shot?"

Did I? "We have something. I'm not sure what it is. If nothing else, I want to support her while she mourns the death of her father."

"I get it, man," he said, "but don't you think if she wanted your support she'd have told you everything?"

Fuck. Anvil to gut. But Luke was never one to tread softly. He was just being a friend.

"Yeah, it's occurred to me."

"You've got it that bad, huh?"

"Honestly, I'm not sure what I've got. I only know she's special. She lied for a good reason."

"It's easy to tell yourself that, Matt," he said, "but when people lie, it's usually not for a good reason. It's usually to cover something up."

"What would she have to cover up? She's a famous super-model who just lost her dad. She probably needed an escape from life."

"Maybe. Just be careful."

"I will."

"You want me to come along?"

I thought about it. Having Luke along would make it easier, but I needed to do this on my own. Riley was important to me, and I wanted her to know that. Having a friend tag along with me wouldn't show her that. No, I had to go out of my comfort zone and prove to her that I was there for her and would help her through the loss of her father.

"I need to do this by myself, but thanks."

He nodded. "Got everything?"

"Yeah. Let's bolt."

We drove the hour to Billings without saying much. I was lost in thought, and Luke seemed to understand.

When he dropped me off, he said, "Go get her, man."

I opened my mouth to protest that I was only going there to offer support, but then closed it and simply nodded as I grabbed my duffel and shut the door.

Go get her, man.

A man didn't hop on a redeye to offer support to a woman he just met.

No.

A man jumped on a redeye because he was in love.

Fuck me.

I'd fallen in love with Riley Wolfe.

And Luke was right.

I was going to go get her.

27

RILEY

I sat, numb, as my brother described what he'd learned about his buried memory.

A woman with cuts above her breasts had escaped from a dark place where my father and our parish priest had been hunting her.

Hunting her.

She was the prey.

"Do you remember her name?" I asked.

"No. I don't think I asked her. Somehow we got the elevator to go up, and as soon as it opened—I don't even know which floor we were on—she ran out."

"Naked?" I said.

"As far as I remember. I never..." Roy closed his eyes. "I never saw her again."

"This was over a decade ago," Reid said. "We'll never find her."

"Probably not," Lacey agreed. "We'll have to concentrate on Zinnia. The times don't match up, so the woman Roy saw can't be Zinnia."

"Unless she came back and threatened to expose them," I offered.

Lacey widened her eyes. "I hadn't thought of that."

"I know my father," I said. "I had no idea this shit was going on, but I can guarantee you that if one woman managed to escape, he never let another escape. He would have taken precautions."

"I suppose it's possible he stopped the hunting games," Reid said.

"More likely he just upped the security," I said. "Like I said, one of the benefits of the life I led was that I knew him better than anyone. I knew how his mind worked. He got what he wanted, no matter what."

"Whether he stopped or continued," Lacey said, "Riley makes a good point. Zinnia could very well be the woman Roy encountered in the elevator."

"I don't know," Charlie offered. "If you'd been hunted by Derek Wolfe, would you ever go near him again? Even for a huge settlement? You couldn't pay me all the money in the world to face him."

"Charlie makes a good point too," Lacey said.

"Only one way to find out," Rock said. "We need to find this Zinnia."

Our server entered the banquet room then. "Excuse me, ladies and gentlemen, but your amuse-bouche is ready." Two others followed him in, carrying trays.

"Chef Gabriel has prepared sashimi salmon on a rye toast point with a touch of garlic wasabi."

The servers distributed the small dishes.

"What's an amuse-bouche?" Rock asked.

"A pre-appetizer," Reid said. "It's French. It means something to amuse your mouth while you wait for your actual appetizer."

Rock rolled his eyes. "You want me to eat raw fish."

"Try it." Lacey smiled. "Salmon sashimi melts in your mouth."

"Only for you." Rock popped the salmon into his mouth, chewed, and swallowed. "My mouth isn't amused."

"Bro," Reid said, "you need a lesson in the finer things in life."

Lacey patted her lips with her napkin after swallowing hers. "I think it's delicious."

I shoved mine across the table to her. "You can have mine, then. I'm with Rock. I don't eat raw fish."

"You don't?" Reid looked shocked.

"Have you ever, in your life, seen me consume raw fish?"

"Well, no, but—"

"Our esteemed father made me try sushi once. Once. I threw up in the ladies room. Never again."

Roy, Charlie, and Reid agreed with Lacey that it was delicious. Whatever. Good for them.

"Now that we're done with raw meat," Roy said, "we need to discuss finding a way into this underground hunting arena our father had."

"If it still exists," Lacey reminded him.

"All I can tell you is that the elevator dropped," Roy said. "I seemed to be underneath what I thought was the lowest floor of our building."

"I've taken a look at the master blueprints." Reid took a sip of his cocktail. "There's a level reachable only by a special elevator, but it's the mechanical floor. Since our building is so tall, we also have mechanical rooms on higher levels."

"I wasn't in a special elevator," Roy said. "It was one of the normal elevators accessible from the lobby."

"Right," Reid said, "and I've gotten confirmation that our mechanical floor houses nothing but mechanics."

"He couldn't have been playing his game on the mechanical

floor anyway," I offered. "Engineers and mechanics have access, and Dad would never risk getting caught by anyone."

"Unless maybe that's part of the game?" Charlie asked.

I shook my head. "You don't know Derek Wolfe."

She opened her mouth, but I gestured her to stop.

"I don't mean that in a bad way, Charlie. Be glad you don't. My father left nothing to chance. That wasn't the way he was wired."

"Agreed," Reid said. "He taught me the business, and Riley's right. He made sure all bases were covered. Always."

"Yeah," I said. "He made sure all bases were covered in his non-business pursuits as well."

All eyes gazed upon me then. My cheeks burned.

"Look, I'm not trying to get sympathy, okay? Please, just don't. Having all of you feeling sorry for me isn't helping."

"She's right." Lacey smiled, or tried to. "You're a strong woman, Riley. You don't need anyone's pity. That's not what this is. We feel bad about what you went through, just like we feel bad about what your brothers all went through. But we don't pity you."

I nodded. I didn't believe her for a minute, but it was a nice gesture.

"My recall isn't perfect," Roy said, "but I feel strongly that the floor I encountered was lower than the mechanical floor. As low as you could get in the building. I could go back into hypnosis and try to get more information."

"Only if you want to," Rock said.

"I want to do all I can. I'm not sure it'll do any good, though. Once I uncovered the woman, it all came crashing back to me. I don't think hypnosis will get me any further."

"What we need now is evidence," Lacey said. "We need to get to the hunting ground at the bottom of the building."

"If it's still there," I said quietly.

"What do you mean?"

"I mean, my father covered his tracks. Once he knew Roy had seen the place, he probably destroyed it."

"He couldn't destroy a whole floor of the building without anyone knowing it," Rock said.

"Sure he could," Reid said. "He built it without anyone knowing it."

The server interrupted us again. "Your appetizer for the evening, ladies and gentlemen. Chef has prepared broiled calamari rings with roasted garlic and red pepper." He and the others distributed the plates.

Once they had left, Rock said, "Raw fish, and now squid?"

"Try it," Lacey said. "What have you got to lose?"

"My lunch." He pushed the plate away. "Doesn't anyone believe in good old beef anymore?"

"I hear beef is up for the entrée," Reid said. "Except for Riley. You're getting tilapia."

I rolled my eyes. "Great."

"You don't eat red meat."

"I do now." I stood. "I'm going to go change my order to the beef entrée. As long as it's not raw, that is." I hastily exited the banquet room, found our server, and let him know what I wanted.

When I returned, all gazes were upon me once more.

"What?" I nearly yelled.

After a few seconds, Rock spoke. "Riley, did Dad ever take you...hunting?"

28

MATTEO

I got a room at a Manhattan hotel I couldn't afford. I hoped it would only be for a few nights. But who knew? It could take a while to find Riley. Sure, she was a big name here, but that meant she probably also had mega security.

To think.

I'd slept with a supermodel.

Me. Matt Rossi. Mr. Small Town Guy who made silver jewelry and did odd jobs for a living.

The velvet box holding the silver and pink sapphire pendant sat in my pocket. Once I found Riley, I'd put it around her neck. After I settled in my room, I took the elevator down to the lounge and found a seat at the bar.

"What can I get you?" a well-dressed bartender asked.

"Beer, please."

"What kind?"

"Whatever you have on tap is fine."

"We have Guinness draft, Stella Artois, Budweiser, Fat Tire, and Dos Equis."

Okay, then. "Bud is fine."

"You got it."

Seconds later, a pilsner glass of good old Bud sat in front of me.

"You want to run a tab?" he asked.

"Sure." I slid him a credit card. "Can I ask you something?"

"Sure enough."

"Do you know Riley Wolfe?"

"The model?" He chuckled. "I wish."

Jealousy speared into me. I couldn't fault him. Of course he wished he knew Riley. She was the most gorgeous creature on this planet.

"I mean, do you know where I might find her?"

"On any magazine cover."

"Where she lives, I mean."

"I assume she lives in the Wolfe building."

"The Wolfe building?"

"Yeah, it's this huge silver skyscraper in Lower Manhattan."

"Where's Lower Manhattan?"

"Dude, did you just get off the bus from Nebraska or something?"

"Just off the plane. From Montana."

He guffawed. "That's something else. And the first thing you do is ask for the most famous model in New York. That's awesome."

I didn't see anything funny about it from where I was standing.

"Wait," he continued. "Here comes someone who might be able to help you."

A young man ambled to the bar. He was pretty-boy handsome and dressed to the nines. Here I sat in my jeans and the one button-down I owned.

"Hey, Fox," the barkeep said.

Fox?

"Hi, Johnny. I'll have the usual."

"You got it." He set to pouring what looked like bourbon, but from a bottle I didn't recognize. "This guy has a question for you."

"Fox" turned to me. "Yeah?"

I held out my hand. "Matt Rossi."

"Fox Monroe. Are you a fan?"

"Of who?"

Johnny guffawed again. "Fox here is a model."

"Oh. Yeah. Sorry. I don't know any male models. I'm actually looking for a female model, though. Riley Wolfe. Do you know her?"

"Riley? Is she back? Last I heard she flew the coop again."

"Flew the coop? What are you talking about?"

"She disappears from time to time. Kind of her MO."

"Oh?"

"Yeah. It irks the rest of us in the industry, but she gets away with it because she's so good. Of course the Wolfe name doesn't hurt either."

"So you *do* know her."

"Of course. She's a pain in the ass for the rest of us, but I have to admit. She's an amazing model. It all comes so naturally to her. The poise and the beauty. She carries herself like the old-school supermodels."

"Old-school supermodels?"

"You know. Cindy Crawford. Naomi Campbell. Christie Brinkley."

I nodded. Was it weird I'd only heard of one of those models? "She is certainly beautiful."

"She got that from genetics. The rest is all her. She'd have an amazing career if she'd stop being such a flake."

I tamped down the anger that threatened. "Seems she already has an amazing career."

Fox took a sip of the drink that Johnny had set in front of

him. "You're not wrong. Damn, this is good stuff. Expensive, though."

"What is it?"

"Pappy Van Winkle bourbon. Fifteen-year. I stumbled upon it by accident, and now I don't want to drink anything else. Good thing I just got that Dolce & Gabbana contract." He signaled to Johnny. "Pour one of these for Matt here."

"No thanks. I'm on a budget."

"It's on me. Everyone should try this once."

"Not really a bourbon drinker," I said.

"You don't have to be. This stuff is in a class all its own. Trust me."

"Okay, man. Nothing like a Bud with a bourbon chaser, right?"

"Don't chase it. Sip it."

"Whatever you say." I took a sip of the amber liquid Johnny set in front of me.

Smokiness and spiciness. Nutmeg. And man, it glided down my throat. No harshness at all. "Wow."

Fox nodded. "Am I right?"

"Just for kicks, how much is this?"

"It's a single."

"I mean the price."

"Ha! You don't want to know."

"Actually, I really do. And before you tell me, thank you. I appreciate the thought."

"It's sixty-five a shot here. Some places charge more."

My mouth dropped open. "Sixty-five? Dollars?"

"No. Sixty-five potatoes. Of course dollars."

"Fuck." I took another sip. "It might actually be worth it."

"No shit. I've tried to find it at local liquor stores and online. Even the distillery, but it's impossible. It gets sold out as soon as it's released, and most of it goes to high-end bars like this one."

"Damn." Another sip, and I was nearly done. No way could I afford another. "I guess you made a bourbon drinker out of me."

"Nah. I made a Pappy's drinker out of you. There's a definite difference." He signaled to Johnny again. "Another for my friend here."

I shook my head. "No, thank you. It's way too much."

"Dude, I just got the contract of a lifetime. I'm happy to treat you."

"You don't even know me."

He cocked his head. "You're right, at that. Tell me about yourself, then. Specifically, why are you looking for Riley Wolfe?"

29

RILEY

Did Dad ever take you hunting?

No wonder they were all staring. I'd been gone five minutes, and during that time, I'd become the subject of their conversation.

I sat down and tried to hold back my irritation. "No, he didn't. And I'd appreciate it if you wouldn't talk behind my back."

Five sighs of relief met my ears.

"Don't you think I would have told you?" I asked.

"We didn't know," Roy said. "You never told us anything."

"We could have helped you," Reid said. "We were adults before you were. We could have gotten you out of his house. We could have petitioned the courts for custody. Or we could have—"

"Stop," I said. "Just stop. We've been through this. You couldn't have. Don't you get it?"

"We can never truly get what you've been through, Riley," Roy said.

"You're right. Be thankful."

He didn't reply right away. I couldn't blame him. Any of

them. Sure, they could be thankful they hadn't gone through the horror I had, but they'd all gone through shit at our father's hands, and I wouldn't deny them their right to hate him on their own terms.

"He just meant," Reid said, "that we would have gotten you out of there. Come hell or high water—"

I shook my head vehemently. "I've thought about that. A lot. And I've concluded that you couldn't have. Don't you see? He wouldn't have let you!"

They all gaped at me, as if the words I'd uttered were incomprehensible.

"Actually," Roy said, "she's right."

"Wait." Reid shook his head. "You just said—"

"I said we can never truly know what she went through, and I stand by that. You said we would have helped, and I agree. We would have. We would have moved mountains. But our father— he would have moved *planets* to get his own way."

"Planets?" Rock scoffed. "You've gone off the deep end, Roy."

Charlie patted Roy's hand.

"I'm not being literal, Rock," Roy said. "I'm only saying whatever we did to help Riley wouldn't have been enough. Dad had all the power, control of all the assets, probably control of the authorities. If he wanted to keep abusing our sister, we couldn't have stopped him. Look where your attempt got you."

"Wait a minute—"

"Rock, please." Lacey stopped him.

"Look where your attempt to stop him got you," Roy said again.

"I was fourteen, for fuck's sake. A kid. I had no control over anything, including my own hormones."

"No, you didn't." Roy paused a moment. "That's my point, entirely. Sure, you were a young hothead, but our father never changed. In fact, he became *more* powerful and *more* egotistical, if that was possible. He was a megalomaniac. Derek Wolfe got what he wanted no matter the cost. No one stopped him."

"Roy is right," I said quietly. "Only he said it better than I could. Trust me. You couldn't have stopped him. Any attempt would have had you wishing you'd never tried."

"Hey, I don't wish—" Rock began.

"I know," I said. "I know you don't wish anything different. I know you'd do it all over again, and I know you two"—I nodded to Reid and Roy—"would have tried if you'd known. I get it. I'd do the same for any of you. But you wouldn't have been successful, and he'd have made your lives miserable, just like he did to Rock."

"We weren't teenagers," Reid said. "Roy and I could have—"

"We couldn't have," Roy interjected. "We'd have wanted to, and we'd have tried, but we wouldn't have been able to protect her. I wish it were different, but it's not."

"So there's no use in any of you feeling guilty for doing nothing when you didn't know anyway," I said. "Had you tried, he'd have made you pay. Big time. So please, give yourselves a break. You couldn't have saved me, and I know you would have tried. Frankly, I'm glad you didn't know. I can't bear the thought of what he might have done to you."

True words.

"Was our father a megalomaniac?" Rock asked. "Or a fucking psychopath?"

"He was a pedophile, for sure," Reid said.

"Only with me." I raised my hand when mouths opened to interrupt me. "Hey, he's a sicko for sure, but he never touched another child."

"Even in his hunting games?" Lacey asked.

"I didn't know about that. All I can tell you is that there were times when I..." Nausea crept into me.

"It's okay," Lacey said. "You don't have to tell us."

"Except you do," Rock said. "We need all the information."

I nodded, gulping down the nausea. "Sometimes he...with others...and their children. Some of them shared. He didn't. He never touched anyone but me and he didn't let anyone else touch me."

"I suppose there's that," Rock scoffed. "But just because you didn't witness him molesting other children doesn't mean he didn't. That doesn't make me feel any better, Sis."

"Me either," I said.

"The woman I saw who escaped appeared to be an adult," Roy said. "She was young, for sure, but definitely through puberty. That doesn't mean she was of age."

"True," Lacey said. "But if she and Zinnia are the same person, Zinnia had to be of age to sign a legal document."

"And if they are one and the same," Reid said, "years had passed between the two incidents. She could have been underage when Roy found her."

"All true," Lacey agreed. "We need to find her."

"The PIs are on it, baby," Rock said. "We need to prepare ourselves to act like the grieving children tomorrow at the asshole's memorial."

"We're losing a buttload of money every day we don't break ground in Vegas," Reid reminded us.

"I don't think any of us care about that at the moment," Rock said.

"Someone has to. We're in great shape, but we can't keep delaying. This is still a business."

"Fine, fine. You and I'll go to Vegas first thing next week and get it figured out."

"Good," Reid said. "We can't put it off any longer."

The servers arrived with our salads—spinach with avocado and tomato and a jalapeno ranch dressing.

I took a bite.

Mmm. Spicy. And delicious.

Not nearly as spicy as the Mexican food I'd eaten in Montana with Matt, though.

Damn.

I missed him.

I missed him so much.

30

MATTEO

"There isn't a lot to tell," I said. "I'm from a small town in Montana outside of Billings called Sumter Falls."

"Oh? How do you know Riley?"

"I don't, really." Not actually a lie. I sure didn't know her as well as I wanted to.

"Not buying it, dude," Fox said. "No one flies to New York from Montana to meet a supermodel without knowing her. Unless he's a stalker."

I nearly spit my sixty-five-dollar bourbon on the bar. I swallowed quickly. "I'm no stalker."

"Yeah, you don't look the type. I had one once. She was a real piece of work." He took a drink. "Still, though, why'd you fly here to find Riley?"

"If I tell you the truth, you need to keep it in confidence."

"Absolutely. Who would I tell?"

"Well...everyone in the modeling industry comes to mind," I said.

"That's not my style." Fox set down his glass and met my gaze. "What's your story?"

"Do I have your word that it stays between the two of us?"

"You do."

For some reason, I believed the young man who was a virtual stranger to me. I wasn't sure why. Maybe I just needed to tell someone about Riley and me. Maybe that would make it more real. I was beginning to wonder if I'd imagined the whole thing.

"She rented a cabin of mine in Montana. That's how we met."

"Oh?" He lifted his brows. Yeah, his interest was definitely piqued. "So that's where she ran away to. Montana."

"Ran away?"

"Yeah. Like I said, it's her MO."

"Why?"

"Why?" He chuckled. "If I had to wager a guess, probably because she's a spoiled brat whose had everything handed to her since the day she escaped her mother's womb."

"Hey, wait a minute—"

"Easy. I mean no disrespect. She's great at what she does. I've already told you that. But she doesn't seem to take her career seriously. Why in hell would she just take off whenever the wind blows, you know? Answer? Because she can. Daddy takes care of her."

"Uh...didn't you hear? Daddy's dead."

"Yeah. That's right. Someone offed him."

"So she's probably mourning him," I said.

"Then why did she run away? To get away from her brothers?"

""Brothers?" She'd told me she had only one brother. So much I didn't know.

"Yeah. Three of them. All big and strong and protective. I met one of them recently. He's the size of a tank."

An artist the size of a tank? Riley's brothers didn't scare me. I could hold my own. Besides, I was no threat to their sister. I was in love with her. Despite the fact she'd lied to me continually.

But was I truly in love?

I knew nothing about her. I'd learned more from a half hour talking to Fox than I had from Riley in the few days we spent together.

Had I fallen in love with an illusion?

"Is she close with her brothers? Her family?"

"I honestly don't know. I barely know her. We've been to some functions together, and we've had some trivial conversation, but she pretty much keeps to herself."

I nodded. "I get it."

Did I ever. She'd invented a whole new identity to keep me from getting to know her. Talk about keeping to herself. Maybe I didn't know her any better than Fox did.

Except she and I had slept together. Made love. It had been quick and furious and wonderful, but I wished with all my heart that I'd been able to show her so much more.

"So why are you looking for her? She made *that* much of an impression on you?"

Had she ever. "Does that surprise you?"

He shook his head. "You aren't the first guy to fall for a pretty face."

I took a sip of my expensive bourbon. "She's a lot more than a pretty face."

"Is she? She seems like the typical heiress to me. Spoiled. Comes and goes as she pleases even though she has commitments."

"Commitments?"

"She was supposed to be shooting in Paris this week. Everyone in the industry knows it. She does this all the time, and her poor agent has to make the excuses."

I finished my bourbon. "I see."

"If you've got some fairytale image of her, of saving the damsel in distress, my best advice is to get over it, Matt. Go home to Montana. Find a nice local girl. Get married and have some kids. Riley Wolfe isn't for you."

"Do you want her for yourself? Is that what this is about?"

He laughed. "God, no. She's too old for me."

Hmm. Good question. How old was Riley anyway? Her fake driver's license had said she was twenty-eight. Seemed about right.

"How old are you?"

"First, I was kidding about Riley being too old me for. I'm twenty-one. I look older, and I won't age quickly, which will serve me well in modeling."

"Only twenty-one, and already you know the best bourbon?"

"I told you. I found it by accident— Wait a minute!"

"What?"

"I was with a woman the night I tried this for the first time a few weeks ago. A woman who married one of Riley's brothers. He was there that night. Rock Wolfe."

"What was the woman's name?"

"Lacey. She's an attorney. A total hottie, but she wouldn't bite because she's ten years older than I am. What is it with some women?"

"Maybe she was in love with someone else. Riley's brother. Where can I find her?"

"Lacey?" Fox dug out his wallet and leafed through it. "I think I have her card. No, I guess not. Sorry."

"Shit. But her name's Lacey, right? An attorney. Last name?"

"Ward, I think, but like I said, she's married to Rock Wolfe now."

"That's okay. It's a start. Thanks, man."

"Any time. Just remember if you find Riley, my name stays out of it."

"You got it. Thanks for the drinks, and best of luck with your Duckie and Bandana thing."

He laughed. "You're a riot, Matt. It's Dolce & Gabbana." He pulled another card out of his wallet. "You ever want to have another drink, give me a call."

"Will do." I stood and held out my hand. "I'm glad we met."

"Yeah, me too. See you around."

I walked out of the bar, clutching the card and remembering the name he'd given me.

Lacey Ward.

My key to finding Riley.

31

RILEY

Though I'd requested the filet mignon entrée, I only ate a few bites. Nothing tasted good to me tonight.

I dreaded the memorial service tomorrow, and though my brothers needed me, I hated being back here. It was all a constant reminder of my father.

On top of all that crap?

I missed Matt.

I missed him so much.

The servers had collected our plates, and Charlie had the floor. Apparently she'd set up the memorial service.

"We need to be at the church at one p.m. tomorrow," she said. "The service is at two. I've got the programs being printed tomorrow at ten, so..."

"What?" Rock asked.

"One of you has to do a eulogy."

Silence descended in the banquet room like a black curtain. A eulogy?

"I'm sorry," Charlie said, "but you guys told me this had to look like a real memorial where you were all devastated. One of you is going to have to step up."

"Not me," I said. "I can't."

"No one expects you to do it, Sis," Roy said.

"I sure as hell can't," Rock said. "I've been away since I was a kid."

"I hate to say this," Reid said, "but that may make you the perfect choice."

"Oh, hell, no." Rock shook his head vehemently.

"Can't Father Jim just say a few words?" Reid asked.

"That's fine with me," Charlie said, "but you told me this has to look like you all care."

"How can any one of us do it?" Rock said. "It's impossible. We all have our issues with the bastard."

"I'll do it," Roy said quietly.

My eyes shot wide. Roy? The recluse? The most introverted of all of us? He was going to speak publicly about our father, who he knew to be a monster? Firsthand?

Charlie touched his wrist. "Are you sure?"

He nodded. "Rock and Riley can't. They suffered too much at his hand. Reid suffered more than I did. I'm the logical choice."

"But you, more than even me, know what he was capable of." I shook my head.. "Are you sure?"

"It was a secret I held trapped inside my mind for over a decade," Roy said. "Freeing it has freed *me*, in a way. I don't expect you to understand. I kept to myself. Partially because of the repressed memories, but partly because it's just who I am. I'm an artist. An introvert. I wasn't there for any of you when you needed me in the past, but I'm here now. This is something I can do for all of you. Please. Let me."

Silence.

Finally, I said, "What can you possibly say?"

"I'll lie through my teeth. Don't worry. I'll make it look good."

"Bro, if you're willing, we'd all appreciate it." Rock smiled.

"Willing isn't the word I'd use," Roy chuckled, "but I'll do it. For my family."

I smiled at my middle brother, the one who looked most like me. "You're amazing, Roy."

"Hardly," he said, "but honestly, a weight has been lifted from me. I feel better now than I have in a long time." He smiled at Charlie. "Of course, this lady has helped me a lot too."

"A good woman can work miracles," Rock agreed.

Both Charlie and Lacey's cheeks reddened.

Servers brought coffee and tea. I inhaled the chocolaty aroma. Smelled great, but not as good as the coffee at the Bean House in Sumter Falls.

"Dessert will be served in a few moments," the server said before leaving.

"I can't possibly eat another bite." Lacey added a touch of cream to her coffee.

"Me neither," I said.

"You hardly ate anything, Riley," Reid said. "Even after you insisted on beef. Are you okay?"

Was I okay? What a loaded question. I hadn't been okay in twenty years.

Except when I was with Matt.

I was okay then.

In fact, I was almost...happy.

What an odd feeling—one I desperately wanted to feel again.

I couldn't, though. My time running had come to an end. I had a family who needed me. I had a career, and I was done making Fredricka jump through hoops. I was going to be the ideal client now. Never again would I welch on a contract.

Riley Wolfe would earn her place in the world of modeling not by her name and face, but by her professionalism.

I was here to stay.

Dessert turned out to be Bananas Foster. How long had it been since I'd eaten dessert? Not long, as I'd indulged with Matt a few days ago, but before then? Years.

I hadn't eaten much dinner, but for some reason, Bananas Foster sounded good to me.

I scooped some up in my spoon and brought it to my lips.

Then I let myself taste it.

The creamy vanilla ice cream, the smooth banana, and the sweet sauce of brown sugar, cinnamon, and dark rum.

Delicious.

I smiled to myself.

How Matt would enjoy this. He lived such a simple life, but he loved good food. If only he were here, sharing this meal with me.

I sighed after swallowing the deliciousness. Better that he wasn't here. My life was a mess. I was determined to fix my career and take charge, and I had a lot of work ahead of me. Plus, I needed to fix my head. Get some therapy. Roy highly recommended his therapist. Next week, I'd call and get an appointment.

I had to get my head on straight. Get my career back in order, before I could share myself with anyone.

I held back a scoff.

Matt Rossi would have found someone else by the time I was whole enough to be worthy of him.

The thought sent a spear of sorrow arrowing through my heart.

I took another bite of Bananas Foster.

This one didn't taste nearly as good.

32

MATTEO

Morning in Manhattan. So different from morning in Montana. Lacey Ward was easy enough to find online. She was a partner at a Manhattan firm, so I called first thing after noshing on a bagel I'd picked up and smothered with cream cheese. Best bagel I'd ever eaten.

I called the law firm as I was wiping the last of the cream cheese from my lips. The receptionist spewed out the names in a sing-songy voice.

"Lacey Ward, please," I said.

"I'm sorry, Ms. Ward no longer works here."

"Oh? Could you tell me where she's working now?"

"She's legal counsel at Wolfe Enterprises."

Of course. She married a Wolfe, so now she worked there. "Thanks. Sorry to bother you." I did a quick search for the number I needed.

I got ready to punch in the numbers, when I made a rash decision. Why call when I could just show up? It'd be a lot harder for her to turn an actual person away, but she could easily dismiss a phone call. Chances were I'd get voicemail anyway.

I breathed in. Out. In again.

I was one step closer to Riley. My heart was beating hard. More like galloping. Was Riley even here? Fox had said she had an MO of disappearing. Had she come back here when she left Montana? I had no idea. No idea at all. But if her father had just died, chances were pretty good.

Instead of catching a cab, I walked several blocks to the Wolfe building with my phone as my guide.

New Yorkers bustled around me, never smiling, some bumping into me without so much as an "excuse me." Man. Why did anyone live here? Everything was so crowded and closed in.

I pondered this as I stopped abruptly when my phone chided me.

"You have arrived."

Okay, then. So this silver skyscraper was the Wolfe Building. It was no Empire State Building, but it was a mountain of steel nonetheless.

I drew in a deep breath and entered through the revolving doors.

Several armed guards greeted me, along with metal detectors.

"Good morning." I smiled.

My smile wasn't returned. "Please place your phone and all metal objects in the container, sir," one of them said.

I complied, and after he nodded, I walked through the detector.

I nearly jumped when the damned thing beeped.

"Come back through, sir," the guard said.

Meanwhile, others were lined up behind me, frowning. I'd angered the masses.

"Please spread your arms," the guard said as he hovered a

wand over me. "Seems good now. Do you have any artificial joints?"

"No." I pulled the silver pendant out of my pocket. "Is this the problem?"

"Yeah. Probably. Why didn't you put it in the container?"

"I...forgot it was there."

"All right. You're good. Go ahead to the reception desk."

"Thanks."

Yeah. A lie. I hadn't forgotten it was there. I just didn't want to shove it into a container with other things that had no meaning.

I headed toward the reception desk.

"May I help you?" one of the four receptionists—the only one who wasn't busy—asked.

"I'd like to see Lacey Ward, please."

"You mean Lacey Wolfe?"

"Yes. Sorry."

"No problem. She hasn't been married long. Sign in there, please." She gestured to an iPad. "Do you have an appointment?"

"I—"

"Wait," she interrupted me. "You can't have an appointment. The Wolfes are all out today for Mr. Wolfe's memorial service."

"Right. I don't have an appointment." I thought quickly. "I just came to ask her about the details of the memorial. You know, so I can go pay my respects."

"You're a friend of the Wolfe family?"

"Yes. I'm a friend of Riley's."

"How nice." She handed me a crisp card with the Wolfe logo at the top. "Here are the details. The service is at two."

I took the card from her. "Awesome. Thanks for your help."

I scanned the card. St. Andrew's Parish. Wake to follow at the Waldorf Astoria.

Apparently I was going to a memorial service this afternoon. For now, though? I had to buy something to wear. Jeans and a T-shirt weren't going to cut it for Derek Wolfe's funeral.

THANK GOD I had a decent credit line on the one card I carried with me. Black slacks, a black silk tie, and a white button-down shirt in Manhattan set me back two grand. What the fuck? That was more than I'd spent on clothes in my entire adult life.

Despite the fact that I was now two grand in the hole, I took a cab to St. Andrew's for the ceremony. I didn't want to take a chance of being late. I arrived at the church and stood with my mouth hanging open.

It was a gorgeous old building, almost like something out of Paris or Barcelona. Granite stones and ornate stained-glass windows.

Okay. New York had something to offer after all—besides Riley Wolfe, that was. I was a western boy, but we didn't have historic buildings like this in Montana. Hordes of people milled around the entrance. Would there even be room for everyone? I pushed through as best I could, finally making it inside.

"Welcome," someone said, handing me a program. "Be sure to sign the guest book."

"Thank you." Then I bypassed the guest book. I didn't even know the man. I was here to see his daughter.

Of course I wouldn't see her now. She was no doubt up front in the roped-off areas. I'd have to find her after the service. I quickly found a pew that wasn't completely filled and took a seat in the back.

I opened the pamphlet containing the program for the service.

Derek Paul Wolfe

He was sixty-five years old. Still a young man. Everything I'd read since I found out who Riley was indicated he'd been the victim of a gunshot. Was he murdered? No one seemed to know yet, though it was presumed he had been.

This obituary made him sound like a saint.

Father, entrepreneur, philanthropist.

An all-around wonderful guy. Who would want to murder an all-around wonderful guy?

Beat the hell out of me.

It helped to explain why Riley had run off to Montana, though. She was mourning. She needed to escape.

And of course she came home for the memorial.

She hadn't run away from me. She'd run toward her home, to honor her father's life. Who wouldn't?

Well, I wouldn't, but I washed that thought away. Being at a memorial service was enough of a downer.

A string quartet was playing something classical. I wasn't a classical music enthusiast, but it sounded like Mozart to me. I could be totally wrong.

I settled in at the end of the row. I smiled at the man next to me. He grumbled under his breath.

Yup. New Yorkers.

All right, then. All I had to do was wait this out. I pulled my phone out of my pocket and put everything on silent, and then, instead of joining in for the hymns and scripture readings, I played a game of solitaire, which was met with a surly frown from my neighbor.

I warmed and slid my phone back into my pocket.

"...was a gifted businessman," a microphoned voice said.

I looked toward the altar. A man—a man who could have been Riley's twin—stood at the lector podium. His dark hair was long and pulled back against his neck. He looked down at notes frequently, as if he weren't comfortable speaking in front of people.

"He instilled in my brothers, sister, and me the value of hard work. We were born to privilege, but we still had to earn our way. Each of us worked for his company when we were young, and he taught us valuable lessons for work and for life.

"But who was Derek Wolfe, really? He was a private man who valued duty, decency, honor, and integrity from the time he was a child to the day of his horrific death. He was born to Alistair and Marnie Wolfe, my grandparents, and was their only child. He studied at St. John's preparatory school in Manhattan before venturing to Columbia for a degree in business. He played sports at prep school and university, as he was a tall and strong man and gifted athletically. He was gifted academically, as well, and was inducted into Phi Beta Kappa at Columbia and was also a member of Mensa.

"A few years after college, he married Constance Larson. Though their union eventually ended in divorce, our mother and father gave us an idyllic childhood.

"As a father, Derek Wolfe demanded the best, and we gave it. He made sure we always knew how lucky we were to live in such luxury.

"If we broke something, we either fixed it or paid for it. How simple it would have been for our father to just purchase a new one. But Derek Wolfe's children learned the value of money.

"His discipline was strict. As children, we sometimes fought against it, but as adults, we understand the lessons learned.

"Even as we grew away from him, he remained a solid presence in our lives and in our mother's. He was always a reassuring presence during difficult times.

"Especially during difficult times.

"Derek Paul Wolfe.

"You knew him as an entrepreneur. A businessman. A philanthropist. An avid golfer and squash player. Builder of an empire.

"My siblings and I knew him simply as "Dad.""

"And we miss him.""

The man nodded and then left the podium.

A few sniffles and soft sobs echoed through the sanctuary. The parish priest then took the podium for what I hoped would be a brief homily.

"Derek Wolfe and I grew up together," the priest began. "Not many of you know that, I'm sure. He was a little older than I was, and I'd come around this very parish on Sundays to beg for a few spare coins. You see, my mother and I lived in a tenement in Hell's Kitchen, and I regularly walked over to the good side of Manhattan to beg and steal. I sometimes crawled underneath the pews to grab a purse that had been left unattended.

"One day, I tried to steal Marnie Wolfe's purse.

"Derek, then about eleven years old, kicked me in the head so hard I cried out in the middle of mass."

A few gasps emanated from the pews.

"Derek's mother scolded him and sent us both out of this very sanctuary with instructions to wait until mass was over and she'd deal with both of us. Of course, she wasn't *my* mother, so I chose to run.

"Except I wasn't fast enough for Derek Wolfe. Roy was right when he said his father was athletically gifted. He caught me and knocked my head into a wall until I saw stars. Then he forced me to walk back to the church and apologize to his mother when she emerged from mass.

"His parents took me home, fed me lunch, and then sent me home with a hundred-dollar bill and a bag full of groceries.

"So began a lifelong friendship.

"The Wolfes took me under their wing, and soon I was attending mass regularly. I attended Sunday school and received my first communion not long after. And I realized I'd found my calling. Someday, I told Derek, I'd become a priest."

He laughed. "Of course the first thing Derek said to me upon that revelation was, 'you're going to give up girls?'"

Chuckles from the pews.

"Yes, laugh," the priest said. "That's another thing Derek taught me. To laugh. Derek laughed a lot, even with a scared little boy who'd tried to steal his mother's purse.

"So when I answered his question and told him my calling was to God and not to girls, he laughed again. But then he said, 'Jimmy, if you really want to be a priest, I'll make sure you're a priest.'

"And he did. He asked his parents to get me into a good school and pay the tuition. When it was time for seminary, Derek was already at Columbia and he paid my tuition and costs out of his own pocket.

"I married Derek and Connie, and I gave first communion to all the Wolfe children.

"To say I owe Derek everything is an understatement.

"Derek embodies the philosophy and lessons of our savior, Lord Jesus Christ.

"In the Gospel of Luke, Jesus, says, 'Blessed are you who are poor, for yours is the kingdom of God. Blessed are you who are hungry now, for you will be filled. Blessed are you who weep now, for you will laugh.'

"Because of Derek Wolfe, I was filled, and now I laugh.

"Live each day the way Derek Wolfe lived. Share your treasures with others. Help those in need. And laugh.

"We may mourn the loss of Derek Wolfe. But I can guarantee you that he's in a better place, and that he's laughing."

Silence, then, for what seemed like hours. Until finally the priest said, "Amen." A pause, and then, "May the peace of the Lord be with you always."

"And also with you," the congregation murmured.

"Now let's share that peace with each other the way Derek would want us to." The priest left the altar and shook the hands of the people in the front row.

And damn.

There she is.

Riley Wolfe.

She was cloaked in black, but I'd recognize her perfection anywhere. She shook hands with the priest while gazing at her feet. Then she sat down once more.

In the meantime, the people in my pew were bustling, shaking hands, and hugging.

The gentleman next to me stuck his hand out. "Peace be with you," he said gruffly.

"Peace to you as well." I shook his hand and smiled.

He didn't smile back.

Once everyone was done hugging and having sex in the aisle —okay, they weren't having sex, but my God—the priest resumed his spot at the altar and began the sacrament of holy communion.

I didn't participate. Not that I had anything against communion, but I didn't want to parade in front of Riley right now. Yeah, I came here to see her, but she was in mourning. Showing up without any warning at all might upset her.

So I stayed in my pew while mourner after mourner stepped to the altar to receive their bread and wine.

Finally, after a prayer and more from the string quartet, the priest gave the blessing and benediction.

I rose and stretched my legs. Old wooden pews were anything but comfortable. I looked down at my feet as the family members passed by, walking down the aisle.

They'd no doubt form a receiving line, and I planned to wait until the end so as not to startle Riley.

More waiting.

I grabbed my phone back out of my pocket. I played more solitaire but had trouble concentrating as my heart was thudding against my sternum at a rapid pace.

Nervousness? More like anxious anticipation.

I couldn't wait to see her.

I'd hold her in my arms, let her cry into my shoulder for as long as she needed to. I'd help her get through this.

That was what you did for the person you loved.

And God, I loved her.

I loved her so much.

The crowds finally dwindled, and I made my way out of the sanctuary. Three men and two women— including the man who'd read the eulogy—stood in a huddle.

The women were both attractive, one blond and one brown-haired, but neither of them were Riley.

I approached them. "Excuse me."

"Yeah?" one of the men said. He had piercing green eyes.

"I'm looking for Riley Wolfe."

"You a friend of hers?"

"Yeah, I am. I want to offer my condolences." I held out my hand. "Matteo Rossi."

"Rock Wolfe." He took my hand. "Riley never mentioned you to me."

"We just met...recently."

"I see. This is my wife, Lacey, and my brothers, Reid and Roy. That's Roy's girlfriend, Charlie."

Riley's three brothers, as Fox had said. I shook hands all around. "Nice to meet all of you. But...where's Riley?"

"She couldn't handle the receiving line thing," Rock said.

"Yeah," I said. "I understand. I'm sure you're all very upset by the loss of your father. I'm very sorry."

"Right." Rock nodded, but his lips twitched slightly.

"You coming to the wake?" Roy, the long-haired one, asked.

"Will Riley be there?"

"She should be."

"Then yeah, I'm coming."

"Come on, then," Rock said. "You can ride with us in the limo."

33

RILEY

I wiped my mouth with a handkerchief that once belonged to my grandmother. My mother had pressed it into my hand before the service, mumbling something about looking my part.

I didn't shed one tear or sniffle once during the service. I just sat, numb, feeling nothing as I listened to my brother spew lies about our father.

He'd been good at it too.

But the worst was Father Jim's homily.

It was more about Derek Wolfe being a paragon of society than about any lessons learned from scripture.

It was a farce. A complete farce.

Especially since we all knew who Father Jim really was. He was as sick as my father had been, and he had to be stopped.

Perhaps all the horror had ceased when my father died, but Father Jim still had to go down.

I didn't have the strength to do it, but my brothers did.

And my brothers would.

They'd been wonderful when I told them I absolutely couldn't stand in the receiving line and hear virtual strangers talk about how great the man who terrorized me my entire life was. They let me off the hook, and I ended up here, behind the church, puking into a rose bush.

The dry heaves had finally stopped, and I got ready to shove the soiled hanky into my purse, but then I regarded it.

The initials CW were embroidered on one corner along with an ornate pattern.

CW. Constance Wolfe. This handkerchief hadn't belonged to my grandmother. It was my mother's.

Connie Wolfe had always been able to spin a tall tale.

My head began to swim, and in an effort not to fall down, I grabbed the closest thing—a large branch of the rose bush.

"Ouch!" A thorn pricked my finger.

A bead of blood oozed onto my flesh. It grew larger, larger, until it dripped down the length of my finger in a tiny red river.

Blood.

How well I remembered blood. My virgin's blood staining the white sheets on my bed. My father whisking them off and then ordering me to cover the bed with clean linens.

I was eight.

Fucking eight years old.

Eight years old and in searing pain. My face stained from tears as I walked outside my bedroom to the closet near the end of the hallway. I grabbed what looked like a new set of sheets and brought them back to my room. I did my best to re-make the bed, but within a few minutes I realized the sheets were too big and my arms were too short.

I fell asleep on top of the mass of linens and woke the next morning, still throbbing in pain.

No one came to help me. Not my mother, for certain, and when I got home from school the next afternoon, my bed had been made and was stretched taut with clean linens.

The new sheets were brown.

Brown sheets for a little girl.

I hated them, but it wasn't until I was a few years older that I hated them even more. The brown would hide any blood. Once dried, it was the same color as the sheets.

The stream of blood continued onto the palm of my hand.

Finally, I blotted it away with the fake handkerchief from my grandmother.

Nice move, Mom. Did you even look at the design on this thing?

Next was the wake at the Waldorf.

I wouldn't be able to avoid people there. I'd have to speak to them, and I'd have to listen to them tell me how much they admired my abusive father, how much they'd miss him, how much he'd done for them and for humanity at large.

He built a lot of luxury hotels, casinos, resorts. So yeah, he created a lot of jobs. He also gave huge amounts to charity, including his own foundation. So yeah, he helped others.

Just not his own.

Everything and everyone was more important to Derek Wolfe than his children.

Especially his daughter.

I shook my head. Guilt swam through me. My brothers had also suffered at his hands. All three of them. But by their own admission, they'd never been sexually abused by the man. Beaten to a pulp, sure. But never raped.

I winced even as I thought the word.

I never let myself say it, write it, even think it, while he was alive.

Now?

Even though I winced, even though I felt the nausea rising in my throat once more, I could think it.

Raped.

My father raped me.

My father stole my innocence.

My father stole my soul.

And now, the wake.

I could bail. My brothers wouldn't blame me. They'd understand. I could easily sneak out to a side street and call a cab to take me anywhere.

Anywhere...

Back to Montana.

Back to Matt.

Perhaps I should never have left.

I could be happy now, in Matt's arms, drinking coffee at JoJo's, sharing a meal at Trudy's, walking the main streets of Sumter Falls and saying hello to everyone I'd met.

But I gave that up. For my brothers.

And ultimately, for Matt as well.

He deserved better than a broken and soulless woman who was still a tired little girl.

He deserved better than me.

I drew in a deep breath and exhaled slowly. My cut had clotted, and I shoved the blood-stained handkerchief into my purse.

Flashing back once more to the blood-stained sheets.

Damn!

How would I get through this?

How would I get through the rest of my life?

Therapy. I'd promised Roy I'd call his therapist, Dr. Woolcott. But I'd break that promise. I already knew.

I was beyond help.

So beyond help.

I walked back into the church. Only a few mourners remained. The church ladies were taking down the altar decorations.

"Ms. Wolfe," one of them said, "are you okay?"

"Of course she's not okay," another admonished. "Her father is dead."

I smiled weakly. I was far from okay, but not because my father was dead. In fact, his death made me more okay than I'd been since I was six years old.

Still, okay was far from the right word to describe me.

Broken. Violated. Completely fucked up.

Take your pick.

"I'll be fine," I said. "Excuse me."

A giant hummer limo had brought us to the service. I walked swiftly out the front entrance. A few people still lingered, but the limo was gone.

My brothers had left without me.

I grabbed my phone out of my purse. It was on silent for the service, so I hadn't heard the ding of Rock's text.

Sorry, Sis. We have to go. See you at the Waldorf. By the way, a friend of yours is with us.

I wrinkled my brow. A friend? Did I even have any friends? I hadn't paid attention to anyone at the service. All the faces were blurred to me.

"Do you need a ride, Riley?" someone asked.

I turned. A young man stood there. He looked vaguely familiar.

"Fox Monroe," he said. "We did a shoot together about six months ago."

"Fox, of course." I didn't offer my hand. "Thank you, but no. I have transportation."

"Good enough. See you in a few."

Transportation. I walked quickly to the subway stop. Today I didn't want to be Derek Wolfe's daughter. I wanted to be another faceless person on the subway.

34

MATTEO

The Wolfes sure knew how to throw a party.

A champagne fountain. Seriously. With real vintage champagne. So my question was...with this kind of cash, why did Riley Wolfe rent my little cabin in Sumter Falls, Montana? She could have stayed at the poshest hotel in Billings.

And speaking of Riley, where was she?

Crowds of people stuffed caviar into their mouths and sipped champagne from the fountain. Riley's brother Rock stood next to me.

"You seem like a fish out of water here, Matt," he said.

"It's that obvious, huh?"

"Only to another fish out of water."

I cocked my head. "You?"

He chuckled. "This is not my scene at all."

This time I dropped my jaw.

"Surprised?" he asked.

"Uh...yeah. You're a Wolfe. You were raised in luxury." But he'd also lived in a small biker town near Helena, Riley had told me.

"For the first fourteen years, yeah. But luxury—at least luxury in the Wolfe household—has its price." He cleared his throat. "How do you know Riley, anyway?"

"She stayed at my cabin earlier this week."

Rock raised one eyebrow. "What? She stayed where?"

"You didn't know?"

"Hell, no. None of us knew where she was. Where's your cabin?"

"A small town in Montana. Sumter Falls."

His eyes softened. "Fuck. Montana."

"You know Montana." I didn't inflect my voice, as I already knew he did.

"Montana's my home, man. It's a long and boring story."

"It doesn't sound boring to me."

"Damn. She went to Montana," he said more to himself than to me. "Good for her."

"I'm not following."

"Like I said, it's a long and boring story."

"I'm listening," I said.

"I'm sure you are, but unfortunately I have to mingle with Daddy's mourning public. Maybe later we can grab a drink."

"But Riley—"

"She'll be along. Give her a break. Today is...tough for her."

"I know that. I'm sure it's tough for all of you. Losing a parent isn't easy for anyone."

"True that. But not necessarily for the reasons you think. Excuse me. Help yourself to whatever you want." He walked away without smiling.

I reflected on his words.

I have to mingle with Daddy's mourning public.

Had that been a note of sarcasm in his tone?

Sure seemed like it.

Was this all for show?

Was this—

All thoughts in my head ceased.

In the doorway stood my dream.

Riley.

And she met my gaze.

Her jaw dropped. She turned and ran back out the door.

Like a jackrabbit, I sprang after her. She stopped at the elevator and frantically pushed the button.

Until I covered her hand with mine. "Baby."

She gazed at her feet as I took her hand, brought it away from the elevator button and to my lips, and kissed it.

Then she finally looked at me, those deep brown eyes so full of pain.

"I'm so sorry," I said.

"H-How did you find me?"

"Are you kidding? How could I *not* find you, Riley? I..." I gathered every last morsel of courage I possessed. "I love you, baby. I love you."

"You love Riley Mansfield. Not Riley Wolfe. Riley Wolfe is...a mess."

"She looks pretty good from where I'm standing."

"Matt, please..."

"Please what?"

"You have to go. You don't belong here."

"At the Waldorf? Drinking champagne to honor your dead father? Maybe not." A wave of sadness swept through me. "I come from a humble background, which you didn't seem to have a problem with a few days ago."

She shook her head vehemently. "That's not what I mean. Those last few days were... God, Matt, they were heaven, but they belong to someone who doesn't exist."

"Riley Mansfield. I get it." I trailed a finger over her perfectly sculpted cheekbone. "I'd already figured out you weren't who you claimed to be. You're not that good an actress."

Her eyes widened.

"Of course, all I knew is that you weren't a business ed teacher in Philly. I didn't guess you were a supermodel and heiress to a billion-dollar fortune."

She smiled weakly. "I can't imagine anyone could guess that."

"Remember when we were in the flower shop and Kari said you looked familiar?"

She nodded.

"She found photos of you in one of her fashion magazines. I did some quick checking and found out your father had recently died. I know you came to me for an escape, Riley, and I sincerely hope I helped. I'm so sorry."

"You did help. You helped a lot. But those days were a fantasy for me, Matt. They're not something I have the luxury of keeping."

"Sure you do. I'm here. Now. And I want to be with you."

"Because I'm rich."

"For fuck's sake." I curled my hands into fists. "You don't mean that. Tell me you don't."

"Why else would you travel almost two thousand miles to find me?"

"Seriously? I just told you, Riley. I love you."

"You haven't even known me a week."

"So?"

She shook her head. "No one falls in love in a week. Except my brothers, apparently."

"What?"

"Rock and Lacey, and then Roy and Charlie. They fell in love quickly."

"There you go, then," I said. "It's possible."

"But not for me."

"Are you saying you don't love me?"

A vise squeezed my heart.

Yes, that's what I'm saying, Matt. I don't love you.

Those could very likely be the next words out of that gorgeous mouth of hers, and I braced myself. Steeled myself. Because they might very well knock me on my ass.

"No," she finally said. "That's not what I'm saying."

The vise around my heart loosened but still maintained a good grip. I wasn't out of the woods yet. Not by a long shot. "What *are* you saying, then?"

"I'm saying you don't love *me*. You don't love Riley Wolfe. You didn't fall in love with Riley Wolfe. You fell in love with Riley Mansfield, and she's an illusion."

"She's not an illusion. She's standing right in front of me and she's just as beautiful as I remember her."

"Only on the outside," she said.

I grabbed both her cheeks, her skin warm against my palms. "Damn it. I don't fall in love with paper dolls. I fall in love with good hearts. And I love you, Riley. I love you so much." I crushed my mouth to hers.

She opened briefly, and the sweetness of her tongue against mine filled me with hope...until she pushed at my chest and broke away.

"I can't. I just can't."

"Why? We had so much fun together. We made love, Riley. Are you saying it didn't mean anything to you?"

She closed her eyes for a few seconds and inhaled. Then, "I wish I could lie to you, Matt. It'd make things a lot easier for you. But I can't. I'm done lying. And the truth is that it meant the world to me."

Again, I breathed a sigh in relief. "Do you love me?"

She closed her eyes once more.

"It's a simple question, Riley. Either you do or you don't. Either way, I can live with it. If you do, we make a life together. If you don't, we can begin a relationship, see where it leads. You already said your time with me meant the world to you, so we have a foundation. We have a start."

She bit her lower lip. "That's the problem, Matt. We *don't* have a start."

"I don't understand."

"You don't want me."

"Bullshit."

"You don't know anything about me."

"I know—"

"Stop." She placed two fingers over my lips. "Just stop. You know what the internet tells you. That's all you know."

"I know you're a mess right now because your father died. I know you're mourning."

"See?" She shook her head, her lips trembling. "That's just it. You don't know me at all. I'm not mourning. I'm glad the asshole is dead!"

35

RILEY

I pounded on the elevator button once more. I drew in a breath, except my lungs didn't expand. No air went in, and my heart pounded like someone was punching to the beat of a bass drum.

"Damn!" I cried. "Come on!"

"Easy." Matt took my hand from the button once again. He didn't kiss it this time. Instead, he covered it with his own and then entwined our fingers together. "Let me help you. Please."

I shook my head. "No one can help me."

"I can."

Maybe he could. Indeed, he already had. Those few days in Montana had been bliss. Bliss I'd never felt in my young life.

A man who wanted me, who treated me well. Who was tender with me. Who gave me a rose. Who wanted to give me a beautiful pendant.

And I'd rebuffed him.

Was it possible? Though I hadn't been around to witness it, both my brothers had fallen in love quickly, and they seemed happy.

Bullshit. No "seemed" about it. They *were* happy. Blissfully happy, despite the turmoil in our lives. Despite being persons of interest in our father's murder.

Could I be happy with Matt?

God, yes, I could.

I did love him. No two ways about it. I was hopelessly in love with Matteo Rossi.

Which was why I couldn't drag him into this clusterfuck.

But I was done lying, so the truth tumbled out of me.

"I do love you, Matt. I do."

That gorgeous smile split his sculpted face.

"But—"

This time he placed two fingers on my lips. "No buts. Whatever it is, we can handle it."

"You shouldn't have to handle anything. Loving me shouldn't be like serving a sentence, but I'm afraid that's how it would be."

"Doesn't matter," he said. "I already love you, and I can't change that. What's more, I don't want to change it, Riley. I want to be with you. I want to make a life with you."

"We barely know each other."

"So we get to know each other. Who says we have to run out and get married tomorrow? We take our time. Learn about each other. Make love with each other. Enjoy each other."

I sighed, resisting the urge to melt into his arms. "You don't know how much I wish I could do all of that."

"You can."

"I—"

Rock walked toward us quickly. "People are asking about you, Ry." He turned to Matt. "Good. You found her."

I raised my eyebrows. "You two know each other?"

"We gave him a ride in the limo," Rock said. "We waited as long as we could for you. Where have you been?"

"I...took the subway."

"The subway?" Rock laughed. "Good for you."

Matt stared at both of us quizzically, one eyebrow cocked.

"You want to come into the ballroom?" Rock asked Matt. "We've got enough expensive food and booze to feed a fucking army."

"Already been," Matt said.

"Come back in, then," he said. "Ry and I have rounds to make."

I went rigid. "I don't want to."

"I know, Sis. I know. But we have to."

"Why does she have to?" Matt asked. "It's obviously bothering her."

"She shouldn't have to," Rock said. "None of us should have to, but we don't have a choice."

"That's ridiculous," Matt said.

I drew in a deep breath and forced my body to regain my model-like posture. "He's right, Matt. There are things you don't know. Things you *can't* know."

"I don't accept that."

Rock met Matt's gaze then. "You have to accept it. You don't have a choice. You obviously traveled a long way to see my sister, so I'm not going to make you leave. You're welcome to come back to the wake."

I sighed again. "Okay. I'm ready. I'm coming."

"Riley..." Matt began.

"My brother's right. I have to go in and face my demons."

"Wait... Demons?"

"Leave it," Rock said, his voice adamant. "Don't make this more difficult for her than it already is."

I placed my hand in the crook of Rock's arm and let him lead me back to the ballroom. I didn't look back.

I didn't look back because I couldn't bear the thought of seeing Matt standing alone by the elevator.

Matt, who loved me, but who didn't *know* me.

Matt, who I loved, when I thought I'd never love anyone in such an intimate way.

"Easy, Sis," Rock said as he opened the door to the ballroom. "Just take it easy."

I put on my runway face. It wasn't a smile. It was a surly look that fashion designers loved. I entered the ballroom as Riley Wolfe, supermodel daughter of Derek Wolfe.

And I got ready to play my part to the fullest.

I'm so sorry for your loss.

He was a great man.

I'll never forget him.

He was so generous. He helped me save my company.

Loved his golf game!

Loved him. What an amazing man.

The words turned inaudible eventually. I simply smiled and nodded and said my piece.

Thank you.

Thank you so much.

Thank you for coming.

Your being here would mean a lot to him.

Thank you. Thank you. Thank you.

Hours passed, and finally I stood alone in the great ballroom with only my brothers, Lacey, and Charlie.

"Great job, silver," Roy said to Charlie.

"You said to do it up right."

"We did," Rock said, "and you did. No one in the world will guess that we weren't the most devoted children on the planet."

I stayed quiet. I couldn't let down yet. If I did, I'd collapse into a heap on this ugly carpeting—who designed hotel carpeting anyway?—and I wouldn't rise for days.

"You okay, Riley?"

I looked up into the blue eyes of my brother Reid. Of my three brothers, Reid was the least likely to ask after me. He was usually into work, women, and himself and had little time for family.

Not that Roy and Rock had much to do with the family, either, but they weren't as self-absorbed as Reid always seemed to be.

Perhaps I'd misjudged my youngest brother. Our father had passed him over in favor of Rock to run the business. Rock, who'd been gone since he was a teen and knew nothing about the family empire.

I'd expected Reid to go out on a booze-and-women bender, but he hadn't. He'd stayed, helping Rock with his new duties as CEO of the company. Maybe he was changing.

Or maybe he wasn't. How would I know? I was hardly ever around.

I really didn't know my brothers at all.

They knew me better than I knew them. After all, they knew my darkest secret now. Not the details, mind you. Those were for my head alone. No one else should have to bear that burden.

I scanned the empty ballroom and looked down at my feet. A program from the memorial service lay on the floor, gray and black footprints shading the white paper.

Derek Wolfe. For so long, I'd thought *I* was my father's darkest secret.

Turned out I was wrong.

Turned out I was dead wrong.

36

MATTEO

Three hours had passed.

Three hours, and still I sat in the lobby of the Waldorf Astoria, waiting for Riley.

I hadn't gone back into the ballroom. I didn't want to make any of this more difficult for her than it clearly already was.

But I didn't leave, either.

We were going to talk this out.

If she needed to cry all night, I wouldn't stand in her way.

But my arms would be around her while she did it.

Damn it, I would not let her bear this alone. Why was she so determined to cut me out? Nothing could be that bad.

Nothing.

Eventually, two people I recognized walked through the lobby. Rock Wolfe and his wife, Lacey.

I stood. "Hey, Mr. Wolfe!"

They walked toward me swiftly.

"Rock, please. Mr. Wolfe doesn't suit me."

His wife smiled. "It certainly doesn't."

"Why didn't you come back to the wake?" Rock asked.

"It was a family affair. Besides, you heard Riley. She didn't want me there."

"Look, man," Rock said. "Riley... She's been through some serious shit."

"I got that impression."

"So you may want to just let her..." He raked his fingers through his hair. "Let her go, man."

Lacey whipped her hands to her hips. "Let her go? Seriously, Rock?"

"Lace, I'm trying to help him."

"Look at him. He's clearly in love with her."

Rock's jaw nearly dropped onto the marble floor. "Huh?"

I didn't have the strength to lie. "I am. I love your sister."

"How is that even remotely possible?"

"Beats the shit out of me." I plunked back down on the plush couch. "I've never felt this way before. She struck me like lightning. Got under my skin."

"I think you might be able to relate, Rock," Lacey said.

"Yeah. yeah. But this is my baby sister."

"She's a grown woman," Lacey reminded him.

"She is, but she's been through so much."

"She has," Lacey agreed.

"Wait a minute." I stood back up. "She mentioned demons. What the hell are you talking about?"

Rock sighed. "I'm afraid she'll have to tell you that when she's ready. If she's ever ready."

"I came two thousand miles to find her," I said.

"You did. And don't take this the wrong way, but are you looking for her money?"

My right hand curled into a fist and I had to stop myself from punching Rock Wolfe's smug nose. "I'll let that go, friend, but only because we just met and you don't know me. But if you knew where I came from, you'd know that money doesn't mean a damned thing to me. I have a great life, though a modest one."

Rock let out a low chuckle. "Brother, I do know where you came from."

I nodded.

"Montana's an amazing place. Big sky country. As close to heaven as you can get. It will always be my home, no matter where I'm actually living. Lace, you mind a quick trip to the bar? I want to buy Matt here a drink."

"You go ahead," she said. "I think I'll go back to the suite. I'm exhausted."

Rock kissed her lips. "Okay, babe. See you in a few hours."

"Nice to meet you, Matt." Lacey waved

Rock turned to me. "Let's get a drink. I'm going to tell you my story."

"I STILL HAVE MY CABIN," Rock said. "And not a day goes by that I don't miss the fresh air and sunshine. Not to mention riding those hills on my Harley. It's freedom, man. Pure freedom."

"So why'd you end up back here?" I asked. "I mean, New York has the Met and all, but it sure doesn't have fresh air and sunshine."

"It's a long story," he said.

"Okay, then. How did Riley end up in Montana? And why was she calling herself Chloe Mansfield?

He widened his eyes. "Who the hell is Chloe Mansfield?"

"Riley's alter ego, apparently. She has a driver's license in that name. Chloe L. Mansfield. That's how I knew for sure she'd been lying to me. When she first told me her name was Riley, she said it was her middle name. I happened to see her ID, which showed that her middle initial was L. It wasn't until the florist in town showed me a spread in a fashion magazine that I figured out who she actually was. But I already knew she wasn't Chloe L. Mansfield."

"That fucking bastard," he said under his breath.

"What? Who?"

"I've told you all I can, man." He finished off his bourbon. "The rest is up to Riley."

"You're really going to leave me hanging?"

"I don't have a choice. Riley has her secrets. We all do, but not from each other. At least not anymore."

"What family doesn't have secrets?" I asked. "Seems pretty normal to me."

He scoffed. "If you heard this family's secrets, you'd realize most other secrets are harmless in comparison."

"Rock—"

"Listen." He signaled the bartender for the check. "Our father was murdered. You already know that. What you don't know is that..."

"What? For God's sake, what?"

"It'll be common knowledge before long. The police won't be able to keep it under wraps. All of us are suspects, including my wife."

My heart plummeted to my stomach. "You mean... Riley?"

"Yeah. Riley, Roy, Reid, Lacey, and me. And here's the kicker. I'm the only one with an ironclad alibi. I was in Montana at the time. But they won't let that rest. They think maybe I had it done."

"But... What about motive?"

He scoffed again, and this time it sounded almost like laughter. "One thing about living in small-town Montana. You don't hear nearly as much news. There are about a hundred people who'd have liked to see my father six feet in the ground, but none more than his own progeny."

I dropped my mouth open.

"That surprises you."

"Well...yeah. Though Riley did mention demons."

"My sister has been to hell and back, like I said. Her demons are real. And they're big. She probably had the most motive of all of us."

"My God... What did he do to her?"

"It's not my story to tell. But if you love her, you're going to need to give her time."

"I... Fuck. Did he...?"

"I won't tell you, but if your mind is going where I'm guessing it is, you're on the right track."

"He hurt her," I said more to myself than to Rock.

"He hurt all of us," Rock said. "But yes. He hurt Riley the most."

37

RILEY

"Get the fuck away from her."

My brother stands in my doorway, something shiny in his hand.

Daddy sits on my bed. My nightgown is up around my chest. Daddy likes it that way. He says I'm prettiest when he can see all of my skin.

"What the hell are you doing in here?" Daddy demands.

"I know what you're doing," Rock says. "You won't get away with it. Get away from her, or I swear to God I'll kill you."

Daddy laughs and tugs my nightgown over my small body. "You don't know what you're talking about."

"I know exactly what I'm talking about. My room is right next to hers. I hear her screams. I hear her sobs. You're going to stop this now."

I did scream, but not tonight. I'm not sure what Rock is talking about. I screamed that other time because Daddy's hands were cold on my skin. When he tugged my nightgown up.

"You're so pretty, sweetheart," he said.

I like being called pretty. If Daddy thinks I'm pretty when my nightgown is pulled up, then I want my nightgown pulled up. I want to be pretty. Mommy says girls are supposed to be pretty.

"Don't you fucking touch her," Rock says. He walks into my room.

I can finally see what the shiny thing is. It's a knife. A big silver knife like Cook uses in the kitchen. She chops onions into tiny pieces with a knife like that.

"Watch out, Miss Riley," she always says to me when I watch her chop. "This knife is sharp. Don't you ever touch it."

"Be careful, Rock!" I cry out. "Cook says that's sharp!"

Still he comes closer, and Daddy stands.

"Give it to me, Rock," Daddy says.

"You leave her alone." Rock's voice cracks and squeaks. Even shakes a little. His voice is lower now, but it still cracks sometimes.

"You little piece of shit," Daddy says.

I don't know what that word means. I don't know the F word either—the one Rock said. The one Daddy and Mommy say a lot when they fight.

Rock still walks toward Daddy, and then...

The knife. It's touching Daddy. Blood trickles through his white shirt.

"No, Rock, no!" I scream. "Don't hurt Daddy!"

I JERKED UPWARD.

I was back at my place. The limo driver dropped me off first. Rock wasn't in the limo. Lacey said he stayed to have a drink in the bar with a friend. Why? There'd been plenty to drink at that stupid wake. Did Rock even have any friends here?

I rose from my couch where I'd been sitting in a daze.

Sitting. Thinking. Remembering.

Remembering how it all began. How Rock got sent away.

Funny. Until Rock told us the truth, I'd forgotten that night. That night so long ago had been buried inside my mind, making room for much more horrific things.

The bloody white sheets.

The new dark-brown ones that I hated.

"Damn it!"

I hurried to my bedroom, threw the blankets off my bed, and then tore off the sheets. "I hate you!" I screamed as I ripped the sheets down the middle.

These sheets weren't brown. They weren't white.

They were lavender, actually.

But I didn't care. I ripped and I ripped and I ripped until I'd torn the entire sheet into two separate pieces.

My breath came rapidly. From exertion or rage, I wasn't sure.

I threw myself on my naked mattress then, and I sobbed.

I sobbed and I sobbed and I sobbed.

I cursed my father. I cursed my life. I cursed Matt for coming here and making me want him even more.

I cursed everything I could never have.

And then I cursed my mother.

Nothing is happening to you that isn't happening to a hundred other girls, Riley. Just close your eyes and think of diamonds.

Diamonds.

Right.

I never wore diamonds. The few I owned were locked up in a safe deposit box.

Thinking of diamonds never helped, Mom, thank you very much.

Weren't mothers supposed to protect their children?

For that matter, weren't fathers?

Rock. The only person who ever tried to protect me. I'd never forgive myself for telling him to stop. If I could go back in time, back to that innocent little girl I'd been, I'd tell my brother to plunge that knife into the bastard's heart.

Then I'd be a different woman today.

My brother might have gotten a few years in juvie, but he'd be fine now. He was strong. So strong.

I sat up.

No.

I didn't actually want that at all. Rock had already paid for trying to help me, and Roy and Reid honestly hadn't known. In fact, they'd been envious of the time Dad spent with me.

They didn't know…

They didn't—

Someone pounded on my door.

I was a mess. The tattered pieces of my sheet lay strewn on the floor along with the rest of my bedding. I glanced in the mirror quickly. My face was streaked with tears, my eyes red and my nose runny.

Well, of course. I was mourning dear old Dad.

Might as well answer the door. I could put on a good show right now. One devoted daughter coming up.

I sniffled and walked to my door, still wearing my black dress. I'd kicked off the uncomfortable Louboutin pumps as soon as I got home.

I opened the door.

And I melted.

Matteo Rossi stood there, his arms open.

I fell into them.

"It's okay, baby," he murmured against the top of my head. "It's all going to be okay."

He was wrong, of course. My life would never be okay. But maybe I could play make-believe for a few moments, much like I did in Sumter Falls only days ago.

Yes, make-believe.

Pretend.

Let's play house, Daddy.

I pulled away from Matt and grabbed two fistfuls of my hair. "Get out of my head!"

Matt maneuvered himself into my apartment, pushing me gently inside and closing the door.

"I'm not trying to get in your head," he said soothingly.

"No, no, no!"

"Baby, please."

"Not you. Not you. *Him!*"

"Easy." He touched my arm gently and led me to the couch where I'd been sitting earlier. "Sit. Come on. I'm going to get you a drink."

"Don't want it."

"Just water, baby. You're dehydrated."

"I'm not."

"Of course you are. You've been crying all day."

He wasn't wrong. I *had* been crying all day. Just not for the reasons he thought.

He found his way to the kitchen. Cupboard doors opened and closed, and then the whooshing of water from the faucet. The clink of ice cubes.

Soon he was back, holding a glass to my lips. "Drink. Come on."

I took a sip and let the cool water wet my mouth and throat. It felt nice. Really nice.

"What can I do for you?" he asked. "And don't say leave."

"I wasn't going to," I said.

"Good."

"I'm a mess, Matt."

"So you've said. I happen to think you're beautiful."

That got a scoffing laugh out of me. "Right now? Please."

"Riley, you could be covered in dog shit and still be the most beautiful woman in the universe. You're a supermodel, for God's sake."

"There's nothing super about me."

"I beg to differ."

I took another sip of water. Then another. My throat felt raw from the sobs, and the water soothed it.

"I love you," Matt said.

I sigh. "I love you too."

"At least we're in agreement on that." He took the glass from me and set it on the coffee table. "What do you need, Riley?"

I let out a soft huff. "Nothing. Absolutely nothing. Look around you, Matt. I'm an heiress. I have everything anyone could want."

"I'm not talking about stuff, Riley. What do *you* need?"

I huff again. "A different life?"

He smiled. "I can give you that."

"I mean a different first twenty-five years, Matt. And I'm sorry, but you can't give me that, and my money can't buy it either."

"That's true. But I can offer you my love. My support. I'll hold your hand and help you get through everything."

I shook my head. "You don't even know what you're getting into."

"I have a general idea."

I glared at him. "It's you, isn't it? You're the friend Rock had a drink with."

"I had a drink with him, yeah."

"Damn him."

"He didn't tell me anything. Other than you're all persons of interest in your father's murder."

And one more huff from me. "Not the devoted children we seemed to be at the funeral, huh?"

"He didn't tell me anything I couldn't find out on my own. You know that."

"Yeah. I know."

"Is that why you used a fake name in Montana?"

"Part of it. Part of me just wanted to be someone else for a little while. Pretend. Have that different life that you and no one else can give me."

"But it wasn't different," he said.

"No. It wasn't different. Not at all. On the outside, maybe, but not on the inside."

"I want to help you."

"I'll say it again. You don't know what you're getting into."

"Maybe not. But whatever it is, I don't care."

"What if I did it? What if *I* killed my father?"

"I don't believe you did."

"You hardly know me."

"All right." He took both of my hands in his. "I'll keep all your secrets, Riley. Did you kill your father?"

I shook my head, sighing. "No. But if I'm going down for it, I wish I had."

38

MATTEO

I believed her.

This woman didn't have it in her to harm another soul.

But if Derek Wolfe had done to her what I was imagining, he didn't have a soul.

He was rotting in hell right now.

Good thing, because if he crossed my path, I'd strangle him with my bare hands.

This woman—this sweet and beautiful woman...

"Riley," I said, "I'm going to help you. I'm going to help you prove your innocence, and I'm going to help you get through all the other shit you're living with."

"You can't," she said. "No one can help me."

"I don't accept that."

"You don't have a choice, Matt. I am who I am, and there's no changing it."

"I think you misunderstood me. I don't want to change *you*, sweetheart. I love you exactly as you are. I want to help you deal with all of this."

"I love you for that. I really do. But I'm a fucking mess, Matt."

"You say no one can help you. I disagree. If you want help, it's available."

"I *do* want help. But I also don't want to go down for a murder I didn't commit, and I don't want any of my brothers going down for it either."

"Rock says he has an alibi."

"He does. He was in Montana, but the authorities think he might have hired someone to do it. Except he had no money. He was living on his own."

"And Reid and Roy?"

"Both alone in their apartments. No one can corroborate."

"And...you?" I asked hesitantly.

"Same. I was alone. Here. The murder took place at four in the morning."

"What about his girlfriend? Fonda something? I read about her when I researched your dad."

"Fonda? She's not implicated. She wasn't with him that night. She and my mother appear to have alibis. Besides, my mother wouldn't have him offed. No Derek Wolfe means no seven-figure alimony payments."

"So you all have a motive?"

"All except Lacey, and they seem to be going after her the hardest. I don't get it."

"Where was she?"

"Home alone at her place as well. Except the security tapes, which would have shown her coming home and going out the next morning, seem to be missing."

"Surely there are security tapes for this place," I said.

"There are. But we all have the money to hire an expert, so the security tapes mean nothing."

I nodded. "Fuck."

"Fuck is right." She sighed. "My dad was into some nasty stuff."

"I can imagine."

"No, you really can't."

"Riley, I know what some fathers do to their little girls. I can imagine, even though I don't want to. If he walked through that door right now, I'd fucking kill him myself."

"You're not wrong in your assumptions." She gulped. "But that's not what I'm talking about."

Rage unfurled at the back of my neck, surging through the rest of my body like a river of boiling blood.

I'd already guessed, but to hear her say it...

Good thing the derelict was already in his grave.

Finally, I gained my composure, tamping down the anger that threatened to overtake me. Riley didn't need that right now. She needed me whole and unyielding. She needed my strength.

"Not your brothers?" I asked.

"He beat the shit out of them, but no, he didn't abuse them sexually."

"Then what? What the hell is worse than what he did to you?"

She shook her head. "I can't even bring myself to say the words."

"Please. I want to help."

"Apparently, he..." She swallowed, closing her eyes. "He killed women. Hunted them, and killed them."

I stared into space, almost seeing right through Riley next to me.

Hunted women.

Killed them.

The words became jumbled in my head.

It was too much. Too much just to know what the psycho had done to the woman I loved. But now? To know he played fucked-up hunting games with others? With fellow human beings?

"H-How..." The words caught in my throat.

"Roy. He saw it once. He... It was a memory he'd buried inside his mind. He underwent guided hypnosis last week and uncovered it."

"Did any... Fuck. Did any of the women..."

"As far as we know, one might have survived. We have a name. Just a first name. Zinnia. It's an uncommon name, but still, what are the chances we can find her? And even if we do find her, we don't know that she's behind the murder. And if she is, I kind of want to let her go."

"I understand, but you have to save yourself, baby."

"I know."

"They're going to look at your phone records. Your emails. Will they find anything suspicious?"

"You mean will they find emails and payments to a hired killer? Of course not."

I breathed a sigh of relief.

"I heard that."

"Baby..."

"Part of you wonders if I did it."

I cupped her cheek, hoping she felt the love through my fingertips. "No, it's not that. I'm just concerned. We have to get you out of this."

"We have to get us all out of this. We need to find this Zinnia and uncover all my father's secrets. Only then will we be able to move forward."

"I can't believe I'm about to suggest this, but..."

"What?"

"Can your family pay off the authorities. Get the case closed?"

She closed her eyes and exhaled. "I can't lie to you. I've thought about it."

"And your brothers?"

She opened her eyes. "They haven't brought it up. But there's this detective, Hank Morgan, who seems bent on finding a culprit. I don't know why. My father was no paragon of virtue."

"Then we figure out this detective's angle."

"We already have the best PIs in the business on this. They're looking for Zinnia. They're looking into Morgan. They're doing all they can."

"Are they loyal?"

"I assume so. They're getting paid a boatload of money."

"Are they the same PIs your father used?"

"I don't know. You'd have to ask Reid, but probably."

"Then they owe their loyalty to your father. Not to you."

"Except my father's dead."

"He is. But his money isn't. There might be a stream somewhere that you and your brothers don't know about."

"What are you saying?"

"I'm saying I don't trust your father," I said. "You have to consider that this is all a setup."

39

RILEY

A setup.

We'd considered that, and we decided that our father was too much of an egomaniac to orchestrate his own death.

I should tell Matt this.

I should tell Matt a lot of things.

But right now...

Right now I wanted—needed—something else from him.

I turned to him and crawled into his arms.

He held me tightly, and my body responded instantly. My nipples hardened and I ached between my legs.

How could this be?

How, when I was just thinking about all the horrid things my father used to do to me?

Still, I yearned for Matt's lips on mine. Yearned for him to undress me, kiss me all over, take me to that amazing place I've only been once.

I kissed his neck and inhaled his crisp, masculine scent.

Intoxicating.

Then I trailed kisses to his mouth and pressed my lips

against his, parting my own slightly, letting my tongue touch his firm lips.

But they remained closed.

"Kiss me. Please," I whispered.

He parted his lips and I slid my tongue between them. But his tongue didn't meet mine. I searched for it, found it, twirled my own around it.

And he pulled back.

"Baby..."

"What is it?"

"After all you've been through..."

"You don't want to kiss me?"

"God, yes. I want it more than air. But—"

I moved out of his arms and slumped on the couch. "I disgust you."

"Riley! Of course not."

"You're thinking about what he did to me. And you don't even know the details!"

"God, no! I'm not. I can't even let my mind go there. I'm thinking of you, Riley. *You.*"

"If you're thinking of me, and my needs, you should kiss me."

"If I'd known, I never would have pressured you in Montana."

"Pressured me? You didn't."

"I wanted you."

"And I wanted *you.* Do you think I would have let it happen if I didn't want it? I know how to say no, Matt."

"But—"

"I said no all those times. He just didn't listen. You *would* have."

"Yes, of course I would have."

"Then get over yourself and kiss me. You want it. I want it. What's more, I need it right now. I need to feel the beauty in the world, and Matt, the only time I've ever felt it was when I was with you."

"Oh, God, baby." His lips came down on mine with a force I wasn't expecting.

I opened for him, and we kissed deeply, passionately.

But he pulled back once more.

His eyes were sunken and sad. "Baby…"

"Matt, please…"

"I… can't. Not until we get you the help you need. I can't take advantage of you."

"What advantage? I'm giving you the advantage!"

"But you—"

"Matt, we've already done this, and you didn't know about my past then."

"But I know now, and if I'd known—"

"But you didn't. I need you, and I know you need me just as much."

"God, yes. I do."

I rose and pulled him to his feet. "We're going to bed."

"Here?"

"Yes, here." I led him to my bedroom.

"What happened here?" he asked.

Shit. I'd forgotten in my lust. My bedding was strewn on the floor, and my top sheet ripped into two halves.

"Nothing."

"Nothing? Come on, Riley."

It came back to me with a vengeance. No more lies. I loved this man, and he deserved the truth.

"I… I tore my bed apart. Remembering…" Tears welled in my eyes.

Maybe Matt was right. Maybe I shouldn't be doing this. Words poured out of my mouth.

"He used to make me put brown sheets on my bed, because any other color…"

Matt pulled me back into his arms. "I get it. You don't have to say it."

"You can't bear to hear it?'

"No, I can't, but I can bear it if you can. I'm trying to protect you, Riley. Can't you see that?"

I pulled away. "I want you to go."

"No. I'm staying."

"If you're not going to make love to me, I don't want you here."

"I'm not going to make love to you. Not after what you've been through today. But I'll stay, and I'll hold you. I'll cook you dinner. I'll remake your bed and tuck you in. I'll lie beside you and protect you. And I'll have a fucking hard-on the whole damned time, because I love you and I ache for you, but tonight is not the night to touch you."

"Even if I want it?"

"Even if you want it."

And just like that, I realized he was right.

Right on the nose.

I didn't want to make love to make love, I wanted to make love to escape.

Matt deserved better than that, and so did I.

40

MATTEO

"I understand," she finally said.

"Tell me, then. What can I do for you? Are you hungry?"

"Not really."

"Did you eat at the wake?"

"Are you kidding? Not a bite."

"Then I'm making you something." He rose and walked into the kitchen.

I followed him. "I'm afraid my fridge is empty."

"We'll go out, then."

"I can't. I don't want to go anywhere. I look like a freak with these swollen red eyes."

He kissed the tip of my nose. "You're beautiful, but your wish is my command. We'll order in. What kind of food do you like? I know you love Mexican."

"Are you kidding? No Manhattan Mexican place can equal the stuff Mrs. Carson made."

"Indian, then? Italian? You name it."

"I don't care. You pick something."

"You got it." I fired up my phone, found an Italian place close

by, and ordered two servings of lasagna to be delivered along
with salads and bread.

"Now," I said. "Let's take care of that bed." I walked to the
bedroom.

She'd torn her top sheet in half. I wasn't sure how she did it.
It was ripped neatly at the seam, which must have taken some
brute strength to start.

I imagined Riley could do whatever she set her mind to, and
her mind had been set on ripping that sheet.

"Extra sheets?" I asked.

She gestured to the bathroom. "There's a linen closet in
there."

I found the bedding quickly and re-sheeted her bed. Then I
put the comforters and blankets back on. "Good as new."

"Thank you," she murmured.

"Did he...? Here?"

She shook her head. "No. Never here. Always on his terms.
Here would have given me too much power."

"Why didn't you take the power, Riley?" I hated myself for
asking the question. I knew better. "God, I'm sorry."

"Don't be." She looked down, unable to meet my gaze. "I
don't know. I'll never be able to answer that question, Matt."

"I shouldn't have asked it. It was unfair of me."

"No." She shook her head. "It was a fair question, and one
I've asked myself millions of times. He had some kind of sick
hold on me." She sighed. "You're right. I need to get some help.
Roy gave me the name of his therapist—the one who helped
him remember what he saw over a decade ago. I was thinking I
wouldn't call her. But maybe I will."

"I'll go with you if you want me to."

"I'd like that." She smiled hesitantly. "I'd really like that."

THE NEXT DAY, after holding Riley all night and nursing a nasty case of blue balls, I went with her to meet with her brothers at the Wolfe Building.

"Can he be trusted?" Reid, the blue-eyed brother, asked.

"Fuck off, Reid," Rock said. "If Riley trusts him, that's good enough for me."

"And me," Roy agreed.

"He's the man I love," Riley said, "and if you want to know how wonderful he is, he took care of me last night. He didn't lay a hand on me."

My cheeks warmed, and I wished she'd shut up. Our personal life was our personal life, but I understood the point she was trying to make. I didn't take advantage of her when she was a mess.

"That's more than you'd have done, Reid, with a woman in a similar situation," Rock said snidely.

"Fuck off, Rock." From Reid.

"Both of you fuck off," Roy said. "Let's bring Matt up to speed."

I sat, my jaw nearly on the table in front of me, as Rock relayed everything.

Everything.

He'd tried to kill his father to protect Riley.

He got sent away.

Roy and Reid—mostly Reid—got the shit beat out of them.

They were jealous of Riley's princess trips.

Until Rock told them what really went on during those trips.

How they'd wished she'd told them so they could stop it.

How they wouldn't have been able to stop it no matter what.

And then Roy's buried memory.

The woman who Derek Wolfe—and that priest from yesterday—had been hunting somewhere in the basement of the Wolfe Building.

I raked my fingers through my hair. My body throbbed with nausea, anger, disgust, repulsion. If it was negative, I felt it as my heart pounded like a jackhammer.

I'd just walked into chaos.

Fucking chaos.

But I'd deal. I'd deal because I loved Riley. I wanted the best for her, and I'd do anything I could to help find out who truly offed Derek Wolfe so Riley could be at peace.

"You can walk out, no questions asked," Riley said. "I wouldn't blame you."

I placed my hand over hers. "Nothing doing."

"Are you sure?" Rock asked. "You look a little green around the gills."

"Can you blame him?" Lacey said. "It was a lot for Charlie and me as well. But this family, all of you, are worth it."

I nodded. "You are. I'm fine."

Rock went on, "You seem like a hell of a good guy, but we're dealing with some major shit here. We don't know what's going to come up. Someone killed our psycho of a father, and we have no idea who. He had thousands of enemies. It could seriously be anyone."

"But it's not anyone in this room," I said. "I believe that with my whole heart."

"You don't even know us," Reid scoffed.

"Do I have to tell you to fuck off again?" Rock said.

"Sorry, bro, but I'm the one who learned this business at Dad's side, and one thing I learned was never to trust anyone."

"If you trust me, you can trust Matt," Riley said.

"It's okay, baby." I squeezed her hand. "He doesn't know me, but I'll prove worthy of his trust. Of all of your trust."

"Good enough," Rock said. "Reid and I have to fly to Vegas first thing tomorrow to deal with some contract issues on the hotel. This holdup is costing us millions per day, and we need to get it taken care of."

"Why don't we all go?" Roy said. "How about it, silver? Want to go to Vegas? We can take in a show."

Charlie Waters, Roy's girlfriend, smiled. "It sounds great, but there's a lot of work to be done here too."

"You know what?" This from Lacey, Rock's wife. "I think we could all use a break."

"What break?" Rock said. "Reid and I will be working."

"True," she said, "and so will I. But Roy and Charlie should take some time. And you too, Riley. You deserve it."

"How are we supposed to take time off when all of you are persons of interest in this case?" Charlie asked. "I don't think I can."

"I can," Roy said, "and if I can, you can, silver. We need it, especially after that farce of a funeral yesterday."

"I just got back from vacation," Riley added. "Remember?"

I squeezed her hand again.

"We're all going," Rock said. "I'll have Jarrod book everything. Suites for everyone."

"If you say so," Charlie said. "I can take care of this instead of Jarrod, if you want, since I'm in the know about all you guys are going through."

"That'd be great, Charlie," Lacey said.

"Then it's settled," Rock agreed. "Vegas, here we come."

41

RILEY

Tingles.

I got tingles watching Matt react first to the Wolfe private jet, to the glitz of Las Vegas, and finally to the suite Charlie had reserved for us at the Wolfe Premiere.

The Wolfe Cinquième Hotel and Casino was supposed to break ground three months ago, and apparently a local regulation was causing a hold-up, along with contractor issues. I didn't know or care. That was Rock and Reid's problem.

My problem at the moment was erasing the crap inside my head so I could have a few beautiful days in Nevada with Matt.

"Baby, I can't afford any of this," Matt said to me softly.

"Did anyone ask you to pay for it?"

"I can't just let you—"

I placed two fingers over his full lips. "I want to. I want these few days with you. We can begin where we left off in Sumter Falls."

He laughed then. "Riley, this is so *not* Sumter Falls."

"True. It's Las Vegas. But we can find tons to do here. Do you like to gamble?"

"Luke and I play poker with a few guys at home. I'm pretty good at it."

"Cool. We can set you up at video poker to test your skills, and if you're that good, we head to the poker room."

"And play against pros? I don't think so."

"Not pros. They stay at the high-stakes tables. You can play at the regular tables."

"With others who are really good."

"Some are. Some aren't. Some get drunk and make stupid moves."

"So you know poker, then?"

I paused a moment. Then, "I watched my father play many times."

Matt stayed silent for a few moments.

"It's okay." I touched his arm. "I have to be able to talk about it. It's just poker."

Finally, he nodded. "Was your father any good?"

"The best. A regular iceman. He had the best poker face I ever saw."

He chuckled. "You haven't seen mine yet."

I didn't doubt Matt was good, but my father had been ruthless. He took big losses in order to make the smallest gain overall. He was frigid. Icy. Unstoppable.

Just like he was about everything in his life.

I doubted Matt could hide his emotions the way my father did.

Because Matt actually had emotions, and my father didn't, so frankly, he'd had nothing to hide.

"You're that good, huh?" I said.

"I don't like to toot my own horn, but..."

I giggled. "Something tells me you *love* to toot your own horn."

"Maybe. Just a little. I have to prove worthy of the beautiful Riley Wolfe."

"You're more than worthy."

Indeed, he was. I was the one not worthy of him, but I didn't say it. I wanted these few days to be fun. A chance for us to get to know each other a little better. A chance to feel real love for the first time in my life.

"What shall we do first?" he asked.

"Whatever you want."

"Well, then, I'm starved, but it's pretty late."

"It's midnight in the city that never sleeps," I told him. "We'll find you some food."

We took the elevator down to the main floor and found a twenty-four-hour sandwich shop. Matt ordered a turkey club with all the fixings, but I passed. I'd been eating like a pig the last week, and I still had my career to consider. Fredricka would kick my butt if I put on any more weight. I did have a bite of his sandwich, though. It was yummy. The first thing that tasted good since I got back from Montana.

"Now what?" I asked after he'd finished.

"I'm good and carbo loaded." He trailed a finger over my cheek. "Now I want to go back up to our room and make slow, sweet love to you."

I shuddered.

I'd begged him two nights ago and again last night. Instead, he held me, which was really what I'd needed.

Now? I was ripe. So ripe and wet and full of aching need for him.

"Please," I said softly. "Please make love to me."

BACK IN OUR SUITE, the king-size bed beckoned.

The white hotel sheets made me pause, but only for seconds. This was now.

This wasn't nineteen years ago. This wasn't even a month ago.

This was now.

I was no longer enslaved to my father in that mind-numbing way.

I was free.

Free to make love with the man I loved.

"Tell me what you want," he said. "I don't want to overwhelm you."

"I want you to overwhelm me. Please, Matt. Show me everything."

He groaned. "God." Then he clamped his lips onto mine.

The kiss wasn't soft and dulcet, like his kisses had been during the past two days. No, this one was full of need and passion, and I met it with all the emotion coiled within me. All the emotion I'd never been able to let out.

We kissed deeply, with desire and passion that had pent up within us the last couple days.

Our lips slid together, our teeth banged, our tongues tangled, and we each moaned, we each groaned, we each hummed into each other as if we were a drug the other craved.

Drugs.

No more coke for me. Matt was my drug. Something I needed now and would never be able to live without.

He undressed me slowly, only taking his lips from mine to gasp in a breath.

Soon I was naked except for my panties, he still fully clothed, standing next to the giant bed.

My heart thudded, and fear swept into me.

Las Vegas.

I'd been here before.

With...

I pushed it away. "No!" I screamed.

"Baby?"

I shook my head vehemently. "I don't mean for you to stop. I was pushing an unwanted thought out of my head."

"You sure?"

"Yes. Yes, I'm so sure. I need you Matt. Please." I unbuttoned his shirt and parted the two sides.

God, his chest. Muscled and fair, nearly hairless.

Matt was beautiful. I wouldn't change a thing.

He went achingly slowly, and I knew why.

He was giving me a chance to change my mind. To say no.

Wasn't going to happen.

Finally, he stood naked, his huge cock jutting out from the light brown triangle of curls. I sucked in a breath at the sight.

This was Matt.

Matt.

No one but Matt.

Matt, who I loved.

"Lie down, baby," he said.

I obeyed and lay down on my back.

"You're so beautiful," he said, his breath catching. "I've never seen anything so beautiful in my life."

"I've never seen anything so beautiful as you." I stared at him, taking in every inch of his spectacular body, every piece of his beautiful soul.

Matteo Rossi was a man worth fighting for, and I would fight the good fight. I'd get over what my father had done to me so this man and I could have the life we deserved.

I'd start by banishing all thoughts of my past from my mind —at least for this beautiful moment.

Matt and I both deserved that.

He lay down next to me, at my side, and lightly trailed one

hand over the swell of my breasts. My nipples responded imme-
diately, hardening.

"So beautiful," he said again, softly. "So damned beautiful."
He leaned over and sucked a nipple between his lips.

I gasped as a bomb nearly exploded between my legs. This
was Matt. Matt who loved me. He loved my body, and because
he did, I did.

No longer was my body something I detested.

I adored it as he adored it. This was what my body was made
for. This and only this. All other crap I'd endured had been at
someone else's choosing and not mine.

This moment was my choice.

My moment.

My love.

He continued sucking my nipple. I threaded my fingers
through his silky blond hair, the feeling against my skin so
exquisite.

My whole body was in flames, especially that hidden part
between my legs.

My pussy.

God, I needed him. In my pussy. Tongue, fingers, cock.

All of him.

"Please," I whispered. "Please."

He dropped the nipple from his lips. "Just tell me what you
want. Anything. I'll give you anything."

And then I knew.

I wanted to suck his dick.

I wanted to do it because I wanted to do it. Not because he
wanted it.

I would take the power, as he suggested.

And I would take that power to give the man I loved
pleasure.

"I want to put my mouth on you," I said, my voice low and

breathless. "I want to touch every part of you with my lips and tongue, and I want to suck your cock.

"God," he groaned. "Are you sure?"

"More sure than I've ever been. Please. Let me do this for you. Let me do this for *me*."

He rolled onto his back. "Tell me where you want me."

"Right there is fine. So fine." I rolled to my side and brushed my lips over his. "I love you so much, Matt."

"I love you too, Riley. So fucking much."

I kissed along his stubbly jawline, down his neck to his broad and muscled shoulder. His skin was warm beneath my lips. Warm beneath my exploring fingertips. I kissed his chest, following along the lines of the muscles and sinew, until I flicked my tongue over a coppery nipple.

It hardened beneath my lips, which turned me on even more.

He responded to me.

To my touch.

I continued my assault on his chest, moving toward his abdomen, sliding my tongue over each indentation of his sixpack. God, he was magnificent. And God, I loved him so much.

His triangle of curls beckoned, and I dived into them, inhaling his musky and masculine scent. I was a mere inch from his cock.

That beautiful cock, a shade darker than the rest of his fair skin, and darker still where blue veins marbled through it.

His head was a shiny knob, and a drop of fluid glistened at the tip.

I gathered my courage and licked it off as he shuddered beneath me.

"Fuck, Riley. Fuck." He squeezed his eyes closed.

"No," I said. "Open your eyes. Watch me. Please."

His eyelids fluttered and then he opened his gorgeous blue eyes. "Whatever you want, baby. Though if I watch, I might not last long. Hell, I'm not going to last long anyway."

"Doesn't matter." I swiped my tongue over his cock head once more. "We have all the time in the world."

And we did, as far as I was concerned. Matt and I were in a time warp, and time had no meaning. If he didn't last long, we'd simply begin again.

And again.

And again.

For this was what I wanted.

He whimpered softly as I moved down from his dick to his muscular thighs. I kissed them, caressed them, appreciated them with my gaze.

Such hard, firm, muscular thighs.

I moved downward still, kissing his knees and calves and then the instep to his foot. I kissed each toe, and then massaged his feet lightly with my hands.

"Damn, Riley."

I didn't reply, simply kissed back up the other leg and then parted his legs slightly so I could settle between them.

His dick throbbed in an invisible rhythm. I felt its warmth even before I touched it.

So warm and inviting.

This was love. Loving all of a person, wanting all of a person, pleasing all of a person. Not just the physical but the emotional. The spiritual.

I took him between my lips and sucked just the head.

He sucked in a breath. "Fuck. Riley. Fuck."

Warmth coursed through me. Pleasing someone you loved—there was nothing like it. It was the ultimate high. The ultimate reward. Giving pleasure instead of receiving it.

I trailed my lips over his shaft down to his balls, which were already scrunched toward his body. I inhaled their muskiness, kissed the soft hair on them, and then sucked one into my mouth.

He groaned, shivering against my flesh.

I released his testicle and sucked on the other, and then I turned back to his dick and stroked its length with my tongue. Its warmth and its miniscule movement, the blood rushing through it pulsing lightly against my mouth.

Until I reached the head, and I sucked all of him into my mouth, as far back to my throat as I could.

Which wasn't far, but that was okay. This was about both of us, not just him. What he wanted and what I wanted, and I knew he'd be pleased no matter what.

I pulled back and sucked him again, and then again, until—

"Riley, stop. Stop now. I don't want to come yet."

I was tempted. Oh, so tempted to keep going, to take the ultimate control over him, but this wasn't just about me.

It was also about him.

I let go of his dick and then met his fiery gaze.

"Take off those panties and sit on me. Take me into your body."

I was ready. My fingers were under the waistband...

And then I remembered what in my passion I'd forgotten.

The burns. The scars. The evidence of my self-mutilation.

I couldn't.

"Now," Matt said, "or I'll rip them off you. Right in two, the way you ripped those sheets."

"No, please..."

But it was too late. He'd already torn them from my body.

My pubic hair had grown in, but not enough to completely hide what I'd done.

Matt's eyes grew wide. "Oh, Riley. No." His voice was laced with sadness. With pity.

"No!" I cried. "Don't pity me. Don't ever pity me!" Tears welled in the bottoms of my eyes.

He reached toward me. "Honey, those cigarettes. I never saw you smoke."

I slinked away, curled into a fetal position on the other side of the bed.

His arms wrapped around me, and although they warmed me, still I shivered with the chills knifing through me.

And I wondered how a man like Matteo Rossi could love such an object of pity.

42

MATTEO

I held her close, tried to ease her shivering.

How could I not have known?

That night back at the cabin, it had been dark in the bedroom. I'd been so full of lust and desire. I hadn't looked closely. Eagerness, need, had controlled me, when I should have been thinking about her. About Riley.

"Never again," I whispered against her silky neck. "Never again will anything harm you. Not even you. Got it? I won't let you."

She trembled against me, choking back tears.

"Shh," I said. "It's okay to cry if you want to. If you need to. Let it out, baby. Let it all out."

She turned toward me then, snuggling into my arms.

And she cried into my shoulder.

AN HOUR LATER, I awoke to the most beautiful sight.

Riley had climbed on top of me and was sinking onto my hard cock.

And God, I was complete.

Complete in a way I hadn't been the first time. This time Riley Wolfe was making love with me. Not Chloe Mansfield. Riley, with all her scars, and I loved every bit of her.

I loved her because she was Riley. Riley, who'd been through so much horror in her short life. Riley, who harmed herself to keep her emotions in check.

No more.

She slid down onto me fully and easily because she was so wet.

"You're so big," she said. "You're burning me inside, but it's a good burn."

"God, yes. Good burn."

And it was good. So damned good.

She rose and sank back on me.

Rose and sank again.

She fucked me.

And I fucked her.

I grabbed both her breasts and squeezed. Then I moved to her nipples and pinched them in alternative movements.

"Matt, it feels good. My nipples. Feels so good. Oh, God. I think...I think..."

She slid one hand over her belly to her clit and caressed it, closing her eyes...

"Matt, oh my God!"

And as she exploded, I did as well, closing my eyes to see the rainbow of colors shattering around me.

You're beautiful.

Come for me.

That's it, baby.

The words from my throat became part of the psychedelic mirage around me, circling me, cleansing me, fulfilling me.

I gripped her hips as my climax roared on.

We came together in a whirl of love and lust and passion, of giving and taking and just being.

Together.

We came together, and I knew, in that instant, that I'd found my forever.

WE WERE both going to be okay.

We slept in each other's arms again, this time without my blue balls. In the morning, I slid into her from behind, and it was slow and sweet.

She sighed into her pillow as I fucked her gently, and our mutual orgasm was soft and light, so different than the last, but no less implosive.

When the contractions in my cock finally stopped, I stayed embedded inside her for a few blissful moments. Then I flipped her onto her back and spread her legs.

"Don't," she said.

"It's okay."

"I'm embarrassed."

"It will heal," I said, "and you're never going to do this again."

"I won't," she promised. "Never again."

"Good. Because this pussy is mine now, and I'm going to finally taste it." I dived between her legs and—

A phone rang.

Not my ring.

Damn it all to hell.

"Sorry," Riley said, easing away from me. "I should probably get that. It might be one of my brothers."

"Mmm," I nuzzled her neck. "Stay."

"I'll be back in a minute."

Then she was no longer touching me. A second later, the bed

shifted with her weight leaving it. I closed my eyes. She'd be back soon, and I was going to go down on her. Eat that luscious pussy with relish.

So I waited.

When several minutes had passed, "Riley?"

She came back to the bed. "Sorry. It was Rock. They actually found a significant clue here in Las Vegas."

"This early in the morning?"

She gave me a warm-hearted smack on the arm. "It's hardly morning, Matt. It's eleven thirty."

I sat up in bed and drew in a deep breath. Sure enough, the sunlight was streaming in the window, and it wasn't the dawn of a sunrise.

"Rock and Reid have been working since this morning, and someone contacted them."

"Who?"

"I don't know yet. We need to meet and get the scoop."

"Okay. Go ahead. I'll take a shower and be ready when you're back."

"Silly." She punched me again. "You're coming with me."

"You sure your brothers are okay with that?"

"Rock and Roy are, and Reid can go fuck himself. Besides, you're part of this now. I want you to be part of it, though I wouldn't blame you if you ran away screaming."

I grabbed her and gave her a deep kiss. "No way. You're never getting rid of me."

"Good." She stood. "Now get up. I'll meet you in the shower."

That was all my dick needed. I was ready to go again.

I headed to the bathroom where Riley was already soaping up her hair. I stepped in with her, amazed at how large the shower actually was. Three shower heads pummeled us with warm water.

Her gaze dropped to my cock.

I grinned. "Ready for more?"

"Always." She wrapped her arms around my neck and I lifted her, pinning her against the tiled wall and shoving my dick inside her heat once more.

She was still wet from my climax inside her, and I pumped, this time frantically, as if my life depended on it.

"Feels so good, Matt," she breathed. "I'm going to come quickly. The friction... Oh my God!"

I felt each shudder of her pussy walls around my cock, and within seconds I joined her in the orgasm, releasing into her everything I had.

Every fucking thing.

Which wasn't much. I didn't have more than a couple thousand in the bank plus my two properties and my silver business.

That was it.

But it was hers. All of it.

Just like my heart.

She slid down the wall, limp in my arms, and we held each other as the water pelted us in warmth. Then we washed each other's hair, which was more intimate than I'd ever imagined, and then rinsed and dried off.

"Ready?" Riley said, after dressing in skinny jeans and a crop top.

"Ready to take you to bed again." My groin tightened. "You look hot."

She kissed my lips. "So do you. I'll take a rain check. Let's go."

ROCK AND REID had booked a conference room at the hotel for the days we were here, and they ordered in a catered lunch.

Once we were done eating, Rock started talking. "I got a

phone call this morning from one of our PIs. He found a woman named Zinnia."

"Where is she?" Roy asked.

"Believe it or not, she's right here in Vegas," Reid replied. "She's a showgirl."

Both Lacey and Charlie lifted their eyebrows.

"A showgirl?" Riley said.

"Yeah, and all the stats add up. Our guy contacted her, and she's willing to talk to us."

"Great," Roy said. "Let's talk, then."

"One problem," Rock said.

"Does she want money?" Lacey asked.

"That was my first thought too," Reid said, "but the PI says no. She just wants anonymity. She'll help us if she can, but she won't talk to any authorities."

"What good does that do us, then?" Roy said.

"She may not know anything," Rock said, "but the fact that she's asking for anonymity rather than money makes me think she may be the person we're looking for."

"I agree," Lacey said. "Who will she talk to?"

"Only one of us," Reid said, "and she prefers that it be a woman."

"But I should go," Roy said. "I might recognize her."

"Agreed," Reid said. "That's what we told the PI. He's checking with her and we're waiting to hear back."

"So nothing until then?" Roy asked.

"Nothing for you. Rock and I have work to do." Reid shifted in his seat.

He seemed uncomfortable. Riley had told me the whole story of Rock being put in charge instead of him. Was that what this was about? Or was something else going on?

Rock's phone buzzed. "Rock Wolfe here," he said.

Pause.

"I think Lacey would be—"

Pause.

"Gotcha. Understood. Tell her thanks."

Pause while he scribbled some notes.

"Perfect. They'll be there." He ended the call. "That was Roark, the PI who found Zinnia. She's agreed to talk to you, Roy, as long as Riley goes with you."

Riley nearly jumped out of her chair. "Me? Why me?"

"She wants a woman there."

"Then Lacey is the logical choice," Riley said. "She'll know what questions to ask."

"That's what I told him, but it turns out she's a fan of yours, and she wants to talk to you."

"But I won't know what to say to her!"

"Won't you?" Lacey smiled. "You'll know better than anyone. If she's the person we're looking for, then she's been through something as traumatic as you have. I think she chose well."

"But I won't know what to say to her," Riley repeated, more softly this time.

"I'll give you a list of things to ask her, like I did for Roy and Charlie when they went to Montana to talk to Leta Romero. You'll do fine."

"I'll be there with you, Sis," Roy said. "You got this."

Riley reached for my hand and squeezed it. "I'll do what I have to do."

43

RILEY

I sat with Roy at a bar in a lesser known hotel off the strip. Still, crowds milled around, and I nearly choked from the cigarette smoke. The bells from the slot machines and the din of conversation swirled around us.

We waited.

Roy had ordered us a couple of sodas. It was three in the afternoon, and neither of us felt up to drinking. Better to keep our heads, though I had to admit a glass of wine would have helped take the edge off.

But maybe I needed my edge. I needed to remember what my father was capable of so I could handle this woman with kid gloves. God only knew what she'd been through. I had the feeling Roy hadn't seen the worst of it that night.

Roy stared at his phone. "She's late."

"Have you considered that she might not show at all?"

"Yeah, I've considered it. If I were her, I probably wouldn't either."

I nodded. "We have to be strong for her, Roy."

"I know. I'm okay. That therapy helped a lot. My mind hasn't been this clear in ages, Ry. It's like a giant weight is gone from me."

I sighed. I envied my brother. I feared I'd carry the weight of my father's sins forever, even with therapy. After all, Roy didn't have to get over what was done to him, just what he'd seen.

Big difference there.

Still, I was getting stronger. Matt helped, and I helped myself too. I'd never burn myself again. I knew that as well as I knew my own name.

Fifteen minutes passed.

Then twenty, and we sat silently, sipping our second round of diet soda.

"Ready for something stronger?" Roy finally asked.

I got ready to nod, when a woman caught my eye. Her hair was jet black and pulled into a tight ponytail high on her head. She wore dark glasses, and she just looked...

She looked the way I felt.

I gestured to Roy. "I think that's her."

"Really? Then it's not the woman I remember. She was blond."

"There's such a thing as hair color," I said. "Does that look like natural black to you?"

"Actually, no," he said. "It's too black. Almost blue-black."

"Exactly." I smiled in her direction. If she was a fan of mine, she'd recognize me, unless this wasn't her at all.

But it was. She inched toward us hesitantly. I patted the seat at the bar next to me.

She shook her head slightly and then sat down at a table in the corner.

Okay, I got it. She didn't want to talk at the bar, where someone might overhear us. "Come on," I said to Roy.

"You sure?"

I nodded. "That's a woman who has something to hide." I walked to the table, Roy following me.

I sat down. "Zinnia?"

She nodded hesitantly.

I stuck out my hand. "I'm Riley Wolfe, and this is my brother Roy."

Her hand was limp in mine, and she didn't take Roy's at all.

"What can we do to help you feel more at ease?" I asked. "Would you like a drink?"

She shook her head. "I'm... I'm a fan of yours."

I smiled. "Thank you."

"I actually did some modeling when I was young, before you came on the scene. I just... You know. Your father..."

"I'm not my father," I said, "and neither is Roy."

"I get that. I always wanted to reach out to you on social media or even email, but I couldn't."

"We're here now," Roy said. "What would you like to say to Riley?"

"Just how much I admire you. Your beauty and your grace."

"Thank you very much." I smiled. "How old are you, Zinnia?"

"I'm twenty-nine. And no one calls me anymore. It's not my legal name anymore. I go by Zee."

Twenty-nine. The right age. "The letter Z?" I asked.

"No. Z-e-e."

"All right, Zee," I said. "I'd be happy to talk to you about modeling, but right now I don't have the luxury of time. Roy and I need to ask you some questions about our late father."

"Could you take off your sunglasses?" Roy asked.

"No, I can't."

"Surely you can't wear them when you do your shows," he said.

"No, I don't. But I'm heavily made up and it doesn't matter."

"What show are you in?" I asked.

"Right now I'm doing *Best of Sin City*."

Best of Sin City. Most likely a topless show, which meant—

"She's obviously not the person I saw," Roy said. "She's not blond, and she'd have..."

Zee met his gaze. "Scars? I have them. And I remember you."

"But how...?" I began.

"Makeup. You'd be amazed what our makeup team can do. Some of the girls I work with have to cover up worse. Lots of bruising and scarring."

My stomach dropped. "You mean..."

"I mean their men beat the shit out of them. Yeah."

"And you?"

"No. No one beats the shit out of me. I'll never be in that situation again."

I smiled, reached forward, and touched her forearm. "Good for you."

"It's a lonely life, but I deal." Then she met Roy's gaze once more. "I never thanked you."

"For what?"

"For saving me. I never would have gotten out of there alive."

"I wish I could have done more," he said.

"There were others," she said. "I saw them..."

"What did you see?" Roy asked.

"Several girls were in cages. They must have been sedated."

Nausea clawed up my throat. I swallowed it down as best I could. "Roy, I don't think I can hear this."

"You can go," he said. "I'll get the information."

I breathed in. Out. In again. "No. I'm staying. I want to be here for you, Zee."

"Thank you. I'm sorry I can't do more."

"How many men were hunting you?" Roy asked.

"I don't know. It seemed like dozens, but I was so scared."

"You signed a document," I said. "About six years ago."

"Yeah. I was broke. I'd just gotten out of rehab, and I needed money to start over. It took every ounce of strength I had to go to your father. I had to show him..." She choked back a sob. "I had to show him the scars. Tell him I could name him and the one other guy. The priest. He... He paid me off. I should have asked for more than I got, but...I just wanted to erase that part of my life."

"How did you end up here?" I asked.

"I'm a good dancer—I took ballet and jazz all through childhood—and I needed a place where I'd blend in. Where no one would ever think to look. I changed my name from Zinnia Rehnquist to Zara Jones. That way I could still go by my nickname, Zee."

"Wouldn't it have made more sense to go by a totally different name?" Roy asked.

"Roy..." I began."

"It's okay," she said. "He's right, and I considered it, but I needed something that was mine, you know?"

I nodded. I understood more than she knew. Her past might be horrific, but it was still *her* past. I felt the same about my own, in the same warped way.

"No one gives showgirls a second look," she said, "unless you're a big name. I'm not, and I made sure I never would be."

"But you said you wanted to be a model," I said.

"Not really. It was my mom's thing, and I'm too old now. Thing is, even if I wanted it, I couldn't take that path. Even lesser models have their photos everywhere. I couldn't risk it."

I shook my head and turned to Roy. "Our father cost her a lot."

"He cost us all a lot," Roy said. "I'm so sorry, Zee."

"I didn't come here for your pity," she said. "But when Mr.

Roark told me all of you were suspects in his murder, I knew I had to say something."

"Yet you say you won't talk to the police."

She shook her head. "I can't. Please don't ask me to."

"You understand," I said, "that if you don't talk to the police, you can't actually help us."

She nodded. "But you have to also understand. I can't talk to the police because I have a bigger motive than any of you."

"Actually, you don't," Roy said. "We all have huge motives. All that really matters is whether you have an alibi, which you probably do. Our father was killed in New York around one a.m. Pacific Time. You were probably performing."

She shook her head. "Except I wasn't. Our show was dark the night of the murder."

"Fuck." Roy raked his finger through his long hair.

"I'm sorry," she said.

"Where were you that night?" I asked. "Maybe you have an alibi anyway."

"Home. In bed."

"Do you have any roommates?"

"Three, but they were all out."

"Fuck," Roy said again. "Though flight records would show you hadn't gone to New York, and if you were performing the day before and after, you couldn't have gotten to New York any other way. You're probably safe."

"We need all information you have," I said. "Even if you don't want to talk to the authorities. We understand. Right, Roy?"

Roy didn't reply.

"Right, Roy?" I said again.

"Yeah. Sure."

"I owe you everything," she said to Roy. "I'll do anything you ask. Anything except talk to the police."

Roy sighed. "I never asked for anything in return. Saving your life was an accident."

"Maybe it was," Zee said, "but you still did it, and I'm forever grateful. I went through a few years of wanting to die, but then I realized that I wouldn't have fought so hard to live while I was down there if I truly wanted to die."

I nodded. "I understand completely."

"So neither one of you are suicidal," Roy said. "That's a good thing, but it doesn't help us out here."

Zee finally took her sunglasses off and met my gaze. "Wait a minute. Are you saying..."

Her eyes were a gorgeous blue, lighter than Reid's but still a clear sapphire. The kind of eyes I always wanted.

I attempted a smile. "I'm saying we all understand. We all had motives, and we're all innocent. That's all I want to say right now."

But would my story help her make a decision to help us? I didn't know, and I certainly wasn't about to confide in a complete stranger. But maybe she didn't have to be a stranger.

"Look," I said. "Can we take you to dinner? My whole family? You can meet all of us and tell your story."

"No. Not in public."

"We're in public now."

She hastily donned her sunglasses once more. Damn. I had to remind her we were in public. Not my finest moment.

My big brother saved me. "It wouldn't have to be in public. We can have dinner in one of our private suites or in a private conference room."

"I'm not sure I could eat," she said.

"It doesn't have to be dinner," I said. "Just a meeting. My brothers are awesome, and my sister-in-law, Lacey, and Roy's girlfriend, Charlie, are great too. Lacey's an attorney, so she can help you as well." I sighed. "Please, Zee. We need to get to the bottom of what our father was doing."

"I... I've told you all I remember. Your father—and I only knew him because I'd seen his picture—and the priest. He was wearing his collar, plus I recognized him from mass."

"Wait..." Roy wrinkled his forehead. "Are you saying you went to St. Andrew's?"

Zee nodded. "For years. He gave me my first communion."

"Did he do anything else to you?"

She shook her head. "Never, which was why I never understood... Why was he there? Why was he with your father?"

"That's what we need to find out," I said. "Father Jim may have had the biggest motive of all to kill my father. And you could be the key to all of it."

44

MATTEO

"I want to marry Riley."

I'd just finished my first Pappy Van Winkle fifteen-year when the words tumbled out of my mouth.

Rock sat next to me at one of the hotel bars. Reid was still working in the conference room, and Lacey and Charlie had gone to the spa for massages.

I expected his mouth to drop open, but it didn't. In fact, he didn't seem surprised at all.

"Are you asking for my permission?"

"No. Not really. I guess... Well, maybe I am. I've known her for all of a week."

"About the same amount of time I'd known Lace when I figured out she was the one. So none of this surprises me."

"I'm just afraid..."

"Of what?"

"Not of anything, really. Just afraid she'll never want to marry. You know, after what your father did to her."

"Riley's a smart girl. She won't let her past color her future."

"But didn't you? You ran off to Montana. Left everything behind."

He took a drink. "I did. And now I'm back. Confronting the past wasn't easy, and certainly not painless, but I'm glad I did it. Riley might only weigh a hundred and twenty pounds soaking wet, but she's a Wolfe, and she's as strong as I am, if not stronger."

"She is that."

"Still, you need to give her some time. If you ask her to get married now, she may run again."

"She ran to me last time."

"She ran *away* last time. Running to you was coincidence."

I signaled the bartender for another. "You're right."

"She loves you, though," Rock said. "I've never seen her look at anyone the way she looks at you."

"You weren't around."

"You got me there. But when I came back after Dad was killed, Riley looked... Not sad, exactly. Not angry. Just...resigned. Like her life was her life and it could never change." He smiled. "She doesn't look that way anymore, and if you have anything to do with that, you've made a friend for life in me."

"Where did you live in Montana?"

"A little biker town north of Helena called Grayforke. You know it?"

I nodded. "Yeah. I've been there a few times."

"Do you ride?"

"No, though I always wanted to. I got my license a few years ago, but I haven't been able to afford the bike I want."

Rock stood. "No more drinking, then." He shoved several bills on the bar.

"Oh?"

"Yeah. You and I are going to rent a couple Harleys and ride this afternoon."

"RED ROCK CANYON," Rock said. "It's short, but we don't have a lot of time. Maybe tomorrow we can do the Valley of Fire."

A ridiculous grin split my face as I put on a helmet and sat on the Harley Davidson Heritage I'd just rented. I planted my cell phone on the GPS stand and plugged in the route Rock gave me.

"Wait until you see these views," Rock said. "Nevada isn't Montana, but parts of it are ridiculously beautiful."

"You've done these routes before?"

"A couple times. Sometimes my buddies and I took a road trip to Vegas, lost all our cash, and spent the rest of the time on hogback riding under the blue sky. Nothing like it."

"Sounds amazing."

"You ever ridden a bike like this before?"

"I test drove a couple after I got my license. Loved them all, but my dream ride is an Indian."

"Let's see if I can't change your mind. Indians are great, but nothing beats a Hog." He strapped his helmet under his chin and then typed into his phone. "Just letting Lace know what we're up to."

"Should I text Riley?"

"Might be a good thing."

I quickly sent Riley a text letting her know I was going riding with Rock. Would she know I meant motorcycle riding? And would that freak her out?

I was all suited up and ready to go, and I really wanted to see how this baby handled. Besides, I was qualified. I quickly added to the text:

Don't worry. I have a motorcycle license and I'm qualified. Love you.

"Let's go," I said to Rock as I cranked my engine.

Man, the sound of those pipes. I gunned them a couple times, and Rock laughed, nodding as he gave me a thumbs up.

We rode west of the Strip to the Red Rock Canyon Conservation Area. From there, we'd follow the thirteen-mile loop.

I almost wanted to pull off my helmet and let my hair flow in the wind, but I knew better. Safety first, especially now that I had someone I loved to keep myself safe for.

Even without the flowing hair, the picturesque sights mesmerized me. The gorgeous orange-red rock formations. The sandstone peaks of the Keystone Thrust. I envied the hikers we saw on the way. They could stop and appreciate the deviation of colors and textures. The reddish-orange turned greenish in places, brown in others. Different from Montana, this land was true desert, though greenery was abundant as well. But it was the sandy brown of the desert that drew me most, perhaps because it was so different from what I was used to.

Rock led the way, and he slowed down at the most beautiful places. I took advantage and stared as well as I could while still being careful on my bike.

Even more than the gorgeous scenery, though, just riding gave me a shot of endorphins. Only my climaxes with Riley were a better high. Who needed drugs or alcohol? A beautiful woman and a motorcycle.

What more did a man need?

The bike ride was too soon over. When we rode back to the Eagle Rider rental place and took off our helmets, a wave of sadness swept through me.

"What'd you think?" Rock asked.

"I think I'd like to take Riley and strap her on the back, and then take off and never come back."

"I hear you. And trust me, I thought about it. I told Lace basically the same thing when we were in Montana recently. She came close to being arrested by a rogue deputy, and I told her we could get on the bike and head to Canada. That I'd never look back."

"But you didn't."

"No. I didn't. That would have left Roy, Reid, and Riley with no inheritance."

I nodded. "You're a good man."

"Maybe," he said. "And maybe not. In the end, though, it was Lacey's decision to come back. Not mine."

"You would have gone?"

"In a heartbeat. You have to understand. I'm in love, just like you are. I wanted to keep Lacey from anything that might hurt her."

"I get that."

"I think you do. So tomorrow? Another ride? Valley of Fire?"

"If Riley's okay with it."

He laughed then, a huge guffaw. "Man, you *are* in love."

45

RILEY

I entered Rock and Lacey's suite and raced into Matt's arms. "I've been worried sick!"

"Why?" he laughed.

"Because I got your text. That's why. You were out on a motorcycle?"

Rock guffawed. "And you weren't worried about me?"

"I assumed you knew what you were doing."

"So did I," Matt said. "I told you."

"I know." I sighed. "I was still worried."

"I'm all in one piece." He kissed the top of my head. "I'll never leave you, Riley. I promise."

"So what's the plan for this evening?" Rock asked.

"We're ordering food in," Lacey said to him and Matt. "Here in our suite. Everyone's joining us, including Zinnia."

"She goes by Zee," I reminded her.

Zee had hesitantly agreed to join us for dinner, though she claimed she wouldn't eat. At least she'd be here, though. Reid was on his way, as were Roy and Charlie.

"What'd you find out?" Rock asked.

"She's the woman we're looking for. In fact, she remembered

Roy. There's a lot she hasn't told us yet, like why she waited over five years to confront Dad, how much money he offered her, and why she signed a confidentiality agreement."

"Your father's dead, so the confidentiality agreement with him is null and void," Lacey said. "But there's still the issue of Father Jim."

"How in the fuck is it possible to have a nondisclosure agreement with someone who tried to kill you?" Rock said. "That's fucked up."

"She was probably desperate," I said. "She might have signed her life away for money at that point."

I didn't know exactly why she'd signed, but we'd ask her tonight, where she was safe. Not in a crowded bar.

I just hoped she'd show.

I had a nagging feeling she wouldn't.

Roy, Charlie, and Reid soon arrived, and a few minutes later, the food. The caterers set it up in the meeting room in Rock's suite, and we began with cocktails.

"So where is this woman?" Reid asked.

"She's late," Roy said, "but she was late this afternoon as well. Give her a little latitude. She's been through a lot."

"So have we all," Reid retorted. "What the fuck?"

"Stop being an asshole, Reid," I said. "She's doing her best."

"Maybe we can throw the authorities toward her instead of us. Talk about motive."

Rock rose and pulled Reid up from his chair. "I can't believe you just said that. You want to throw one of his victims under the bus?"

"We're *all* his victims, Rock, in case you forgot." Reid deftly disengaged himself from Rock's hold.

"Fuck you, Reid." This from Roy. "You got the shit kicked out of you. So what? You lived to tell the tale. This woman was

hunted, for God's sake, in some kind of twisted game Dad and
Father Jim played."

"Is that any worse than what he did to our sister?"

I stood then. "It's way worse, Reid. I'm alive."

"So is she."

"But others aren't. How many women did Dad *kill?*"

"Wouldn't there be news stories about missing women?"
Charlie asked.

Lacey shook her head. "Derek Wolfe probably owned the
news. He got stories buried and made sure anyone who cried
about it was well compensated to shut up."

"Motherfucker," Matt said under his breath.

"You got something to add, Matt?" Rock said.

"No. Sorry."

"You're one of us now," Rock said. "Feel free to speak."

"I just don't get it," Matt continued. "How the hell does
someone get so sick?"

"Beats the shit out of me." Rock shook his head. "How late is
she now?"

I checked my phone. "A half hour."

Roy sighed. "We should never have let her out of our sight."

"She should be easy enough to find." I smiled. "Anyone want
to go to a show tonight?"

"I already thought of that," Roy said. "The show's dark
tonight."

"Crap." I plunked back down in my chair. "Roark probably
has her address. We could go see her."

"We could, but let's not." Rock took his seat as well. "She
needs some time. We've got tails on her. We'll know if she tries
to run. Let's give her space, let her think about what she wants to
do. If she's the kind of person I'd like to think she is, she'll do the
right thing."

"As much as I hate to say it," Reid said, "I actually agree with Rock. By the way, bro, don't threaten me again."

"Then don't be such an ass."

That got a chuckle out of Reid. "I'm sorry. I feel terrible about what this woman has been through at our father's dirty hands. But damn it, I've worked too hard at this company to end up going down for that bastard's murder."

"None of us want that," Roy reminded him.

"I know. I get that, but I'm the one who worked by his side, learned this business and brought in innovations that even he didn't come up with. And now..." He shook his head. "I guess I'm still not over him choosing Rock over me." He held up his hand. "Don't say it. I know that's nothing compared to what Riley and this Zinnia went through at his hands. I'm not being selfish. Or maybe I am. Who the fuck knows?"

"You have every reason to be upset," Rock said. "This isn't what any of us wanted. Just leave the asshole gene at the door. Got it?"

Reid nodded. "As long as you do the same."

"Touché, brother. Touché."

"Let's eat," Roy said. "I don't think she's coming."

I sighed. Though I wasn't surprised, I'd held onto a flicker of hope that Zee would show up.

She didn't, though, and I knew, better than anyone, that she'd try to run.

I just hoped we'd be able to catch her.

46

MATTEO

I didn't know this Zinnia, but my insides ached for her, almost as much as they ached for my Riley.

My Riley. I'd already asked her brother for her hand without telling her my intentions.

I had to tell her something else first.

Charlie had ordered a lavish Indian buffet, but it all tasted like dirt to me. Riley picked at her meal as well.

"You okay?" I asked.

"Yeah. I just…"

"I know. She'll be okay, and so will you."

"I'm not worried about me." She smiled. "I have you now."

"You have me forever, but I'm no substitute for therapy."

"Oh, I know that. I'll get what I need. But what I really need and want right now is for this to be over. I want my father's case closed."

"We all do, Sis," Rock added.

"We seem to have the evening free," Lacey said. "Any of you have plans?"

"Not a one," Roy said. "We could catch a show or something."

"Count me out," Riley said. "Matt and I already have plans."

I lifted my eyebrows. "We do?"

"Sure, we do. What do most couples do in Vegas?"

"I don't know. Play blackjack? See a boobie show?" I laughed.

She smacked my arm, not lightly. "Don't be a moron. Couples get married! That's what I want to do!"

I nearly fell out of my chair. Had Riley Wolfe just proposed to me? In front of her whole family?

All other eyes in the room were wide...and staring straight at me.

I met Rock's gaze. I couldn't read it. He was as surprised as I was. Hadn't he told me to go slowly with his sister? To give her time?

Now what?

Should I give her time? That would mean turning down her proposal, which might hurt her. I didn't want to hurt her.

And damn, I didn't want to turn her down either.

I'd marry this woman anywhere and anytime.

Since she'd chosen Las Vegas, why not go all in?

"You want to get married?" I asked her. "Are you sure, baby?"

"I've never been more sure. Please, Matt. Marry me."

I stood and pulled her toward me, kissing her lips hard. Then I lifted her in my arms. "Absolutely, Riley. Let's get married!"

But how would her brothers react?

I imagined a punch to my face. Or a hearty pat to my back.

I didn't imagine what I got.

Roy stood. "That's an amazingly good idea, sis. You want some company?"

Riley, still in my arms, met her brother's gaze. "At the wedding? Of course. You're all invited."

"Yes, at the wedding, but I thought I might stand up there with you. How about it, silver?"

Now Charlie's eyes went even wider. "You mean...?"

"Yup!" Roy dropped to his knee in front of Charlie. "Marry me. Please. I love you so much."

She smiled and wrapped her arms around his neck. "Yes, of course I'll marry you, Roy."

"A double wedding, then." Lacey smiled. "How wonderful!"

Even Reid joined in. "Hmm. I'm the only one without a date for this momentous occasion but I'm sure I can fix that up in no time." He glanced through his phone.

"You have women here in Vegas?" Rock asked.

"Bro, I have women everywhere."

Then a knock on the door.

"Probably the caterers to clean this shit up," Rock said. "I'll get it."

I helped Riley gather our dishes and trash together. Damn. I'd just gotten a marriage proposal. From a supermodel. A supermodel I was madly in love with and who loved me back. Yeah, we had problems to deal with. Big ones.

But I had a ridiculous grin on my face anyway.

Tonight I would marry the woman of my dreams.

Tomorrow we'd deal with the rest.

"Where should we get married?" I asked Riley.

"Whichever chapel is closest. I can't wai—"

Her mouth dropped open.

Rock stood in the doorway to the meeting room with a woman.

"Zee..." Riley said.

"I... I'm sorry I didn't show up. I mean... I'm here now."

"Of course." Riley walked to her and touched her hand lightly. "We're glad you're here. This is my family. My fiancé, Matt Rossi, and you know Roy. That's his fiancé, Charlie, and my other two brothers, Rock and Reid. Then Rock's wife, Lacey."

She nodded nervously. "N-Nice to meet you."

"Hey," Riley said. "I'm sorry we've already eaten, but would you like to join us tonight?"

"For...what?"

"A wedding! Matt and I are getting married, and so are Roy and Charlie."

"I'm not suitably dressed..."

"That's a fabulous idea," Charlie said. "And you're dressed just fine. This is a come-as-you-are thing."

"We're all going like this," I said. "Right?"

"Yeah. Sure." Roy said. "You should come with us."

"But I—"

"You can be my date," Reid said.

Riley's eyes shot wide open.

So did Zee's.

"You'd be doing me a favor," he said. "I'm the only one without another half for this occasion."

"I couldn't."

"Sure you can." From Riley. "We all want you to come."

Zee smiled. Sort of. "I guess. I don't have any other plans."

"Then it's settled," I said. "Let's get married, Riley." I pulled her close and whispered into her ear, "I need to talk to you. Alone."

AFTER WE EXCUSED ourselves for a minute, I stood with Riley alone in the hallway. She fidgeted with her fingers, biting her lower lip.

I opened my mouth, but she pressed two fingers to my lips.

"Don't. I know what you're going to say."

"I'm pretty sure you don't."

"I do. You didn't want to embarrass me in front of my family. You don't want to—"

This time I quieted her by leaning down and pressing my lips to hers in a searing kiss. She opened for me, but then broke the kiss after only a few seconds.

"Don't," she said.

"Honey, I love you. I want to marry you. Tonight. But I can't have any secrets with my wife, and there's something I never told you about my past."

"Your past doesn't matter to me."

"I know that, and yours doesn't matter to me. But I have skeletons too, and I don't want to go to the altar with you before you know about them."

"Your parents..." she said.

I nodded. "My childhood wasn't exactly idyllic."

"What happened?"

"Nothing compared to what you've been through, but it's not fair of me to make you go in blind. I have a few hang-ups myself." I drew in a deep breath. "My mother committed suicide when I was in high school."

Riley gasped, bringing her hand to her mouth. "Matt, I'm so sorry!"

I cupped her cheek. "I'm okay. It took some time, but I'm okay. She suffered from depression most of her life, and I guess one day it got to be too much. My father didn't help things."

"What did he do?"

"He was a drunk, Riley. And not a nice one. He didn't beat up on either of us, but he did a lot of damage to our home and to others' property when he was on a bender. After my mother died, he went crazy. He..."

"Oh, Matt. What happened?"

"He killed a man, Riley."

She went white in the face. "Oh, God. Not you too?"

"Having an asshole father? Yeah. But honey, I'm okay."

"Do you see him? Ever?"

"Once a year I make the pilgrimage. That's all I can stomach. Anyway, after my mother died and my dad was locked up, my uncle got custody of me. He saved me. I was an angry kid. I didn't make it easy on him."

"Why didn't you tell me?" she asked.

"I don't talk about it, and the people in town know better than to bring it up around me. Then, once I found out what you've been through…"

"No. Don't. Your past is your past just like mine is mine. There aren't degrees of horror."

I didn't argue the point, though I disagreed vehemently. She had strength enough for both of us. I pulled the pink sapphire pendant out of my pocket, then, and placed it around her neck. "I wanted to give it to you in Sumter Falls, but you wouldn't take it. I offer it to you now. It's no engagement ring, but—"

"It's better than any engagement ring. It's perfect." She melted into my arms.

And I was complete.

My story wasn't a hundredth as horrible as hers, but now she knew.

And now we could be together.

47

RILEY

T acky.

So tacky, this chapel, but I was in heaven, despite what all of us had been through. I was in love, and I was happy.

I couldn't help giggling as I picked out a bouquet from the display.

"Is marrying me that funny?" Matt asked.

"God, no. I'm just thinking of the look on my mother's face if she were here."

"Should we call her?" Roy asked.

"Only if *you* want to. I certainly don't." I fingered the flowers. "I like the white roses. Which one do you like, Charlie?"

"The roses are gorgeous, but I'm going to go with the lilies, I think."

"Whatever you want." Roy smiled.

The others had already taken seats in the chapel. I couldn't get over Reid. Just an hour ago, he'd been ready to take Zee down to save his own hide, and now he was escorting her to my wedding.

My brother had always been a womanizer, and he was no

different now. An attractive woman came along, and he went for it. Classic Reid Wolfe. He wasn't called the Wolfe of Manhattan for nothing.

I just hoped he understood that Zee was troubled. Surely he wouldn't try to get her into bed. Not when we needed her cooperation. The last thing she needed was a love-her-and-leave-her guy like Reid taking advantage of her and then flying the coop.

After all, once Rock and Reid had concluded their business here, we were all heading back to New York.

On the other hand, Reid knew how to cozy up to a woman and make her comfortable. Perhaps that was exactly what Zee—and the rest of us—needed.

But then I stopped thinking about Reid and Zee.

I thought only about Matt, who looked magnificent with his blond hair hanging below his shoulders, his buff-colored shirt clinging to his muscles and his ass looked delectable in black jeans. I was wearing the same thing I'd worn all day—a miniskirt and camisole with denim mules. Comfy and casual.

Roy and Charlie looked great as well. Roy had pulled his hair back into his signature sleek ponytail and wore dark jeans and a white button-down, no tie. Charlie wore jeans too, along with a creamy silk blouse and strappy silver sandals.

"We don't have rings," Charlie said.

I tugged at the sterling pendant around my neck. "This is my ring."

Charlie gasped. "Oh! It's lovely."

"Matt made it," I bragged. "He's a silversmith."

"Really?" Roy said. "Too bad you don't have your wares on you. It would solve our ring dilemma."

"No dilemma." Lacey walked briskly toward us. "Every chapel in Vegas sells wedding sets."

We all laughed, and ten minutes later, we were outfitted with genuine ten-karat gold-plated rings.

Wagner's "Bridal Chorus" pumped out of the organ at the front of the chapel, where our Elvis-impersonating minister waited.

"That's our cue," Roy said to Matt. "We'll see you ladies in a few."

I turned to Charlie and smiled. "Welcome to the family. I hope you know what you're in for."

"We don't really know each other, but I love your brother more than anything."

"I know you do. Ready?"

She nodded, and we linked arms. Together we strolled down the short aisle to meet our fate.

Rock and Reid pulled the corks out in unison from two bottles of Dom Perignon.

"To the happy couples," Rock said. "I hope you're all as happy as Lace and I are."

After the newlyweds were all served, Reid carried a flute of champagne to Zee. He was ever the gentleman. In that moment, I adored my brother for what he was doing for her—making her feel at ease in a strange and stressful situation. Maybe she'd open up to him. To all of us.

"Speech!" Lacey called. "You first, Matt."

"Me? Why me?"

"Because you're the newest member of the family," Rock said.

He smiled. "I'm not sure what to say, except that I love this lady—my wife—more than I ever thought I could love another person. Thank you for proposing to me, baby. I'm happy to be Mr. Riley Wolfe!"

Everyone laughed, and then I spoke.

"I'm just as happy to be Mrs. Matteo Rossi. Thank you for everything." I clinked my glass to his and everyone took a sip.

Roy stepped up next. "I'm really glad to be here. In this moment, without all the shit that's been dragging me down for so long. Silver, you've made such a difference in my life. I love you more than anything."

Charlie blushed, and her eyes—yeah, they were actually silver—sparkled. "Thank you for seeing me, Roy, and loving me."

Glasses clinked once more, and we all hugged and kissed and shook hands in a mass of lips and limbs.

Zee stood alone, not touching anyone.

"Excuse me for a second," I said to Matt. I walked to Zee. "Doing okay?"

She nodded. "I've never had Dom Perignon before. I don't drink much."

"There's plenty. Want some more?"

She shook her head. "Thank you for letting me stay."

"Of course. In your own way, you're one of us."

"Am I?"

"We're all victims of my father. Maybe not in the same way you were, but in other ways."

"I'm beginning to understand that."

I smiled at her. "Thanks for showing up. I thought you might have run."

"Why would you think that?"

"Because I've done it before. I've run to get away from something. But there's no escaping the past, Zee. You can only accept it, deal with it, and move on."

"I've tried. For over ten years, I've tried."

"Talking about it will help."

"Will it?"

"I don't mean talking to us, though I hope you will. I mean talking to a professional."

"I could never afford that."

"You can now. I'll see that you get everything you need."

"I couldn't impose."

"Are you kidding? If I can't help someone my father hurt, what good is my inheritance?"

"But it's *his* money."

"Correction. It's *my* money, and I want to use it to help you."

"You don't know what you're getting into."

"Trust me. I do."

Reid approached us then with another flute of champagne for Zee. "Moving in on my date, sis?"

I laughed lightly. My God, my brother could turn on the charm. Already I could see Zee weakening.

I didn't want her wobbly-kneed over my womanizing brother. I needed her strong. Strong and willing to tell her story.

Reid tapped his pocket. "Phone's buzzing. Excuse me, ladies." He stepped away.

"He seems...nice," Zee said.

"He's a good guy at heart."

"He's so handsome, too, except for..."

"Except for what?"

"He looks so much like his father. *Your* father."

God. I hadn't even considered how much we all resembled our father. But Zee was right. Reid looked the most like him.

"I'm sorry," I said. "I didn't even think about that."

She didn't reply.

"You have to understand," I continued. "None of us can think like that, or every time we look into the mirror, we're reminded of the man who did such heinous things to all of us. To you. To so many others."

"What did he do to Reid?" she asked.

I sighed. "I don't fully know, and even if I did, his story isn't my story. You'd have to ask him."

"I can't. I don't even know him. Yet you're asking me to tell all of you my story."

I sighed again. She had a good point. "Zee, this isn't about us or even about you. It's about clearing all of our names. None of us is willing to go down for his murder when we're all innocent."

"I get that."

I looked around the small room. Reid and Rock were in a corner in heavy conversation. Probably about the phone call Reid just got.

Damn. Probably more bad news.

But you know what? I wasn't going to deal with bad news tonight. It was my wedding day. My wedding night. "Would you excuse me?" I said to Zee.

"Of course."

I walked straight to my husband. "Time to go," I said.

"Oh?"

"It's my wedding night." I smiled at him. "And you're not going to get any sleep."

The Lone Wolfe.

Ha! Great pun, huh?

Within less than a month, my three siblings had all met their life mates and gotten married.

Not in the cards for me. I was the Wolfe of Manhattan, always with a new lady on my arm. Now, though, since all my siblings were off the market, I was indeed the Lone Wolfe.

The phone call I got after the wedding was from the NYPD detective on our case, Hank Morgan. Consequently, Rock and the rest of them headed back this morning on the jet.

Again, not in the cards for me.

Someone had to stay here in Las Vegas and deal with our damned luxury hotel and casino. *Money is money.* Words of wisdom from the bastard who'd fathered me.

Sure, all of us were being investigated for the fucker's murder, but someone had to take care of business.

That someone was me.

Always me.

I wasn't CEO of the company, but only I could deal with the

contract mess here in Las Vegas. Story of my life. Under-appreciated to the max.

The rest of them were called back to New York for more questioning.

I wasn't going down for his murder, and neither was anyone else in my family. Not on my watch.

Zinnia—or Zee—seemed to be the key.

I just had to get her to talk.

The Wolfe of Manhattan.

I'd never met a woman I couldn't seduce.

So I'd seduce her.

And oh, she'd talk.

WOLFES OF MANHATTAN continues with *Rake*, coming soon!

A NOTE FROM HELEN

Dear Reader,

Thank you for reading *Runaway*. If you want to find out about my current backlist and future releases, please visit my website, like my Facebook page, and join my mailing list. If you're a fan, please join my street team to help spread the word about my books. I regularly do awesome giveaways for my street team members.

If you enjoyed the story, please take the time to leave a review. I welcome all feedback.

I wish you all the best!

Helen

Facebook

Facebook.com/helenhardt

Newsletter

Helenhardt.com/signup

Street Team

Facebook.com/groups/hardtandsoul

ACKNOWLEDGMENTS

Thank you so much to the following individuals who helped make *Runaway* shine: Christie Hartman, Martha Frantz, Theresa Finn, Karen Aguilera, Angela Tyler, Linda Pantlin Dunn, Serena Drummond, and Marci Clark.

ALSO BY HELEN HARDT

ABOUT THE AUTHOR

#1 *New York Times*, #1 *USA Today*, and #1 *Wall Street Journal* best-selling author Helen Hardt's passion for the written word began with the books her mother read to her at bedtime. She wrote her first story at age six and hasn't stopped since. In addition to being an award-winning author of romantic fiction, she's a mother, an attorney, a black belt in Taekwondo, a grammar geek, an appreciator of fine red wine, and a lover of Ben and Jerry's ice cream. She writes from her home in Colorado, where she lives with her family. Helen loves to hear from readers.

http://www.helenhardt.com

Made in the USA
Middletown, DE
26 November 2020